Foreword,

December 1st 2014- I was sitting on what seemed to be a plane that had only be used a handful of times. It smelled new, the lights, a dim blue and it was half full. I was traveling to the PAC 12 football Championship game for an anniversary (my wife and myself love football). On the flight I began to listen to music and I began thinking of a story. I wondered how many people on this plane were thinking of someone, a someone they may be in love with. A someone that they had always wanted to be in love with, and for some reason they either had lost them due to circumstances or never had the courage to ask. Opened Sky is the story I thought about that night.

I would like to thank everyone that has had his or her hand in Opened Sky, at times it has been stressful, scary and doubtful. To Drop Dead Designs, thank you for an amazing cover.

To all of you with or know someone (like me) with an autoimmune disease keep fighting. I know there are days that it is hard to continue the fight, your mind and body are fighting itself. Pick something to take your mind to another place. If you know of a loved one that has an autoimmune disease, stay strong with them.

I will say this to you, the reader. Thank you for taking time out of your life to read this story. I truly love this story and hope you do the same. The places that take place in this book are real (people are not). I have been there, touched and felt these places. Find me on Instagram @authormrmurphy702.

Thank you,
Michael R Murphy (MRM)
@authormrmurphy702

July 25, 1995

The sky threatened to open. Thunderstorms, a reality in Eastern Oregon during the summer appear, damage crops and machinery faster than a raging river in the spring. The silver, dusty earth that nurtured the golden stocks of wheat from the spring planting vibrated. A machine chewed through the field. Steel paddles and razor sharp sickles cut them down. Hot, dusty work.

In the past, drivers did everything they could to get away from it. Cabs were merely platforms, providing protection from only falling off, becoming a casualty to the machine they guided. This one-the one Ben operated-came with a cab lined with glass; a driver could see the outside, cutting through the dust. Air-conditioning made work almost comfortable. Controlling the long header making sure that the elevation matched that of the grain; the field decimated row by row, the seeds shot to the collection hopper; the excess kicked to the back, and bailed for straw.

A day consisted of quick stops, loading the gold cargo into a truck, and continued until either the machine stopped functioning, or the sun started to disappear- much like the grain.

A radio crackled in the cab. "Ben, about done for the day, time to shut down. There is someone waiting for you at the house." Harvesting for him the last two summers, he didn't have a home like many people. His uncle willed him in.

Attending a small college on the other side of the state, the time in the field, was a welcome diversion, that brought Ben peace and let his mind complete mathematical computations. The machine slowed to a crawl. Clouds turned red in the distance.

In charge of a half-million dollar machine, something he monetarily couldn't replace made him nervous. Radio chatter only happened when he stopped. Surveying the dust on the outside of the cab, feeling the hum of the engine in his seat, his heart skipped a beat.

"Starting in now. Who?" Ben tapped the steering wheel with his fingers. Waiting for the response. Not many knew where he lived.

"Supper will be ready, you will see."

His uncle, always short on words. Described the inner and outer workings of farming and life with small bursts.

The combine came back to life, the header's hydraulics made a low pitch hum as it pulled itself into the air. The field was left of a small dirt road not wide enough for anything beside the combine. A plume of dirt signaled something was moving. A vehicle meeting him needed to pull over into the ditch and let the beast pass. Ben didn't particularly like driving, he hated it. So many things can happen when you drive. The protection it offered made Ben feel at ease.

Work today was relatively close to the house. No need to leave them in the field tonight. He began to think of the possibilities of who waited for him.

Metal sheds once off in the distance now derelicts of darkness. The lights highlighted only mere feet of the sheds, only summer let them be brought out into the opened sky.

The lights brushed the yellow paint of his uncle's New Holland. Ben pulled his next to it. Switches flicked powered down the once loud carnivore of plants, becoming as still as the black night.

Ben breathed at each metal step. His feet hit the dark small, oily rocks that made the parking pad. Facades of the ranches buildings, were highlighted with orange lights. In the distance a thunderstorm outlined the topography of the area which included flat land, a few hills and even fewer trees. A hot breeze swept through the area.

The lights of the ranch house appeared a football field away. His feet on the pebbles, the steps true, in sync, had taken the last two years to reveal a normal cadence. Steps not his own echoed off equipment sheds.

A flashlight pendulated in front of him taking a deep breath, the owner of the flashlight closed in. Ben stopped. The steps came closer, softer. A word flickered through his mind. Thirty-six months separated the past to the present. "Leannan."

His body shook, his scalp felt numb. "Hello?"

"Hi Ben."

Warm, soft lips met his own. He knew the taste of her lipstick. The flashlight once illuminating the night now shone on the owner of the lips. The face of a woman, three years older than his. Ben took a breath, his stomach clenched into a tight ball of conjecture.

"Amanda."

"Hi, you're dusty and sweaty."

Mouths met again, her hands fell on his chest.

"Your aunt says dinner, or supper, is almost ready." She looked at the sky, stars showed in the night. "You need a shower before that."

The shower of the secondary bathroom had room for only one person. Ben craned his neck, following the water from his short, dark hair to the drain. Water around the drain ran clear, then dark, and then clear again.

Steam hid the butterfly and flowered wallpaper before the bathroom fan was turned on. A towel covered Ben's torso as he traveled across the hallway. A typical ranch house, the living room and kitchen separated the master bedroom on one end from the guest rooms on the other.

The door to his room creaked open. Amanda, waited for him— her long blonde hair and hazel eyes beckoning. Her figure fit, a volleyball player in college until graduation ended her career last year. Now she studied law at the University of Montana.

"You shouldn't be so startled."

"Sorry, I didn't know you would be waiting for me. And my aunt and uncle?"

Amanda tugged at the towel.

"How long have we been off and on? A year-and-a-half? They're fine with it. If they weren't, they wouldn't let me leave the dining room table and walk in here."

Ben placed himself next to her. Touching the back of her head. Amanda rested it on his shoulder. Her finger traveled down a long grooved gash. "Your scar on your neck is looking better."

Ben exhaled. Pain accompanied not only that but the other scars, screws, and pins in both of his legs. "They still hurt, everyone of them."

Amanda craned her neck. "I'm sorry, lover."

Ben's chest fluttered up and down. "Don't."

Amanda pleaded softly. "How long? How long until you forget?"

Ben settled his lips on her forehead. "I'm sorry, are you hungry?"

The oval dining table, ready for dinner, rested in a nook. Ben imagined the table being made for it.

His aunt had always known what to cook and when to cook it. The mashed potatoes Ben slopped down on the plate went well with the steak she grilled. *Meat and potatoes, what he always wished for.*

"Didn't know you were coming."

"I'm driving to Portland to meet Alice."

Forks, butter knives-everything dropped at the name, Ben rolled his eyes, scars started to burn.

"My god she is back in the States?" His aunt wondered.

"She and I talked on the phone a couple of days ago. She loves flying for the Air Force. I was going to surprise you. But I wanted to stop and see Ben."

His aunt's eyes gleamed; they didn't have children of their own. Ben and his sister, Alice were theirs.

"This is wonderful news! How long will she stay?"

Amanda gently cut her steak. "A couple of days."

"Her room is ready, wonderful news. How long has it been since you've seen her, Ben?"

Twirling the fork in his potatoes, he finally had an answer.

"Long enough, I guess."

Uncle decided to change the subject.

"So how long in law school?"

"Well I just started last year. So I would say another four years."

"You miss playing?"

Amanda glanced at Ben. "Volleyball? I miss, being on a team. Lot of good times and some wonderful friends. But that's over."

"Excuse me, I need to go outside. Thank you for dinner."

Ben entered the night flashes of lightning encircled the farm. *What the fuck am I doing, forget her, forget her.* The kitchen door shut. Ben looked back, Amanda walked to him.

February 1993

Steam from the locker showers coated his skin-sweat dripped from his hair, the hat of the hockey team he could only dream of playing for on backwards. The locker room itself was quiet-for the moment. Forty-five minutes before, a group of teenage boys huddled with their basketball coach, a trip to State had been earned. Ben's basketball team played without feeling for most of the year. The last eight games-the team became one, winning all eight, giving the school the first trip to State in twenty-five years.

Why couldn't this be hockey? Basketball? He only played it to stay in shape for hockey. Another thought of why came into his mind, then another. His father, a massive basketball fan-hung on every foul, basket, win and loss. Ben liked playing the game, yet something was missing, he missed the grass and the cold of fall playing football, when wood smoke filled the air. He missed the coldness of the ice, and the heat of playing hockey. The other glimmer that dashed in his mind-girls. Girls were easier to communicate with while on the court, other sports, placed him further away from the spectators.

Ben zipped his dress pants, shirt and tie placed as his father taught him when he first became a Varsity player-sophomore year. That seemed a lifetime ago. He smoothed his hair around the cap-lifted his duffle bag and traveled to the exit.

The green and yellow of the court reminded him of Green Bay Packer colors, a color palette he never liked. He preferred Black and Gold, much like his own teams colors. Not only was the court the color, every other seat-green or reflected the color scheme.

Most of the fans had vacated the gym, yet at the end of the final bleachers stood a collection of four people. Ben felt a smile creep onto his face. His mom, as always, clutched her purse with conviction, speaking vibrantly with someone she knew from the area. His dad was next, wearing a baseball cap. Ben took a breath has he approached.

"Ben! Great game."

His mom, always the optimist would let Ben know that he had great games. A quality that he loved about his mom, he leaned in for a hug, her head reaching the middle of his chest.

"Thanks mom, I think I did okay tonight, right dad?"

Dad studied games with deep thought. Ben always knew how long his dad would pause after asking the question if he deemed it a good or poor performance. If he extended his hand then it was an exceptional night. Ben felt his hand consumed by his dad's.

"Outstanding tonight, how many, 24 points, right?"

"Something like that." He again smiled, a minute later a mass leaped on his back.

"Brother, you kicked ass tonight."

"Oh yeah, sis." Alice jumped down, he didn't expect she would be at the game. He saw her during the national anthem. A junior at Rocky Mountain, a private college in Billings, saw her for the first time since Christmas break.

"Still doing that pilot shit?" Ben knew she wanted to be a pilot since high school. It was a stretch on the family finances to send her to college, yet they managed.

"Oh yeah, one year to go." Her dark wavy long hair, swayed.

"Nice, how was the drive?"

"Seven hours just to Missoula then another five to get up here...not my favorite, but seeing Flathead Lake is always nice."

"Seeing the lake is sweet, maybe this summer we can go and stay at the cabin." A hand grasped his shoulder, Ben spun and met the owner, accepted an embrace, before a hand was extended.

"Devin, it's nice to see you, taking care of my sister?" Ben made note of his hair receding slightly.

"Likewise, man, and yeah I'm taking care of your sister, she's not getting rid of me anytime."

"I don't think that will happen, what since eighth grade?" Ben smirked.

"Exactly." Alice retorted. "Have you decided where you are going to college next year?"

Ben chuckled. "You guys can have Billings, I'm going to the University of Montana, closer to home, but…I should get on the bus." He noticed Alice's face, slump. 'What is it?"

"I thought you were riding home with us, I mean I'm sure you want to play "which cheerleader will come to the back of the bus," but ride home with us."

His face started to burn, true he wouldn't mind if one of them would sneak back. A "game" he had seen, from the time he started to play sports that involved buses. He reached what everyone called "second base" for the first time in the back of a bus. "It's tempting, we can stop at the McDonald's along the way, instead of a gas station, but since we are going to State, I think I would like to ride with the team."

His dad interjected, 'That sounds like a good call, we will see you at home."

Ben hugged Alice. "Love you sis, we will talk when we get home, stay up."

Chapter Three

Ben placed his bag in the storage compartments under the bus. The crisp night evaporated as he entered the bus-smell of snack food and diesel fumes mixed into a something he always remembered. The trophy sat face up on the assistant coaches' seat, touched it as he passed. Along the route to his seat-in the back of the bus, came a smattering of "great game" and "we did it." He smiled and sat, let out a long breath. Bumps formed on his skin. "I can't believe we did it." His head reached the back of his seat, his eyes closed. Two weeks until the State finals in Billings where Alice and Devin lived. The largest stadium and city in Montana: The Metra, could seat close to 5,000 people.

* * *

He could feel when the bus rounded the corners along Flathead Lake-when they stopped for snacks at a gas station. Sleep is what he needed, the last four days were long, the inside of the bus-low volume.

* * *

The bus entered Missoula, the lights reflected off of the interior, almost home-time to sleep in a real bed, not a hotel room with three other players who would flatulate at will.

Ben noticed the bus slowed, turned and stopped into the K-Mart parking lot. He looked at his watch 12:13a.m. A multicolored light-blue and red began to streak along the windows of the bus, then stopped. Holy shit, we just got pulled over. The atmosphere changed. Someone stepped on the bus, and Ben thought he was talking to the head coach. A very tall wiry man, exited the bus. He noticed everyone had awoke and whispers at what could have happened, ricocheted the buses interior.

The coach re-entered the bus, his cowboy boots shuffled along the floor, they brought much needed weight to his frame. Ben became alarmed, even though there weren't cheerleaders in the back that was for sure. Ben's eyes looked around, met other eyes-each grew concerned as the coach came closer. The tall man bent down to ear level. Ben's body stiffened.

"Ben, you will need to come with me, off of the bus." The tone the coach used was unlike anything Ben had heard in the last year.

Ben met his eyes. "Is everything ok?"

"Please, you need to come with me. Your bag will stay ok, trust me."

"Okay." The walk from the back of the bus was slow, he could feel his legs buckle. He approached the front, the cheerleaders looked at him-Ben could see, that outside, a highway patrol car waited for him. "What the fuck?" "Ben, correct?" The officer asked. The night was silent-no wind, cold and brisk. The officer was much to the same height as Ben, yet many years older. Ben sensed his coach next to him.

"Yes..."

The officer looked at his coach,

"Are you traveling with me?"

"Yes."

The officer looked at Ben, "We need to go."

As Ben locked the seat belt, lights from the patrol car came alive-speed began to pick up. "Where are we going, what happened?"

His coach's voice filled his ears. "Ben, we're going to the hospital, there's a…"

Chapter Four

The car stopped at the Emergency room entrance.

"This way Ben," the patrol officer said as he exited the vehicle.

"What is going on?" Ben exclaimed as he followed.

The officer covered distance darting around nurses, doctors and other patients. "We need to hurry...damn it." He pressed the elevator button-; three elevators and all were far above on floors three, twelve and twenty-three. "Do you think you can use the stairs."

"Please tell me what is going on." Ben recognized the fear in his own voice.

The officer grasped his shoulders. "We need to go, what happens next is out of everyone's hands, do you understand me?"

Ben stiffened as if stuck in deep snow. "Yes the stairs."

Stairs seemed to be the easiest stairs he'd ever done. At the top, the officer flung the door open and they entered a waiting room. A doctor came running down the hall. "No…no…no."

The officer's shoulders slumped, and he turned to face Ben.

***

Ben leaned forward in a faux leather chair and looked at his silver Casio watch. The watch far from waterproof the crystal showed water damage from the summer, he had jumped into the Bitterroot River after Alice. 3:00am. The room lit low, machines beeped and glowed. He approached the bed, the figure on it motionless. "Alice." he whispered. "Do you hear me?"

He placed his hand on hers. She felt warm. One of her eyes bandaged, the other appeared swollen shut. The coach, returned after the ensuring team reached home. Ben could sense his stature next to him.

"I will be in the waiting room tonight, but if you need anything, let me know."

***

Ben spent the night in a chair holding Alice's hand. His heart quickened with a unknown clusters of beeps. The sun illuminated the room, and he moved to the window and peered through the shades. Red and orange clouded the sky over the mountains. It's Sunday. We should be home waking to the smell of bacon and eggs. Today was different; sleep was restless. His aunt from Oregon arrived an hour ago, had left to get something to eat. He looked at Alice, remembered all of those times in their life they fought over shit that didn't matter.

As morning segued into another night, Ben returned from the restroom. His aunt, nagged him the entire day to eat, he declined. He made his place at Alice's side, placed his hand around hers, put his head back in the chair and closed his eyes. "Fuck. I'm going to lose my sister, this is my fault."

He woke to the machines making a different sound, his hand stiffened, pressure from the grasp of another-Alice. Nurses appeared in the room, a doctor entered. They nudged him as they worked to bring Alice into consciousness. Within moments the doctor looked at Ben, the grip of her hand strengthened.

"She's going to be okay, can I talk to you outside?"

Whatever the doctor wanted to talk to him about had to be important. Ben shuffled outside; Alice was coming back to him slowly.

"Alice is going to be okay…right?" Ben asked.

"The swelling on her right eye will go down, the patch on the other will be removed in a couple of days, her throat will be dry, speech will be raspy. I'm not sure."

"I know." Ben replied.

"Would you rather someone else, maybe me or your aunt, tell Alice that her parents and the other gentleman, are dead?

There is no shame in that, no one would think lesser of you…I know it's been rough."

Rough. Rough was the word someone used when you placed your foot on a river or lake rock that was not yet smooth. *Rough* was the word people used when someone placed their hand over bark on a tree in the forest. Rough- was the word people used to describe Montana winters. This was more than that, this was an all-out nightmare. One, he would never wake from.

Chapter Five

With the state tournament a little over a week away, Alice had not spoken since she'd "woken" up. Every day Ben would hold her hand, in the morning and evening, each time the grip became intense. He had appeared at school, then decided he should be with Alice.

He started to fall asleep, the chair creaked with his movement, a foreign sound, a sound small, soft; a voice. Ben first thought it was a dream, yet the voice persisted. He stood, and looked at her. She turned her head to follow the squeeze of the hand. Her eye swollen and bandaged, the machine dictating pulse began to beep with quick responses.

"My…hand."

"Yes." Ben responded.

"Ben."

Ben leaned over to comfort her. "It's me Alice, you will be okay."

Alice's voice appeared in his ear.

"Can you get Devin for me please."

Ben's skin tightened.

"Please, Ben, I want to talk to him."

He closed his eyes as Alice struggled to form words and sentences. Wetness fell off of his check and onto her forehead.

"Ben?" She asked.

"Alice…Devin."

His sister was the most intelligent person he had ever known. Even though she couldn't see, her mind was intact.

"Ben…tell me." Her voice came out in a tiny squeak.

He didn't know how to say it, or when was a good time, but words poured forth. "Mom and Dad, Devin, they…"

Alice laid still for a moment, her mouth curled down, her cheeks turned red. "I don't believe you, I don't, it's your fault…your fault."

* * *

Three days before the trip to Billings Alice was discharged from the hospital. She hobbled on crutches with a broken leg, the only visible scar. Ben attended school enough to travel with the team. Between the two of them, complete silence soon formed. One decision that they made-to stay at a friend's house and not their childhood home.

"I never want to sleep there again," she told him multiple times.

Their aunt would stay there and, now Alice was out of the hospital, contact the lawyer and make arrangements for the funeral. She would take Alice to Billings for the tournament, talk to her advisors at Rocky-she needed to know about her grades for her classes.

Ben lay on the friend's couch and watched the nine p.m. edition of ESPN's Sportscenter. The front door opened and closed. Alice entered the living room, he had told her to sleep in the guest room, he would sleep on their couch. She hobbled

in, her green Rocky Mountain hat on backwards.

"Alice?" Ben asked.

"What?"

Ben rolled his eyes. "When can we talk again?"

Underneath her hat, a train of long hair once came under-now

there was none. "You cut your hair?"

She looked at him, her face pale, eyes slit with pain.

"What's it to you?" She traveled slowly down the

hallway.

"I, I just wanted..." Ben stared at the ceiling as sleep

evaded his mind. Thoughts about childhood, the last years and

moments. A piercing scream from Alice's room awoke his dreams of

the past.

Ben, startled, ran down the hallway and found her

sitting in bed.

"Alice, what is it?"

He placed a hand on her arm. She slapped it away.

"Motherfucker don't touch me."

"What? Alice it's me, Ben."

Alice screamed. "I know who you are."

A fist connected with his chest as he sat on the edge

of the bed. He deflected her punches with his arms. "Alice,

stop."

"You're the reason why I'm like this, Devin and our parents are dead. You should have been in the car too maybe things would be different if you did…get away from me."

"Alice that's not fair." He noticed two silhouettes in the door way-friends that were gracious enough to allow them to stay.

"You know what I wish," Alice asked.

Ben closed his eyes, body and mind tired of fighting. "What do you wish?"

"I wish, that some day, you will be in love with someone and they leave you, it will be your fault…just…like…this."

"You don't mean that."

Alice unleashed a pitch of voice Ben had never heard "I do, with everything I am now, I do and I will do anything to make that happen, I hate you, you should be dead."

One of the friends grabbed at his shoulder. He pulled himself away from Alice and ventured outside. He sat on the concrete steps that lead to the front door, and wept.

Chapter Six

Ben placed his head against the bus window, trees flashed by. He only traveled to Eastern Montana once. Inside he felt excited to view new vistas, people and places. Whispers persisted in town, how would he play? Was it a risk for him to play? Ben closed his eyes and saw only the pity in people's eyes.

Four hours passed, the bus left Bozeman and the mountains behind. As they did so, Ben noticed his relaxing. He could see where the Great Plains began. Wide swaths of land, dotted with yellow grass and plateaus. Clumps of trees signaled where rivers and streams flowed.

From the front of the bus, Coach stood up, placed the speaker handset to his mouth.

"We are about an hour from Billings, it's 1 p.m. So we will practice at Eastern and then eat, go to the motel, we all know our first game is tomorrow at noon."

Ben was confused, and looked to another player. "Where are we practicing?"

"Eastern Montana College."

"There's another college besides Rocky?"

"Yeah, you didn't know that, I mean doesn't."

Ben heard, maybe the quiver in his voice. "Yes, she does."

Chapter Seven

Ben placed the ball on the floor, on one knee he gave the laces on his high-top shoes a snug lift. The gym was empty-bleachers were pulled back, black and yellow colors toured the floor, Eastern Montana College colors. Ben looked around, not bad, bigger than his high school gym-yet didn't feel large. A slow breath exited his lips. It was time to stop the thought of moments, moments he had no control over.

All of the practices during the year seemed slow compared to today, other players as well as the coaches sensed an opportunity. This is what each city in Montana strived to do, go to state in any sport or activity. There was no doubt amongst everyone on the floor, that, tomorrow most of the town would be there-school was cancelled for two days-it gave inhabitants the time it took to drive to Billings, find a hotel and rest. Ben could feel practice for himself, was elusive the last weeks. He placed his hands on his knees to gather air at the end of a shooting drill.

A whistle blew, the team separated into three lines at the end of the court, coach instructed on what drill they would end practice on-the three man weave. The weave required speed, agility and communication to accomplish. Ben stepped up with his group, the door opened on the opposite side of the floor. Three women entered, dressed in black. He felt his lips move, the feelings of before practice, broke. It's time to have some fun.

Feet moved at an exhilarated rate, the ball moved back and worth as each player dove behind one that the ball went too. In the key, Ben cradled a pass, jumped, placed the ball on the glass, slapped the back board with the same hand. He landed on one foot then the other, his body rigid.

One of the women passed as Ben left the court. He noticed she wore an Eastern Montana Volleyball T-shirt, blonde hair...she was cute.

"HI." Ben felt his faced flushed.

"Hi." The blonde laughed. She disappeared through a door.

"Smooth." A teammate let him know.

"Yeah thanks, just wanted to see."

"You should have waited downstairs with us before practice, a redhead was lifting weights. Man she was killer. Long hair, tall, legs up to here. Damn."

Ben motioned to the door where the blonde had left. "I mean she was cute right?"

"I would do her."

Ben laughed. The coach blew the whistle, signaling practice was over. Time to go back to the hotel. Time to blot out memories that hurt.

★★★

The hotel smelled as any other carpeted floors with vacuumed lines. Cold air entered his lungs as he placed the bag on the bed he claimed. Luckily, coach paired him with a freshman manager-he would have the bed all to himself. The manager traveled into the room, placed his bags on the luggage rack, the light of the bathroom turned on and off.

"You okay?" Ben asked, as he examined the ceiling, lying on his back.

"Yeah I'm okay, just."

He had only seen the freshman in practice and around school, conversing, something they had not.

"Just what?" Ben questioned.

"My mom, always checks the bathroom, first thing as we get into a hotel."

Ben turned his head, to see the manager sit on the opposite bed, he looked tired and shocked.

"I know man, it's okay, it's okay." Ben felt his voice slowly quiver.

"But?"

"I saw that the hotel has an arcade, I'm going to give it a try."

"Nice." The manager exclaimed. "I brought my Super Nintendo if you want to hook it up."

Ben grabbed quarters from the wallet, changed into athletic shorts and a school t-shirt, "Now that, is awesome see when I get back."

Chapter Eight

The door closed, Ben journeyed to the lobby, took a left at the stairs and found himself in the "arcade." The "arcade" consisted of one game, *1943*. The game, an older arcade game-a World War II fighter tried to avoid other planes, and bosses. Familiar with the game, he recognized there was no end-you played until the quarters ran dry. *"Not what I was thinking of an arcade, oh well."* He placed six quarters vertically on the lower right corner of the screen. Ben felt the thunk of the quarter as it went in-the game was on.

A quarter, in the arcade world could have a lifespan of seconds. The first coin found this time marker, his plane exploded on the screen at fifteen seconds. "Shit". Another went in, thirty-seconds later, the plane annihilated in a hail of red bullets. The next quarter was the same. He closed his eyes, and slipped in another.

This time he found the rhythm, the plane darted around larger planes, collected power ups that sprayed the entire screen of bullets. A boss appeared, Ben guided his plane shooting turrets on the larger plane. His vision noticed a coin placed next to his, a second later a smaller plane on the screen came up from behind, impacted his plane and exploded.

The new coin signaled a new player wanted the next game. "Dude, not funny." He called this blindly, not knowing who owned the coin-He was confused when he saw the owner. A girl, shorter than him, dark hair placed in a ponytail. She smiled, which exposed a cluster of perfect teeth.

"You had it until the very end, that boss is tough." She said.

"I…I…I'm sorry, I didn't know."

"So you would have said something different if you knew I was a girl?"

"Well." He tried to find the right word, he knew this was a losing conversation. "Well, yes, I would have, maybe." He felt his eyes role, "*maybe*." What the fuck was that? *"Maybe?"*

"It's okay, can I play? Or am I going to watch you die again?"

"Funny, yeah you're up, I'll watch."

She began to play, immediately he noticed she was better than him, and better looking. He glanced at her, green painted fingernails, a green and yellow jacket with matching pants-she had a nice butt. He looked back at the screen, her plane made a move that he had tried but failed.

"Damn." He said.

"What the move or? I can see you in the screens reflection."

"Oh sorry...I mean."

Her plane exploded.

"You're good."

She turned, exposed her perfect teeth. "That's why I play *Nintendo*...well it was fun, got to go."

She passed and flicked her ponytail, hit him as she traveled up the stairs. The next game ended, Ben made his way to the room, *Who was that?* The key placed into the door and turned.

***

A basketball bounced on the floor of the Metra, Ben looked around, grey concrete built the arena, rows of red backed seats, more concrete separated the lower and bottom bowl. Black girders high above encased the ceiling. It was unlike anything had played on, holding 4,000 fans for basketball games. It was the largest venue in Montana, he was to be in the middle of it in an hour. His hand went to the floor, it was cold to the touch, perplexed Ben looked around, how could it be cold? A worker walked over to him.

"It's cold due to ice underneath."

"Ice?" Ben questioned.

"For the Bulls, the minor league hockey team."

Ben could feel his face move. "Excellent."

"They only play here, they practice in the Heights."

Having traveled to Billings once to see Alice he knew of the Heights-it was an extension of Billings, over the Rimrock Plateau.

"Good luck this weekend."

"Thanks."

His mind began to think, maybe this would be a better place for him than going to the University, the house he grew up in would be sold, over hearing his aunt insured that. It was okay, he thought, there was nothing for him there. The only obstacle was Alice-*did he really want to be this close to her?* There was no way that he wanted to attend Rocky, Eastern seemed more his style. School had always been just that for him-*school*. The thoughts of moving filled himself as his name was announced and echoed around the Metra, the state tournament had begun.

Chapter Nine

Halftime brought the team into the locker room, it was a quick half, they had made work of their opponents 40-16. Relieved at how the team continued to work as a team, Ben smiled-most of the year they were individuals, now a team. A knock on the door signaled the five minute warning-the second half, moments away.

Ben traveled to the court-he completed a lay up, a group of green and yellow jackets passed. His mind realized it was the same color the girl had worn the night before. In the middle of the color, he could see her. Today, her hair was in two braided pony tails-he continued to look at her, his concentration pierced by the second half horn.

He always liked to scan the crowd before the beginning of every game and half-to see who was there, who wasn't, and if he could smile at anyone, just for the fun of it. He remembered what his dad told him long ago, *"If you weren't having fun playing, then why play?"* His eyes scanned as he stretched, to the right of the opposing bench he noticed a figure in crutches, wearing Rocky Mountain College colors, it was Alice. Her hat on backwards, he thought she should have had a smile on her face, they were winning-yet her eyes were piercing. His hands cupped his knees, he looked over his left shoulder-noticed the girl from last night, a cheerleader, and began to stretch for the next game.

State tournament, he had heard of-yet never experienced, a time all to itself. The day between each game seemed to last longer than the season-the team shuttled between lunch, game and then dinner. Worried the next game would be a loss, the loser bracket begged for teams. Once a team found themselves in the bracket, they had no chance of winning the state championship-a true double elimination tournament would see a team make it through, this was different.

A sigh of relief exited his lungs as the last moments of the semi-final game ended. The game, close until the fourth quarter, had them pull away 82-68, clinching the first spot in the championship game. He turned to watch Alice-like the other two games watched, intently rooted for the other teams that played against him. He knew why, wished it could be different.

Ben wished he could talk to Alice and the parents he missed. That they could be here to watch their town be one game away from a state championship-the town had always whispered and wished for. In truth he, for the last two games had played just strong enough, just enough to win. After the congratulations on the bench from players and the two coaches, Ben moved past the baseline-with his teammates.

A sea of colored green and gold appeared in the seats above and along the baseline. He had tried to "see" the cheerleader the preceding day, after dinner he walked the halls of the hotel, maybe he could see her in a hall-at the vending machines, or somewhere. One lap, became two, which lead to five-in all he would finish ten laps around the hotel. At the arena however, he could and did see her, the baseline walk almost completed-she was there and looked at him. He could see by how her face reacted that she might be happy that it was him, or maybe it was his face that reacted. Ben passed her, braided ponytails perfect on each side, dark eyes, a bright smile. She winked, he felt his face become warm. It stayed warm, until the cool water in the shower washed it away-all of the players congratulated each other, one looked at Ben.

"Who was that?"

"Who?" Ben questioned.

"That cheerleader you walked by, she wants you."

"You're full of shit." Ben replied.

"No I'm serious."

"I don't know who she is, just met at the hotel."

He laughed. "You're fucking me right? Damn I need to walk around besides playing Nintendo. You know she's from Colstrip right?"

Ben knew that she was from Colstrip, the colors gave it away. A town east of Billings, a town where they mined coal. He had never been there, yet he had seen pictures of the machines that were used. They were quite possibly the biggest machines in the state. Why he was asked, and then it hit him.

"If Colstrip wins this game, we play them for State."

Chapter Ten

Fuddruckers rested across the road from the hotel-a favorite of the players-a hamburger could be topped with almost any imaginable condiment, paired on a buttery bun. A victory dinner for sure, made them forget the next night, a night that could change their school forever. Ben placed his tray, filled with a bacon cheeseburger and fries on the table. The television played ESPN, he watched as the days sports highlights were recounted. A bit of the burger was good indeed. Through the highlights and the burger he hadn't noticed someone had placed a tray next to his, moved a chair-and sat down.

He noticed as other teammates began to look at him, each after the accident, had given him his own space. This look was different, a look of curiosity. His eye followed theirs' and looked at who had sat down.

"Can I sit here?"

He felt his face again, get warm. "Yes. Where is the rest of your team?"

"Oh the coaches after we won ordered pizza, or we could come over here with an advisor."

"So you guys won." He noticed that she began cutting her cheeseburger with a knife and fork.

"Yes we did, it's awesome. We play you guys for State, it's going to be great."

"Yeah it is." He gathered his thoughts to ask a question. "I'm Ben, what's yours?" He had looked for a school jacket, there wasn't any.

She laughed. "I know you're a senior, and I know your name...but thanks for telling me. My parents would kill me if I..."

Ben felt himself blink. The word, parents, rustled his mind. He looked at her, words that came from her mouth were muted, she stopped. He had to say something, anything.

"I don't understand." Ben muttered.

"I said a senior and a sophomore don't mix in my parents eyes."

"Well the team looks like they are walking back." He took a breath, a sophomore? She couldn't tell me her name? What bullshit was that?

"Once last question, senior, I mean Ben."

"Go for it."

"Where are you going to school next year, I'm curious."

Sophomore would mean the next year she would be a junior and then the year after a senior. Maybe in college that would work, just maybe-however, the University of Montana was almost the entire state away from Colstrip.

"The University."

"I see...good luck tomorrow."

* * *

A clock, an object everyone notices during the day-each wondered how much longer to a specific aspect of their life, the end of the work day, to end class, even, how much time one has left on the planet. Ben eyed each clock, in the room, at the restaurant for lunch and dinner. How much time before the team traveled to the Metra, how much time it would take him to lace his shoes, how much time it would take him to think of Alice-time, how much to devote to his parents.

The team boarded the bus-time slowed, as if it knew what he wanted to do. To play and win-for himself, his parents, Alice. He sank into the bus seat, he saw her face in his mind, how much he wanted to talk to her...how much he wanted to tell her about a random cheerleader, how much he wanted to tell her that it wasn't his fault. The past weeks had seen him try, to no avail. Alice was going through more than he could imagine. True he had lost his parents, much the same as her-she witnessed their final moments, and lost someone she loved.

The parking lot was filled with cars, more than in the past two days, it would be packed for the state championship game. In the bus there was once laughter, as it turned the corner-the players noticed a Montana Highway patrol car lead them into their parking spot-all became quiet.

A locker room before a "regular" game, at times, a boisterous battlefield of hormones. Tonight, like on the bus, all were quiet and focused-this was the last game most would play competitively. Everyone could hear the crowd outside-Ben laced his shoes, the last piece of the uniform, and placed a towel over his face. Sweat rolled down his temples due to his nerves, something he had learned to control, but tonight were out of control. He breathed deep into the towel, exhaled and inhaled, his heart slowed-the locker room door opened with a thud. Coach was never known for long speeches and tonight was no different.

"All right boys, here we go, just play your best." He clapped his hands and led the team out of the room.

Chapter Eleven

The hallway separated the locker room and the court, dimly lit-the court at the end of the tunnel acted as a beacon. Ben took a breath, and another, light became brighter. His foot felt the edge of the playing surface and began to run. "Holy shit." The roar of the crowd could be felt inside the body. His hands grabbed a ball, felt the smoothness of the sides, began to dribble and looked around. It amazed him-the population of the entire state seemed to be in attendance. The bands played at a higher volume than normal.

Ben placed the ball on the glass of the backward, turned as the net swallowed it. He glanced down the court, there she was, the cheerleader and all business, school colors painted on her cheek- fuck why is she not older, I don't even know her name. Jitters seemed less with each shot, he looked up at the clock, hanging from the rafters, framed perfectly at center court-fifty seconds to go. The seconds ticked away, even if he wanted to slow time, it was impossible. The game, like life would start no matter if he was ready or not.

Coach gave the final pep talk, Ben walked onto the court, shook hands with the Colstrip players-positioned himself for the opening tip. A referee from the scorers table appeared with the game ball, Ben glanced over his shoulder, eyes fixed on the figure he looked for. Alice stood where she had been at the last game, her hat on backwards, wearing the usual Rocky Mountain attire, and her crutches. Unlike the last games someone stood with her, a blonde. He thought he recognized her from somewhere, he shook it off -the game ball tossed in the air.

Throughout the half when he concentrated the most, the crowd disappeared, not until timeouts or being subbed for, did he notice sounds from the crowd. Ben looked over to Alice with each shot made-her glance cold. When Colstrip scored she would take a hand off of a crutch and high five the woman that stood next to her. The score clock ticked to twenty seconds in the half, it's time to see if she truly hates me.

The ball passed to him as he passed half court-he sized up the defender- Ben crossed over, which left the defender flatfooted. His mind thought of the clock-the baby blue stripe of the three point line approached, the smoothness of the ball licked the fingers as it traveled toward the orange hoop. He began to backpedal, eyes not on the ball-yet on Alice. He could see her expression, her mouth moved, *motherfucker*. Ben turned away from her stare, whatever. The guard that assisted with the play chest bumped him as they left the court, with the team he walked by the Colstrip cheerleaders, he felt ashamed, he forgot to look for her.

Halftime ended in an instant. Ben placed his foot on the court and looked up at the scoreboard, they had the lead 48-39. Damn, didn't know we were up by that much! He dribbled a ball around the key, peered to see the cheerleader-their eyes met, a smile crept into the side of her mouth. He felt the same, let's get this game over so I can talk to you.

Colstrip stormed back and at various times had the lead. Time outs were called, Ben began to feel the power of the crowd that elected their favorite, Colstrip to win. He decided much of the crowd was pro Eastern Montana, no one cared about a school from the Western side of the state-no matter how good they were, or seemed to be.

Ten seconds-all that separated Ben, his teammates and his town from a state championship began to count down-the game was tied. Ben grabbed a loose ball-dribbled it, laid it up on the glass-he looked at Alice and raised his hand to shoulder level-fist pumped down the court. She returned his gesture with one of her own. A faint sound circled into his mind-a whistle, Colstrip had called a time out. The pitch of the crowd made conversing on the court difficult. His coach signaled for them to sit down.

"Okay, here we go.." His coach exclaimed, voice cracking. "This is what we have to do, attack the ball when they inbound, do not, I repeat do not foul. This is it, Ben hang back and watch for whoever gets the ball, again do not foul. Okay let's go, team on three."

Ben stood at half court, studied the crowd all-silent. He closed his eyes, his heart raced. Love you, mom, dad, I'm sorry Alice. He could see the ball being inbounded, a teammate slipped, the ball handler came closer, to his right-the mental clock disappeared. Shit. He jumped, swung his arm-felt the dimples of the ball graze a finger. He looked back-there is no way that fucking ball is going in, we are winning this game.

The roar of the crowd knocked him to his knees-the ball hit the backboard and went in. In a moment he could feel his eyes become moist, a tear hit the floor. He looked over to Alice-her hat flew off as she tried to jump. He felt his elbows and forearms touch the court, it was cold-against his body-tears became more, flowed faster. Ben felt pressure on his back, a voice in his ear.

"You couldn't have played any better, that was a lucky shot..."

Ben placed himself onto his knees to understand who spoke to him-it was the cheerleader. He got up and untucked his jersey.

"Thank you...but you should be with your team, you won."

She smiled, "I know, but I just wanted to say...well...hopefully I will see you at the University some day?"

His stomach tightened, a small chuckle erupted from him. Ben placed a finger around his eye. "Sorry."

The cheerleader stepped closer, "There's nothing to be sorry about. Damn it, I have to go."

Ben noticed her eyes, her smile, and he stepped closer. A hand came around the cheerleader and pulled her back. "Laurie let's go."

A crowd of students and players, swarmed around her-she was gone.

Chapter Twelve

A crystal table lamp glowed off the walls, illuminated the small bedroom. Ben gazed at the clock, the time in large white block numbers-1:00am. Two weeks had passed since the Championship game, still hadn't left his mind. The room reminded him of home, small, and a waterbed much like his, enveloped the room. He would be forever grateful to the friends, who had no children of their own, took him and Alice in.

Sleep, scarce since the game-a thought mulled his mind. It wasn't the shot that ended the game, Alice, or anything about what happened on the floor that kept him up. It was a girl, the cheerleader from Colstrip, that sparked his mind.

A month passed, he gathered his thoughts-how can I contact her? She was much younger, however at some point, they could meet in college...maybe someday.

Pieces of lined white paper-cradled on a brown writing board awaited the pen in hand. Ben, during study hall, ventured into the library and asked for the Montana High School Association encyclopedia-a listing of every Montana school address- Colstrip High School.

The pen dashed the paper, an essay this was not. Draft after draft, Ben studied and shot into the trash, maybe if I would have made one more shot we would have won. A long deep breath exited his nose, the decision was made, to write with his feelings.

Laurie,

It was nice to meet you, I am hoping this letter is okay with you. I don't really know how else to contact you. If you get this you can write back at any time. I have enclosed some stamps for you to write back, so you wouldn't have to ask your parents for them. I have been thinking of the University of Montana...maybe I should go to Eastern Montana College instead, to be closer to Colstrip. I am not saying that we are a couple or anything like that...but it would be nice to know that we could possibly see each other in Billings at some point, it would be easier than Missoula. I understand if you don't write back, but maybe you will.

Ben

The morning sun glinted off the silver mailbox, as the letter slipped away into darkness, he looked at the mountains, a thought came to him- two months to graduation.

***

Ben frequented the mailbox daily, a week passed, then two, a month-the mailbox was empty of letters.

He walked the halls of school slowly, students filtered around him. Ben placed himself in the assigned government seat and looked at the assignment on the board. His gaze turned to the students in the class-he talked to them, they talked to him, he felt he wanted to be somewhere else, most of his friends were admitted to the University of Montana. He raised his hand, the teacher acknowledge his gesture with a glance.

"Yes, Ben."

He noticed his voice was slow and unsure. "I would like to go to the career center please...need to check on...something."

The teacher hesitated, and then shook his head in agreement. "Of course, take your time."

The center cradled a selection of college course catalogs from around the region. Ben fingered through them until he found what he hoped was there, a book from Eastern Montana College. The application was in the middle, he completed it and mailed it.

Two weeks passed, maybe mail stopped at Bozeman and didn't travel to Eastern Montana. However absurd, the letter labeled Eastern Montana College arrived-the words "Welcome" began the letter. Relief entered into his lungs. There was only one person that needed to know.

***

Gym air was hot and humid, the feeling of sweat gathering and rolling into his armpits, crept into his mind. He looked into the crowd, many people he recognized, so many knew his life, so many he would never see again. He began a solitary and silent goodbye to each of them, Ben stopped at a face.

"Benjamin Arthur Meagher", the principal read his name with precision.

Ben looked at Alice's expression, a smile appeared, and she made a miniature clap. Her hair short, face red. An elbow belonging to a fellow senior found his ribs. The school career seemed too fast, elementary, middle, then finally, high school. Times he wished to be grown up, merely fantasy until now. Time to stop thinking you weren't an adult, now is the time to become one, now is the time to make decisions, decisions that could impact his life.

He found the chair, again looked at Alice, using a finger to press the corner of her eye. The last time they truly talked- Christmas break before their parents, and Devon were killed.

"You have Devon, college...everything."

"Ben...what do you want in your life. You can't play sports forever. You will need to choose a passion...do you have one? And no, girls don't count."

That was it sports were his passion. Math came natural, devoted to it? Not in the slightest.

***

Ben traveled through the lines of family members, each congratulating their seniors. In the middle of the group, he found Alice. Standing with Aunt and Uncle, she began to walk toward him. His mind raced of possible outcomes of the meeting, his body braced.

"Congratulations...you did it." Her voice smooth and soft.

His eyes looked into her eyes, they were dark. Fingers at his side twitched.

Alice spoke again, confidence echoed into his mind, not sadness. "Can we talk tonight?"

***

Light of the stars illuminated the football field-the coolness of early June encircled their short laden bodies. Bleachers creaked as they stepped, and again when they sat.

"How are you, haven't...haven't talked to you in awhile." Ben asked.

"I don't know what to say."

"I love you, you are my sister, you cheered against me at state Alice, what do you want?" Ben questioned.

"I want...us to talk again..."

"Why?" Ben thought of the ways he could be trapped in this conversation. "That cheerleader at state, do you know who she is?"

The question took his mind and body by surprise, he saw her eyes, hair and face. "Why should you care?"

"I guess, this was a bad idea, I just wanted to talk."

Ben closed his eyes. "Her name is Laurie and I haven't talked to her since that game, I even sent her a letter to Colstrip." He shrugged his shoulders. "I guess that was pretty stupid of me to do, how did you know about her?"

"I was at the game…remember?"

"The game you cheered against me?"

Ben noticed a pause from her hands flexed around her knees.

"I need to tell you something. I am seeing somebody to help me, with, what happened. I do not want to hate you. I'm sorry I, it's been really hard for me."

Ben noticed the glitter in her eyes and nodded. "I'm going to the University."

Alice protested. "What! You have to go to college."

Ben shook his head, he needed to stop the moment quickly.

"Alice, it's okay, I decided on Eastern and not the U."

"Eastern Washington?"

"No, not Eastern Washington why would I go there, Aunt and uncle don't live close, and you don't either. Eastern, Eastern Montana College."

"Oh my god, that is great, we can see each other sometimes, and I know people at Eastern, but."

"But?" Ben asked.

"I'm thinking if we ever need to get to our aunt, well it would be nice if we had new cars. Mine is so old, and yours is an 84'. I wonder if she would let us?"

He looked at her, a smile, the first in months appeared. "Let's ask."

Chapter Thirteen

Ben pulled into the dorm parking lot in his new 1993 Ford Ranger, Alice pulled up next to him in her new Jeep. Move in day-a hot August Saturday with temperatures racing into the nineties. At least they didn't have many things to place in Ben's dorm room. Ben got out of his truck and grabbed his suitcase, hockey bag, and a milk crate full of office supplies and toiletries. Eastern Montana College had two dorms. One was for upper classmen and was six stories tall. Ben's dorm was bigger, twelve stories, and housed a mixture of floors--coed, non-coed, upper classmen, and athletes. Ben already received a letter from the college with the name and contact information of his roommate. He tried calling a couple times, but was never successful. As he entered the building, Ben felt the energy of the students and their parents--freshman wanting to let go, their parents clinging to them.

Ben and Alice reached the foyer of the dorm and waited for the elevator. Alice smiled at her younger brother.

"What?" Ben noticed the dryness of her stare.

"I'm just looking at you, I'm seeing someone different than before."

"Well don't look too hard. Somebody might think we're doing each other." "Don't worry on that. Have you forgotten I've gone to school for the last four years just down the road?" "And?"

"And I know people who go here. Don't forget that." Alice ended the conversation with a smile and playful punch on his shoulder. She smiled at the sight of the elevator finally opening.

They were the first in the cramped, hot elevator. Ben wasn't sure if the air conditioning was broken or if this was freshman hazing at its finest. Ben pressed the sixth button before he and Alice were pushed to the back of the elevator by incoming students and parents. Most of the freshman who crammed in the elevator got off on the fourth floor. He'd heard the best way to flunk out of school was to live on the fourth floor. Ben needed as few distractions as possible. More students, all women, exited the hot and humid elevator, their perfume mixing with the hot air. The fifth floor was known as the nunnery--no men allowed. When the doors closed, six individuals remained. In a few short seconds, the doors opened on the sixth floor. Ben exhaled. From a sound system somewhere on the floor, Tag Teams' "Whoomp! There It Is" echoed off the brick walls, "What room are you?" Alice asked, almost laughing. Fourth was the floor of doom, but it didn't seem sixth would be much better.

"It's 633. We have to go to the RA's room to get the key." A sign hung in front of them with an arrow pointing down the hall. As they walked, Ben detected his bags weight with each step. Finally, ten doors down the hall, they reached the residential assistant's room. The role of the RA was to keep the floor in order and to guide the students from making huge fucked-up mistakes that could change their lives forever. Or to drink with them, which was *forbidden*. Then again, so was sleeping with residents. Ben knocked on the door, and it swung open. Derek, a junior, was physically fit to the extreme. He stood in the doorway with a car-salesman grin. Ben would later find out that Derek ran every morning and competed in marathons for fun. Derek joked that he ran so well because he was Native American, and they had been doing it since the sun had come over the horizon.

Ben slowly stuck out his hand, trying to seem confident. Derek returned the handshake with a powerful grip.

"I'm Ben."

"Very nice to meet you man," Derek said, reassuring Ben that everything was going to be okay, while also smiling at Alice.

"This is my sister, Alice. She goes to Rocky Mountain."

"Oh, outstanding. What are you majoring in over there?" Alice responded as quickly as she had been asked, "Avionics, I'll be graduating with my pilot's license soon." She smiled.

"That's awesome! I might have seen you around." Derek laughed and smiled. "It's possible." Returning to Ben, Derek began the crash course of college dorm rooms.

"Okay Ben, you're in room 633, which is across from this hallway-between the bathroom and the shower, take a left, and it's the second to last door on the right. Here's your key. Let me know if you need anything. Usually everyone comes out around eleven to watch Beavis and Butthead. Remember this hall is coed, and the washers and dryers are on the women's side." "Thank you, so much." Ben shook Derek's hand again, with a professional grip, and followed his directions. As Ben turned the key thoughts of his parents and Alice, maybe, appeared in his mind. One last face turned his thoughts as the key turned, Laurie. The opened door revealed a blast of stale air as it hit his face.

"Hmmm, I guess you don't have a roommate yet," Alice said. She punched him on the arm.

"Thanks for saying the obvious." Ben thought about punching her back, but he knew her second punch would be harder than the first. The dorm room was equipped with two single beds, a long desk, two closets, a sink, and a window that enveloped one wall. They stepped into the room and opened the window. The airflow helped the staleness, but it was too hot outside to leave the window open for long. "I guess I need a fan," Ben murmured.

"Yeah I think you do." They started to unpack; being careful not to place anything on the other side of the room, assuming a roommate might arrive at any time. The two left for the nearest Target, where they bought a fan, a six-pack of soda, and a small refrigerator. It was nearly six in the evening before everything was unpacked to Alice's satisfaction. "Hey, Ben, I think I'm going to go." "No problem, Sis. Thank you for everything. I really appreciate it."

"You're all I have, Ben. Of course I would help you. Call me if you need anything, and remember to stay around Billings the first night, okay?"

Ben blushed. "What, you think I'm going to drive somewhere?"

Alice raised an eyebrow. "Do I have to answer that?" She started to leave the room and stopped at the doorway.

"Alice, what is it?" "Ben?" "Yeah, Sis." "Mom and Dad would have been proud."

Ben had tried to forget what had happened seven months ago, but that hadn't happened, yet.

"You said you wouldn't do this." Alice walked out, and Ben closed and locked the door. He lay on the bed and fell asleep quickly--it had been a long day.

The next morning, Ben heard a slow, soft knock on his door. The sun was barely visible. He slowly got up and cracked the door, finding Derek peering back at him. Ben was surprised to see him, since they'd only met briefly the day before.

"Hey, I thought you might be up for a little run this morning?"

He brushed his eyes clear. "Yeah sure, that sounds great. Just a second."

Ben soon found himself outside the dorm and stretching in the shade of the cottonwood trees lining the interior of campus.

"Derek, so how far?"

"Today, I'm thinking about three miles. You up for that?"

Ben didn't know if he was or not, but he didn't want to look weak in front of his RA, "Yeah sounds good."

"Look man, I'll take it slow."

The run took them past a canal that flowed around the edge of campus, by the hospital, and up a road that led to the top of the plateau behind the college. When Derek finally stopped, Ben's lungs burned and his breath short. He placed his hands on his hips and closed his eyes. "Nice view, isn't it?"

Ben had been so concentrated on staying conscious during the run, he hadn't noticed where they were.

"Wow, yes." He gazed at the view from the sandstone cliffs that lined the plateaus encircling the city. Like most of the Montana's cities, Billings was situated in a valley made of rolling hills and sandstone plateaus. The bodies and peaks of mountains were visible on the horizon.

"So Ben, do you want to be single?"

He didn't know what to say or if Derek was imparting college knowledge.

"No, I want a girlfriend, maybe, it's just she's younger."

Smiling, Derek replied, "Still in high school? This is college and no, not that. Do you want a single room? Your roommate isn't coming."

Ben felt embarrassment sting him. He shouldn't have to ask Alice for approval. "Yeah, I think that would be nice. If it's going to cost more, need to ask my sister. She handles our money." They began a slow descent down the road to the campus below.

"So your sister and you are the only ones?"

"We are. My parents were killed in a wreck this past winter."

"I'm sorry, Ben. I only have a dad. My mom passed a couple of years ago, cancer. So I can understand a little."

"Thanks, it hasn't been easy."

They were almost back to the dorm, the sun now radiating its heat. Derek changed the subject.

"A word of advice?"

"Of course."

The pair stopped. Ben glanced at Derek, then to the path they had taken.

"Take everything slow. Do your work in class first, before anything else. Professors do their jobs. I don't want you to flunk out at semester. You seem smart, and your sister seems very smart."

Ben thought for a moment. "A word of advice?"

Derek was taken aback, "Sure."

"Alice, she looks nice and plays nice, but sometimes she's not who you think she is."

Derek nodded. "Aren't we all?" Ben looked up at the brick side of the dorm, reaching to the sky. "True. Breakfast?" They ate breakfast in the dorm and parted ways for the day.

Chapter Fourteen

Aine strode out of her educational philosophy class-- already boring her on the second day of class-she needed this class to graduate. For the end of August, the sun flickered hot on her pale skin. She picked up speed and reminded herself, that the everyday workout with the volleyball team was forty minutes from now. Aine always liked showing early. It cleared her mind of the extraneous noises of college and life. She noticed a smaller blond woman, dressed much like herself--black sweatpants and a t-shirt--patiently waiting for her in the middle of campus. Aine slowed.

"Hi, Amanda."

"Nice accent today. You sound Irish. Are you getting taller?"

"I wonder why I sound like that? I'm not sure, little one, I haven't measured myself today."

"Watch who you call little. I'm a junior, and what are you?"

They spoke in unison. *"Sophomore."*

Aine had always reveled in bantering with Amanda. Aine was a true sophomore volleyball captain. The team respected her, even though she wasn't from Montana, or even North America. Amanda stopped.

Aine eyed her. "Amanda?"

"You see that kid--boy--man--over there?" Aine's gaze followed Amanda's gestures.

"I see someone who looks lost?"

Amanda grinned. "I'm sure it's a freshman, he looks like a beached whale. Not that he's fat, just-- Should we help?"

Aine sighed and looked the boy over. "He's a freshman. They all figure it out. Did anyone help me?"

"Yeah, I did."

Aine looked down at Amanda. She was losing patience, glaring at Amanda with her dark green eyes, and she let Amanda know with her thick Irish accent. "We have a workout to do."

The pair ventured into the weight room and started their workout. They loaded the bar for a warm up set, and Amanda stepped behind the bench to spot Aine's presses. The moment Aine lifted the bar off the rack, Amanda asked, "Do you think he's cute?"

Aine exhaled and locked out the rep. They were silent for the next ten repetitions. Amanda grabbed the bar and guided it onto the rack. She breathed deeply and sat up.

"Who?"

"Freshman, that boy, whoever he was. Do you think he's cute?"

Aine exhaled again. "I guess, I don't know. Why?"

Amanda stepped around the bench. "I think I'm going to find him, maybe, maybe ask him out?"

Aine watched her reflection in the mirrored walls, her fiery green eyes, her molten face. For a moment, her gaze ran across her red hair. "You can do whatever you want. I need to lift heavy today."

When their workout sessions ended, Aine went to her room, throwing herself onto her bed. Her room was large, the biggest style the college had to offer, and it was all hers. She liked living alone--she never had to ask a roommate if she could stay up late to finish homework or paint her nails. She pulled out an education textbook and grimaced. She wasn't in the studying mindset. She closed the book and grabbed her swimming cap, goggles, and swimsuit.

As she entered the pool area, Aine observed the usual scant gathering of swimmers, which was more than acceptable to her. She wanted to get away from people and, more importantly,

Amanda. They had been friends since Aine's freshman year, but the morning had unnerved her. Amanda was dedicated to men, the team, and school, in that order. Aine had never seen her without a boyfriend or someone she was dating. She picked the far lane of the olympic-sized pool and crawled in, the cold water stinging her body. Aine closed her eyes and told herself to forget everything that had happened during the day. She had always loved the freestyle stroke, where her long, muscular body made it easier for her to glide through the water. The breast stroke, on the other hand, made her work harder. As she emptied the water from her goggles and blew small bubbles in the water, her muscles began to feel fatigued from the lifting session. She glanced across the water at a well-muscled boy getting into the pool. She felt water in her ears and titled her head, making sure none of her red hair was showing. After one more lap Aine climbed out of the pool. As she turned the shower on, water cascading down her suited body. She pulled off her cap, and long, red hair drifted down her back as the shower wall received her hands.

I can't do this.

Water flowed over her head, her thick hair becoming heavy as her emotions. Aine took some time gathering them. She departed the showers, traveled back to her room and picked up the push button phone, reaching for a phone card. After a few moments, seeming to last an eternity, her mom answered.

"Mum, I know it's three in the morning for you, but I need to talk. Please."

* * *

Ben had a long day. College classes were interesting, but you didn't have to go if you didn't want to. He noticed that some students just didn't want to. Every class he took notes, even if others didn't, and would study his notes whenever he had time. Day turned into night. The floor had been loud, the early September air stifling. The air conditioning hadn't been working well so he decided to go to the pool. He had found it during his first day on campus. The pool was quiet, with very few swimmers. Diving into the cold water, he felt at ease--his mind was flooded with memories of summers at Flathead Lake, its waters fed by ancient glaciers. The lake was as cold as it was deep, yet he'd always relished days with his parents in their cabin. After two laps, Ben paused and noticed long feet complete with black nail polish, and the long legs sprouting from them. He could only see her back, but Ben noticed her athletic body, curvy build, and a single strand of red hair escaping her cap. He didn't have a cap or goggles. When the pool began to sting his eyes, he decided to get out. Ben went back to his room, studied for a few minutes, then ventured over to Derek's room.

"You wanting to watch something?" Derek asked.

 Ben nodded. "Sure."

"You okay?"

"Yeah, I'm okay."

Chapter Fifteen

The coaching-volleyball class met every Wednesday morning from 7:30-9:30 in the athletic complex. The tall, old volleyball coach taught the class. For the first two weeks of class, they met in a classroom. Today was their first day in the gymnasium. For a small college, Eastern Montana's athletic complex was huge--two gymnasiums, racquetball courts, weight rooms, and a pool. The class straggled in, some yawning. None seemed to have showered--it was too early. Eastern Montana College was a small, Division II school, and allowed the women's volleyball team to practice during the class. In the middle of the floor, the team was setting up the net. They uncovered the holes at center court and slid the two steel poles into them. The net was up quickly and was ready for play.

The coach finally blew the whistle, and the team warmed up with soft hits and passes. The volleyball coach gathered the class on the baseline and gave instructions. The class divided into pairs and passed to each other on the sides of the court.

In theory, a volleyball pass was easy. In practice, it was more difficult. The coach gave them cues--knees bent, arms out, hands palm-on-palm, shoulders shrugged. This stance exposed the flat part of each forearm. "Later on this semester," the coach said, "each bad pass will cost you a lap, but for today we will do it until I'm satisfied that you can do it." Ben swore he must have been in the military.

What have I gotten myself into? Ben had learned, from watching volleyball and from dating some of Alice's friends who had played in high school, that volleyball can be as complex as any other sport. You just have to be good at it.

The pairs began the passing drill. A moment later, Ben looked up and immediately stopped passing. He had heard what sounded like a battlefield cannon, a thunderous boom, followed by a grunt and silence. The setter set, and then a hitter smashed the ball down with so much force it struck the floor like a bomb. As he watched, a red ponytail swayed back in forth as she glided along the floor. Her muscles in complete harmony as she struck the ball with elegant and brutal force. She looked like a caged tiger, stalking its prey and then striking. Unlike the other hitters, who stopped after one hit, she hit, ran back, and repeated five in a row, releasing a muffled grunt with each hit. Ben was in awe.

He wasn't the only one watching. The hitter held the entire class's attention. The coach blew a whistle, and everyone turned. "You all did well today. Who would like to practice what they have learned?" No one made a sound.

Ben had never cared what others thought of him. In high school, he'd made friends with everyone--smokers, jocks, geeks, and everyone in-between. He stepped forward and raised his hand.

"What's your name?" the coach asked.

"It's Ben, sir." "Excellent." The coach nodded and directed him to half court.

"Okay, so you are going over to the passing side. Stand where that passer is standing, get into position with your tripod, and then return a hit." Ben replied, "Okay, I might be able to do that." The coach smiled dryly. "Sometimes passers and hitters work as a team during practice to get better. Who would you want as your hitter?" Ben stuttered his answer. "The tall, red-haired--person, sir." "Are you sure?" He asked.

"Yes, sir," Ben said with a smile

The coach growled at Ben, "Then get over there, and be ready please."

"All right class, we will see a hitter hit to a passer and the passer return the hit." He turned to the redhead. "Captain, are we ready?"

She looked back at the coach, her perplexed expression slowly fading into a smile. She pulled her ponytail tighter, slid her mouth guard into her mouth with her tongue, and nodded.

Captain. Ben looked up at the ceiling and whispered to himself, "Am I going to die?" The coach gave Ben a thumbs up, and he returned it. They looked like they were at a funeral, and he was a family member of the deceased.

A player tossed the ball to the setter, who set it perfectly. The captain took her steps and jumped. Everything moved slowly. Her tight ponytail swayed to the left, then to the right, and finally up over her head. Ben forgot to watch the ball as he followed the orbit of her ponytail. The ball slammed against his shoulder and lit it on fire. The coach yelled, "I forgot to tell everyone, my mistake, if the ball is over your waist in that position, it is going to be out so get the hell out of the way." Ben wondered why the coach was trying to make him feel comfortable. Ben kept his feet in the same position, but stood taller and rotated his shoulders. *Damn, my shoulder is killing me.* "Are you ready?" the coach asked. Ben nodded. This time, he watched the ball instead of her hair. The volleyball rocketed off his forearms and over the net. Ben's mouth dropped open. The class gasped and gave him a golf clap. "One more?" the coach asked.

Ben nodded and gave him another thumbs up.

The redhead nodded and held two fingers together. Ben didn't know what that meant, but he noticed the setter back setting the ball, before the captain swung around toward center court. Then the ball was hurtling toward him, glancing off the side of his face, and knocking him down. He lay on his back for a moment, then rolled onto his chest, elbows on the ground, knees tucked beneath him. He felt a hand on his back.

"Are you okay? Your name's Ben, right?" Ben gasped and struggled for words. "Yeah, I'm okay. I'm going to get up in a second."

The hand patted his shoulder, and its owner whispered, "I'm Amanda, a player. She didn't have to do that to you."

"No, it's okay. I'm an idiot, should have got the fuck out of the way."

"You're gonna need some ice." Amanda signaled to the coach that Ben was all right, and the coach addressed the class. "Okay everyone, I think we've had enough for this week. I will see all of you next week. Remember to do your two-page paper on what we did today."

Ben stood up headed toward the foyer. Passing students gave him pats on the back, asking if he was okay. He nodded and responded generically--*thanks, I'm okay*. Just before leaving the gym, he noticed blond Amanda carrying a bag of ice.

"You're okay, right?"

"Yeah, I'm fine. Probably a little headache and a bruise. Thank you."

"Here's a bag of ice, Ben. I'll see you around, and again I'm sorry."

"It's okay, really." Ben smiled

Amanda was cute, but as he left the athletic complex, *Who the fuck is the captain? And is she single?*

Chapter Sixteen

Ben heard a knock on the door of his dorm room. He was still nursing a headache from the volleyball smashing into his skull this morning. As he'd ventured through campus for the day's classes, he could swear everyone knew what had happened. He opened the door and found Amanda on the other side.

Since practice, she had changed into a black and gold university tee and beige shorts, and her hair was in two perfectly equal braids. Ben stumbled over his words. "Amanda, right. You helped me after I got my ass kicked this morning."

"Well, you didn't get your ass kicked. Unless your ass isn't where it should be."

Ben noticed Amanda peer around him for a glimpse inside his room.

"Oh, come in. Please, sorry. First girl, I mean woman, to be in here." "Don't worry, I don't do anything with freshman guys."

"Oh, okay." He was being stupid, but Amanda was cute. She sat down on the first bed, where his roommate would sleep, if he had one. Ben closed the door and crossed the room, sitting opposite her in a college-issued plastic chair.

"Nice room, Ben. It's so homey." Amanda smiled. Her teeth were perfect. "Thanks. It's okay, I guess."

"I was just joking with you. It's not that great of a room. You need to do something with it."

"Like what?" "Well, for starters, this bed. Either send it to storage or combine it with your mattress to make one big bed. The room would be nicer with a bigger bed or more space, either one." Ben nodded. "The walls are, well, too white. Put up some posters or something. Remember, your room is an extension of you." Amanda stood up and reached for the door, then paused.

"Candles are against dorm room policy," she said, "but they smell nice, and sorry but you boys smell all the time. There are seven more things you need to know. First, about the captain. Her name is *Awn-ya*. Spelled A-I-N-E. Two. She's from Ireland, although she won't say where. Irritating. Three. She's a raging bitch. Four. She's a sophomore. Five. Stay away. Six.

She lives in the big dorm room on the top floor. And seven? Movie. You and me on Friday night, okay?"

Amanda swung the door open and left, waving to him before disappearing down the stairwell.

Ben didn't know what to think. Was college always this crazy? He heard Kyle screaming down the hall. When Ben went to check on him, Kyle shouted, "Just scored a hundred and twenty points on Tecmo Bowl!" College was not what Ben had expected, and he kind of liked it.

***

Friday night arrived in a flash. Amanda met Ben on his floor, and they rode the elevator down to the foyer.

"You know where we are going, right Amanda?"

She stepped closer to him. "Yeah, It's on Broadwater Ave. The dollar theater."

"That's right, yeah I think I can get us there."

"We're going to see Disney's *Aladdin*. I mean, if that's okay?"

She flashed her dark brown eyes in his direction.

"Yeah, that sounds great. I haven't seen it."

"I think your one of the few that hasn't."

The door to the elevator opened, and they exited onto the first floor.

"Hi, Amanda." Amanda took a breath and spit out her words quickly. "Aine, Hi." She glanced at Ben. "I'm sorry. Aine, I'm sure you remember Ben. Ben, this is Aine."

Ben extended his hand, trying to be a gentleman. Aine smiled slowly and shook his hand. She smoothed her ponytail with her long fingers. Ben watched her thick, black fingernail polish against her red hair. Aine crossed her arms over her chest.

"I hope you have a good time. The team will probably be watching "The Last of the Mohicans" later, if you and Ben want to join."

"We might. I'll see you later, Aine."

Ben nodded. "It was nice to meet you, Aine." Aine smiled slightly and headed toward the stairs.

★★★

Ben was enjoying the movie. He looked at Amanda, and she looked back before placing her hand on his and her head on his shoulder. He continued to watch her.

"What?" Amanda whispered.

Ben shook his head. How cute she actually was, bordering on beautiful. Yet he thought of someone else the rest of the movie.

When the movie ended and they exited the theater, Ben saw a familiar face.

"Alice?"

"Ben, wow, it's been a crazy couple of weeks. How are classes?"

"Well classes are fine. They were strange to begin with. Not like high school, you know."

Alice nodded. "Uh huh. And? Who are you with?" Alice scanned the crowd, but Amanda found her first.

"Alice?"

"Amanda? You're here with my brother?"

Amanda stood alongside Ben and brushed his hand with hers.

"This is your brother? You never told me he was this cute." Ben glanced back and forth between them, finally glaring at his sister.

"You and Amanda know each other? You never told anyone about me?"

Alice laughed. "Well, no not really. And I told you I knew people. Amanda and I have known each other for a while."

Amanda started to turn pale. "Alice, I'm so sorry for what happened. I know we haven't talked in a while." Alice's eyes darkened and turned sluggish. Ben changed the subject.

"So who are you here with?"

"Friends, but I should go. I will talk to both of you later, okay?"

* * *

When they returned to the dorm, Ben and Amanda stopped in front of the elevator.

Amanda toyed with her key. "You want to come up and watch the movie?"

"That is a welcome offer...I think I'll go to my room. Seeing Alice, I just feel like being alone. I'm sorry."

Amanda nodded. "I haven't lost my parents or anyone I really loved. It has to be hard for both of you. It's okay, we have the entire year." Amanda kissed his cheek and started toward the stairs. Ben took the elevator.

Chapter Seventeen

His eyes noticed the elevator light not moving past the third floor on one bank, and the other seemed to be stuck on five. His right hand rubbed his eye, a 4 p.m. class of world history had most of the class staying to talk to the professor. The others found the liberal art buildings stairs, but Ben had decided to think about the lecture and wait for the elevator. His thoughts raced to the last time he waited for an elevator. The door opened with a loud bang, he felt himself jump. He thought of moving into the elevator, two large carts held televisions and had blocked his way. A woman darted around the opened elevator door-began pulling a cart out.

"Oh hello." The woman, startled looked at Ben.

"Hi, do you need some help?"

She paused; he noticed her eyes covered his body.

"Sure, always love help, grab the other cart and follow me."

Ben felt his hands around the metal poles that made up a side of the cart and pulled, heavier than he thought and more cumbersome. The wheels, needed to be coaxed to move, a shove, rocked the wheels back and forth, finally the cart was clear of the elevator-pulling the cart, Ben caught up with the woman.

"Over in that room, here's the ticket, place it on the VCR when you wheel it into the front of the room."

He looked over the ticket, room number, name of the professor requesting it and for how long. The room was dark as he entered, his finger felt for the light switch to the right of the door. The room quiet and peaceful, a squeak from the wheels signaled it needed lubrication.

"Right there, next to the podium." The voice came from the opened door-the woman had placed her cart in a room and had come back for him. The cart positioned as she requested. Ben exited the room, in the hallway-two more carts.

"Do you need help with these?" Ben asked.

"You definitely like to help." She looked at the carts and then back at him, "Why not."

The elevator stopped at the bottom floor of the building, the doors pulled open. Ben pulled out a cart and she did the same. As he exited the elevator he noticed the basement wasn't a basement at all, at least not in the form that he thought of. It was a grey painted concrete wall to the left-to the right, framed in soft yellow light, an art gallery. It felt organic and quite soft.

"Never knew this was here."

Wheels continually rattled as the carts traveled down the hallway.

"Art museum, really cool, this is a place to get away, just relax."

"Need to come down here more."

The woman stooped and looked at him. "You want to work, wheel carts all over the campus, it's fun really, during the summer and fall it's great, winter sometimes it's a pain."

Ben confused at the new thought-"Work study?" "I didn't qualify."

"Let's put these away and talk to the boss."

The "boss" was an older man, much taller than Ben, he seemed soft and gentle, yet his eyes commanded respect.

"Could use you a couple hours a day, nothing more or less, welcome aboard." His long slender hand, placed out. Ben reacted slowly and did the same. "Just don't fuck up." The boss filled the room with a thunderous laugh.

***

Friday, September 23rd 1993, emblazoned across the Billings Gazette sports page. A ticketless morning had greeted Ben on his 8 a.m. shift. The front page, just news, the sports page appeared, eyes began studying the headlines. He remembered a year ago when his name was in a paper. He brushed off the thought, a long time ago it seemed the upcoming games had their own box. His mouth moved with each matchup for the night. *Billings West vs. Skyview, Stevensville vs. Libby.* He stopped and read the next game. *"Colstrip vs. Laurel."* A mind blister popped, emotions from months ago erupted. He could see her face, her smile and hair. *Laurie, I have to go.*

The afternoon was slow and methodical-classes and time stopped. He played the meeting with Laurie in his mind hundreds of times. *Should I go? Should I not go? Will she even care if I am there? What will I say to her?* The last class ended, Ben traveled back to the dorm. The floor was full of activity-a Friday night, had begun. Ben walked down the hallway and looked into a room, continued and stopped. "Welcome to the Jungle", blared from the boom box, but when the owner noticed Ben he pressed stop.

"What's up?"

"Not much man, I'm Ben by the way, I live on the other side."

"Sweet, I'm Kyle."

Ben hadn't stopped for the music, it wasn't his favorite, yet the grey console by the TV was a Super Nintendo, and by the looks of the room, the Dallas Cowboys were his favorite team, and that meant video game football. "You play Tecmo?"

Kyle's mouth curled into a smile, "Fuck yeah, love it, want to play?"

"You want to go to a high school game after?"

"Sure, always like to get out."

***

Ben took a right on the interstate, pressed down on the accelerator. The pickup found it's rhythm, the new engine picked up interstate speed. Warm for September, the windows rolled down to let the air consume the cab. He noticed Kyle look over.

"So why exactly Laurel?"

The question made Ben uneasy. Should he tell him the truth or make some story up about loving high school football, decided to see what he really wanted to know.

"The truth?"

He noticed Kyle nodded his head slowly.

"Well yeah."

MRM / Opened Sky / 75

If the cab was any bigger, Ben could make up a plausible answer and Kyle would hear the "*truth*." He liked Kyle, seemed a good person and wanted to let him know the past.

"So last March I met someone."

"Okay, so what does that have to do with a high school… oh." "Oh I got it, she's still in high school."

Ben felt ashamed for telling the truth. "She's a cheerleader, for Colstrip."

"Wow! I would have never guessed any of this, I mean it isn't something I woke up today and said, I'm going to go to a football game, a high school football game non the less. Not because I wanted to, I mean I want to, but with you because you met a cheerleader from Colstrip, in March, this is crazy."

The rant made Ben laugh, the truck coasted to the stop sign off the interstate. "I met her at the basketball state tournament, I have tried to forget about her, just can't."

"That's cool, no judging man, if it's meant to be, it's meant to be. I mean in like twenty-years, you will be thirty-nine and she will be thirty-six, thirty-seven maybe, what's her name anyways?"

"Laurie, her name is Laurie."

***

"Where do you want to sit? The Colstrip side or the Laurel side?" Kyle asked as they paid and began walking toward the field. The sounds and smells brought back memories of last year. It was only last year that his parents were still alive, Alice was a sister he could talk to, it felt like a century had passed.

"A stalker I am not, maybe just walk around the twenty." He noticed the field-roped off from forty-five yard line to the opposite forty-five.

"Okay, I'm cool with that, love football but never played."

Traveling around the closest end zone, Bens' mind told him this could have been a colossal mistake, or one of the greatest thoughts he had. They crossed the twenty-year line, Ben stopped. There she was, ten yards away. She was stretching with the other cheerleaders-her hair exactly as he remembered.

"You okay?" Kyle asked.

"That's her."

The game became fast and intense. Ben noticed both teams were well balanced, the fans as loud as he remembered. Ben watched Laurie for most of the night, being careful not to catch her gaze.

"Dude Colstrip has the ball on the two with two seconds left. We should go to more high school games, this is pretty exciting."

"I think that was him." Ben felt his voice tighten.

"What?" Kyle questioned.

Colstrip, called a time out-the quarterback had taken off his helmet.

"That's the same player that made the half court shot over me."

The teams lined up to snap the ball; Kyle placed his hand on Bens' shoulder. "Well at least you can talk."

Colstrip snapped the ball, the quarterback plunged into the end zone, the game ended. *This is it, time to see Laurie and what could come of it, if anything.* "Dude?" Kyle's hand still on his shoulder. When the team came over to the sidelines, Laurie and the quarterback embraced.

The ride to the dorms, quick and silent. Ben placed his finger on the controls of the elevator.

"Sorry man, if you want to talk or anything."

Ben looked at Kyle, it seemed that the night had given him something, a true friend-yet had taken, Laurie away.

"I think I would like to be alone for a bit, thanks man."

Each floor had a balcony, looking over the campus and the sandstone plateaus in the distance. The air was chilly, but humid- a calm September night. Ben rested his hands on the railing and looked out toward the city. Laurie and his sister were out there, somewhere. Laurie was on a bus back to Colstrip.

If he only he could have talked to her-why didn't I say
something? Maybe it wasn't what it seemed, maybe. He blocked it
out of his head. I need to forget about her, obviously she
forgot about me. The mind told him that wasn't fair to her or
him, *how would she know that he came to Eastern? How would she
know that he would be there tonight?* He could see every building
and the campus walkways wide enough for snowplows. A sound of
rustled curtains came from behind, his mind still focused on
Laurie, the view. Ben noticed the tightness of the railing, so
someone was with him.

The light of the night exposed a slender finger, tipped
with black nail polish rested on grey railing. Ben looked up,
his throat tightened.

"Hi." He felt his voice stutter and soften.

Red hair pulled into a ponytail cascaded down the back of
the individual. Black shorts, accompanied flip-flops and a tank
top.

"Is this a bad time?" The figure asked.

"I don't think we have ever really met, except for the
ball that hit my shoulder, you are Annya?"

He noticed she laughed at the remark, exposed a smile-his
palms began to melt into the steel. The night air became warm.

"Awn-ya, don't worry, you did okay."

Nodding his head, Ben looked out over the landscape. "It's a really nice view."

"I've always liked it. The first time I saw Montana, it was on a night like this, clear and warm."

He struggled to understand certain words because of her accent, but he loved listening to her. She was so different from anyone he knew. "So how was the movie you watched that night?" he asked.

"I didn't watch."

"Oh, you were going to. Sorry."

"Amanda was upset, After we talked, I just went back to my room."

Ben eyed the railing. "I didn't mean to upset her."

Aine nodded. "She will get over it, always does."

Ben reacted like he always did in uncomfortable situations, by asking questions.

"You're from Ireland?"

Aine placed her elbows on the railing and leaned over. "I am, how could you tell?"

In thinking for moment he began to respond. "Well."

Aine gave a quick laugh. "I'm joking you, my accent, but, I'm sorry I hit you with the ball, I didn't intend to hurt you, just wanted some fun I guess."

It was more than that. He had played hockey, football, and baseball in high school. He knew all about the fear of showing weakness, but he had never been on the bad side of a display of strength. Ben tried to pay attention to her words instead of her body, flip-flops, black shorts, tee shirt, and her, red ponytail. "I just needed to duck, I guess. What year are you?"

Her green eyes watched him. In the bright moonlight, he could see a line of freckles dotting the bridge of her nose.

Aine's eyes narrowed, a slow smile came into view. "A sophomore, what year did you think?"

His throat became dry and tightened, a lump grew. "I thought... Truthfully, I didn't know." Ending his sentence, he felt his eyes role. "I just blew this."

Again a smile crept onto her face. "It's okay." A nervous laugh entered the conversation. "I'm busy with school and the season, what would you think about doing things some time?"

Ben stuttered, not anticipating what she had asked. "That sounds fine I guess." His mind examined each word out of his mouth, *Fine? Seriously fine?* In a rush, trying to relax. "That's great, I mean more than fine."

She pushed away from the railing, turned back to him and smiled.

"See you around?"

"Yeah, around."

Aine disappeared into the dorm, leaving Ben in the warm air, I'm sorry Laurie, he whispered, his hand went to his shoulder where the volleyball had slammed into his shoulder.

Chapter Eighteen

He looked at the clock, 6 a.m. *I need to get up, class is at 7.* Staring at the white fake ceiling tiles that every dorm room on campus had, he went over the early morning happenings in his head. *Did that really happen? Is she probably the most interesting girl, I mean woman I have ever met. And her body, athletic, tall, perfect. I'm going to blow this.*

A quick shower lead to hurriedly moving down the stairs to meet Kyle. A daily ritual had started to happen, they would meet to walk to math class, and suffer through a long class. Both found seats side by side in order to chat.

"Dude," Kyle whispered.

"What?"

"Let's count how many times in ten minutes he says the word *what.*"

Ben laughed quietly. "Okay."

The professor was from India and ended every other sentence with *what*. In ten minutes, both of their papers were covered in tick marks.

"Time," Kyle said.

They each counted silently, trying not to laugh.

"Kyle, I have seventy-four."

"What, I have seventy-five. You missed one."

"Whatever."

The next topic was lunch. Each day they took turns making a sheet of places to eat and the pros and cons of each choice. *McDonald's not the greatest tasting, but cheap, Wendy's: tastes good, but more expensive. Taco Bell: well, it's Taco Bell.* They shuffled the note back and forth, ranking each spot. The cafeteria never made the list, but for some reason Kyle added it today. Ben nodded. "Campus, why not?"

"Sounds good," Kyle said. "Dude?"

"What?"

"That's ninety, *whats*, by the way. You stopped counting."

Ben shook his head. Kyle kept him on his toes, anyway.

***

Lunchtime was consistently busy, and the food was consistently decent. Ben and Kyle grabbed food and found a table. Ben attacked his pizza, and Kyle took a giant bite out of his mushroom and Swiss burger.

"Can I sit here?" Amanda's smooth voice asked.

"Yes, you can," Ben said. "Kyle, this is Amanda. Amanda, Kyle."

Amanda nodded, but she didn't take her eyes off Ben.

"How's your day going, Ben?"

"Okay, I guess." He used his fork to peel the toppings off his pizza and gnawed at the crust. "Had math, not very exciting. Just talked and thought about food."

"Well, that's interesting."

"What is?"

"What you just did to that pizza."

"Kind of strange I know," Kyle said.

"Would you like to do something tonight, Ben?"

Kyle punched Ben's leg under the table.

"I'm not sure. I will let you know if I'm not busy."

"Okay."

Ben's heart fluttered when he noticed Aine walking into the cafeteria. Her hair fell to one side, and her smile made him want to talk to her. He felt embarrassed, and placed his head down to look at his plate. He didn't know how to play the college game, of who likes who and how you deal with it. Something he could ask someone about with more experience, his RA would be a good person to start with. Amanda, was out of the question to ask. He liked Aine, without a doubt, but how did she feel?

***

Night cooled campus. Fall was in the air, but it would be a few weeks before leaves fell from the trees. The floor had just watched a "Beavis and Butt-head", an episode he had never seen, Frog Baseball. As he arrived at his door he turned the key to his room. The lights above the large mirror, gave off a light that relaxed him.

Needing more air, the wall sized window opened. *That's better.* As the morning began the night was ending much the same way, counting the ceiling tiles and remembering the night before. He closed his eyes-thought about the way she moved and looked the last times he had seen her.

A faint sound from the door awoke him, the red numbers on the clock, showed 1 a.m. Hearing a knock, he placed his hand on the silver doorknob and turned. His insides began to flutter.

"Hi, sorry I'm down here again."

"Aine, no it's fine. We just finished watching Beavis and Butthead and I was just relaxing."

"You guys and them, I just don't understand."

"Yeah well, so."

"Milk?"

His eyebrows moved, mouth crumbled. "Milk?"

Aine smiled. "Milk as from a cow, do you have any?"

Still confused, not knowing why she needed it. Did she want to drink some? "Well I."

Aine placed a finger around her hair, flicking it behind
her ear. "Ben."

He looked down at her other hand, which grasped a blue box.
He felt stupid in not understanding what she was asking. "Oh
yes, your making."

"Mac and Cheese, yes I am hungry, and." Her eyes
glowed a green as bright as any forest in Montana. "I need
milk."

"I have it, I mean some."

A small refrigerator had the essentials he liked, cheese,
milk and orange juice. He moved the milk carton side to side.
"About a half, that should be enough."

Aine had come into the threshold, peering around the room.
"You need some posters or something, these walls are too white."

His eyes moved with hers. "I have heard that before, just
haven't gone to the mall. Here is the milk."

"Thank you."

He felt her smile as Aine walked out of the room, and
placed his hand on the door. "Have a good night." He murmured.

"What?" Aine shook her head. "Your not coming with
me?"

Confused Ben looked at her. "I."

"Are you hungry?"

He nodded, *even if he wasn't* he would have lied and *said yes.* "sure."

"Let's go up to my floor?"

How the words rolled of her tongue made him wonder if everyone from Ireland sounded the same. If so, he should have moved there. As she moved down the hallway, Ben locked his door. It was more than her accent, how her body swayed, her smile. He had only talked to her once, and not in length. Wanting to talk to her more, tonight his chance had come.

A pot banged on the small floor stove, pocketed next to the living room and balcony.

"You know what I hate about making this stuff?" Ben mentioned.

"What the powdered cheese?"

"Well that too, just the wait time for the water to boil."

Aine nodded, "Long yes, but better than Ramen. I will be right back, watch the water."

"Have it under control." As she left, he used his shorts to wipe his palms dry. *Damn it, don't be nervous, it's okay, just be you. I've had girlfriends before, relax.*

Water began the dance in the pan, the box ripped open, golden pasta cascaded in the pot.

"See that you have made it before."

"After football practice, when." He caught himself; a memory from the past invaded his mind.

"You okay?" Aine stood next to him. His eyes traveled up to hers.

"I'm fine, just, that book you came back with, guessing not for fun?"

Her eyes closed slightly. "No, Ed Psych, not fun."

Powdered cheese and milk was placed over the top of the pasta, melding the ingredients together.

The large book was placed between them, opened, as they sat on the simple blue cushions of the couch.

Aine took a bite and placed her fork into the bowl, closing the book. "Holy hot."

"Very, but good." Ben retorted. He noticed that she smiled again. His stomach churned. *Was it because he was hungry? Or was it because of her?* "Your floor is very quiet."

"Most of us have practice in the morning."

He nodded in agreement, placed another bite in his mouth. "So why are you up?"

The fork danced around her bowl, stabbed at the golden bits. "I haven't been able to sleep the last weeks."

"That sucks with playing, you're extremely good." He could tell what he said hit something in Aine, the light completion, turned a pale red.

"Thank you, I am a different person playing than what I am off the court. That's the reason I haven't slept."

Cutting into the conversation, a door creaked from the staircase, and closed. Ben heard someone turn the corner. Straining his neck to see. "Amanda...Hi." Her facial expression told him what he needed to know, she was hurt. Even if Aine told him that she would get over it.

"Ben...Aine...what are you two doing?"

"Well..." In a moment his nerves stammered his throat, swallowed a deep ball of saliva.

Aine countered. "Were just talking Amanda."

"So I see...hope you have a good night...Ben." Speaking with a cordial yet fierceness that made him feel uneasy.

Why is she mad at me, were not seeing each other. Are we? We went to see a movie, does that qualify as seeing each other. His head began to spin as he glanced at Aine.

"I'm going to go, I'm sorry."

"See you around?"

Handing the bowl over, a finger glanced his. "Of course."

Chapter Nineteen

Crunch of leaves weighed underneath Ben's feet as he finished the last class of a Friday. A warm autumn sun highlighted the deep, blue, open sky. He took a breath and smelled the air and the leaves, reminded him of the October's of his past, elementary, middle and high school. How the sun, touched his skin, the breeze cool, yet warm. Leaves that began to decompose gave off an aroma that could never be explained; he thought; only experienced. Thoughts, highlighted his parents, this was the first time he had smelled the leaves and felt the autumnal sun without them, he paused and picked up a maple leaf. The corners were perfectly crisp; the color an offset orange, a voice startled him.

"Dude?"

He looked, focused on his friend and for a moment forgot about his parents. "What's up Kyle?"

"What are you doing tonight?"

"Just staying in I think, might do some studying." He chuckled, as if that would happen on a Friday night. "Why?"

"The women are playing Rocky tonight, there...why, aren't you going?"

"Why would I be?"

Kyle stopped talking for a moment and smiled. "You my think you are being smooth, some people have seen you with Amanda and the tall volleyball player…she's from England?"

"Ireland, Aine is from Ireland."

"See you do know her name.." Kyle snapped a finger.

"Doesn't your sister go there?"

Quickly an image of Alice appeared in his mind-playing in the leaves when they were younger, the first football game she was a varsity cheerleader, their parents. "She does, and?"

"And? Dude? We're going."

He traveled up the back stairs to her room, telling himself he wasn't going to knock. It could be awkward he thought, also another awkward moment he thought of was watching her play. This was college and not high school, the players had more to play for than their town or city. He hadn't watched her play. He didn't want to feel embarrassed when she or even Amanda would look into the crowd. Her door was complete with a corkboard and dry erase marker that adorned it. Ben placed the maple leaf on the corkboard. Sure to not make noise he left the way he came.

* * *

As they entered the court, Ben noticed the floor was much different than the one at Eastern. A golden bear took up most of center court, along with deep green inlays that made the boundaries of it. *So this is what my sister has been paying for?* The school was private, looking around he had for a moment, lost sight of Kyle that had darted up the bleachers, into a section of other floor residents, waved to him and found a seat.

"Nice floor." Kyle remarked.

"It's pretty sweet."

"Is your sister going to be here?"

Ben grimaced. "Not sure, don't really care, why?"

"No reason, just wondering."

Each team's starting lineups were announced. Ben slowly looked at Kyle when Amanda and Aine's names were said feeling his face warm, sweat on his body. *Why did I let him talk me into coming to this game? Why do I feel so stupid?* He had played sports all of his life, family members and girls had always come to watch him play. It was different when he went to watch anyone else play, spying on someone with other spectators, and feeling embarrassed when they didn't play well.

It didn't take long to understand whom, was the better team. Aine dominated the net from the onset of the game. Ben inwardly smiled as she scored each point, noticing how quick she

was on her feet, the strength in her legs. He knew first hand the power she could inflict on the ball, yet seeing her talk and encourage her teammates-something he had never witnessed, impressed him. She continued to talk even on the bench. A hand was placed on his shoulder, a voice whispered in his ear.

"Brother, nice to see you."

Ben exhaled a deep breath. "Wondered if you would come."

"I didn't know you would come over. Should have told me."

"It's okay I didn't want to bother you."

Kyle interrupted, "Hi, match point."

Eastern, looked to close the match out in three games, Aine was to serve. In following her steps, he noticed a glance that she gave, a slow grin, ponytail swayed as she turned to serve.

"What was that?" Alice noted.

"Nothing." Ben shot back.

The spectators began to clap, as Aine palmed the ball.

"Stay away from her Ben. You hear me? Stay away."

"I can't hear you."

The visiting section cheered as the game ended on an Aine ace. Ben looked at Alice, glanced at Kyle.

"Let's go."

Night settled onto the city as Kyle pulled the car out of the parking lot. In looking out the window Ben felt his friends eyes on him.

"You hungry?"

He thought for a moment. *What have a done to my sister to deserve this? She's the only family I have that is alive, except for my aunt and uncle, why is she like this?*

"Sounds good, what do you think? Hardee's, Burger King?"

"Hmm, how about Domino's, we can bring it back to the room and play some Tecmo Bowl?"

That was a great thought, anything to forget his sister, but not watching Aine play. "Awesome. Let's do it."

★★★

The foyer of the dorm during the week was devoid of anyone. On Friday nights to the end of the weekend it was alive with activity. Residents and non-residents asked them for a piece of pizza or even to pay for the entire order as they entered the elevator, the smell filled the space.

"My room or yours?" Kyle asked.

"I think my chances of winning are better in my room."

Kyle laughed. "Why? Because your TV is an inch bigger?"

His was larger, Ben thought. A 20-inch television he had purchased not long ago. It made his room feel like home. "My room it is."

The elevator doors opened, expecting a large group watching television, they stacked the pizza boxes, one on top of the other to hide how many there were. The floor was quiet, the TV off.

"Everyone is out I guess, drinking in their rooms." Kyle pronounced.

Ben turned the corner to his side of the hallway-toward his room. He could feel a long smile begin to form across his mouth and his scalp began to tingle. If he would have looked at his arms, goose bumps would be visible.

"Ahh. Dude?" Kyle whispered.

He saw her, sitting on the floor, Aine's knees pressed against her chest, head placed on them. She twirled something in her finger, as he ventured further down the hall Ben could tell what it was-the maple leaf from the warm afternoon. Again, he could hear his friend behind him.

"Dude?" Kyle clutched one of the pizzas, motioned to hand the other to him.

"Sorry, man."

"No need to apologize. I will see you in the morning. She's more important than Tecmo...any day."

Ben smirked. "Thanks, man."

Each step came closer to her, she was still focused on the maple leaf, still twirled it in her hand.

"Hi, I have pizza if you want any?" *Damn it, is that normal talking?* He thought. His palms moist.

Aine lifted her head. "Thank you for the leaf…it, can we talk?"

"There isn't anyone out on the balcony, we can go there."

Aine shook her head. His stomach sank, *I did blow it, why can't I talk to her?*

Her voice was slow and soft. The ridges of her accent, numbed his mind. "No balcony, I want to, *talk*." Ben stuck out his free hand and offered it to her. As he placed the key into the door, Aine's frame rose next to him, his heart fluttered.

As she entered the room Ben heard her say, "Who do you have in this bag?"

For a moment, he asked himself what bag is she talking about? Yet he realized in moments. "Oh that, sorry I was checking my hockey equipment. I should have put it back, sorry, didn't realize I would have someone in here tonight."

Aine placed herself on the sink counter, her feet close to the floor. "Ice Hockey, you play?"

"At times, in two days I have a beer league pick up game I guess, you want to watch?"

Aine smiled, "maybe."

"Pizza?"

In a moment Ben took a piece and began nibbling at it, stopped, placed it back into the box when she didn't say anything. "Are you okay?" Aine, twirled the maple leaf, as she studied it.

"Thank you for actually watching me play today", she said softly. "I know you have come to the games before, but I think you always have your head down, or looking in another direction, something different...can I ask why?"

He closed his eyes, recounting how he felt at the game, not knowing that she had actually paid attention to him at the other games. "Well, this might be weird, but feel embraced when I watch other people play, just I don't want them to mess up and feel horrible. I don't know, you are a great player, sorry, just something I have always had a weird feeling for." This is where she leaves, he thought, this is where she decides that whatever is going on, he isn't worth it.

"But you play, how is it different?"

"I guess because I'm in control, if I screw up then it's on me."

Aine laughed. "Yes well, that is true, have you ever asked your mum and dad about what they feel like when you."

Her voice trailed off. Ben could see his parents faces during all of his games. Never did they look embarrassed for him playing. They were always there, Little League to high school championship games, both of them were there. At times he could see stress on their faces, yet they never would talk to him about the plays that didn't turn out well, always the positive ones-even if he didn't agree with them. In a moment, wetness consumed his eyes. He couldn't believe this was happening, she would surely leave now.

A hand touched his shoulder; the sound of flip-flops on tile filled the room. He opened his eyes to a soft green pair of eyes, they looked at him with concern.

"Ben did I say something?"

She didn't leave; she is here, in front of me. This is so much different than high school. He wiped his eyes. "I'm sorry, I should have told you I guess. It's not like we have really talked. I mean about things, god you probably think I'm stupid."

"No I don't and I never said that, what is wrong."

"My parents aren't alive, they died in the spring, a car crash, after one of my basketball games, I only have my sister. She goes to Rocky."

Aine looked at him, her eyes were moist, her face turned a slow red. He could feel her touch tighten. "Ben, I lost my dad when I was fifteen. It's never easy. Just believe they are with you. Your parents like my dad will never come back to us, if you think of them and believe they are here with you. They will never be truly gone."

A slow nod came from Ben. "It hurts."

In a moment her arms reached around his back, head rested on her shoulder. He smelled her hair, lavender.

Her voice in his ear made the strains of hair on his head tingle. "I know, you will be okay, I promise. Thank you for the leaf, it reminds me of my, dad, thank you."

The days that passed led Ben to think that college was much different than high school. No one could tell him when to study, who to see, or when to see them. In walking through the liberal arts building, at times, he saw Aine. She would reflect his look with a smile, he wondered if she remembered the conversations they had.

***

The smell of sweat and ice tickled his nose, that after time a hockey player gets used to, and even loves. It fills pores of equipment and fabric. Being always first in any locker room, the bag no longer weighed on his shoulder-deposited on the floor. A room medium sized, with black benches encircled two doors, one to the ice, the other to the showers. It was warm; he always loved how it encircled the muscles. Yet he hated the warmth when the game was over-the last thing he wanted was to feel even warmer than his moisture soaked equipment and body did.

A silver zipper echoed off the walls as the teeth opened the bag, he noticed his hand trembled as the equipment was lifted from the bag. It was picked in the order that it would be placed on the body. Each piece had its own function, a medieval knight on ice he had always thought. After the last loop in the right skate he took a breath, almost finished he told himself. He had played most of his life, still hated the process of pants, shin guards, shin socks and skates, the top protection was so much easier he mused.

Forty-five minutes later his left skate and then the right found their purpose on the almost frozen ice. The Zamboni gave a fresh coat of water, which froze, on the ice, filling cracks and gouges. Ben had from the first time he had ever skated, loved the hum of the blades, then the violent crack as he pushed off. His body rocked back, he adjusted his back-avoiding a fall, *it's been almost a year* he told himself.

The other players, men to be more precise, made him feel small. In feeling more of his surroundings, he looked toward the stands across from the benches. They were small, a smattering of possible girlfriends, wives and children all bundled in winter clothing, to watch a "ballet on ice", as he remembered Wayne Gretzky once stating what hockey was to him. He looked again as his right skate crossed over his left, no Aine yet; he scrunched his nose, crossed over one last time and stopped at center ice with all of the players.

A bearded man, came out of the circle to address everyone. Ben estimated he was at least two feet taller than him.

"Gentlemen, thank you for coming tonight. Before we start, next game same time next week. Also, we do this every time we play for the new players. Name and what you do." There was a groan and laugh from everyone. Ben was silent. The assortment of different jobs was a cross section of the city. Police officer, lawyer, teacher, cook, garbage man, nurse. He finished with saying who he was and student. The man in the middle continued. "I didn't hear professional hockey player." Both teams filled the rink with another chorus of laughter, and banged their sticks on the ice. "Remember we all have jobs in the morning. Make sure we have fun and play clean. I want all of us to play next week. In gripping his stick a panic crossed his mind, I've never been really hurt before, could tonight be it?

At the start, the game was quick, checking was not allowed, yet collisions are always a constant. Some players had played together before evident of their crisp passing and back and forth banter.

"Rookie." A man skated toward Ben on the bench. Not noticing the approach, he felt embarrassed, swung his leg over the board and headed onto the ice.

Almost falling face first on the ice, Ben regained his balance and took a breath. Damn it. I've been on the ice before. Breath escaped his lungs on the fourth time up and down, he glanced at the bench and signaled for a sub. His ass hit the bench, lungs burned, the stick kept his body from collapsing. A glove hit his right knee that belonged to the bearded man. Ben glanced up at him.

"You okay, Rookie?"

Ben nodded his head. His response came out as he inhaled and exhaled. "I'm okay, just have to get back into it."

The man chuckled. "I understand, I didn't start playing until I was 38, now I'm 52. Some are better than others, believe me. You will get there, quick if you continue to play."

Ben exhaled, calming his heart and body. "Thanks."

The man shot back. "Line change, let's do it."

The clock showed 30 seconds left in the first period. A puck deflected off his stick, an opposing player cradled it and accelerated toward his goalie. "Fuck" he told himself as he began to give chase. The skater was faster, yet the man that had talked to Ben on the bench was just as fast. With a quick crossover he hit the puck with his stick, kicked it free towards the goalie. Ben dove crashing into him, the puck nestled safely between them.

Opening his eyes, the smell of ice and equipment cleared any mental fog. A hand reached down at his own, Ben was pulled up to his knees, breath came back to him.

"Alright?"

Ben thought for a moment, the bearded man again asked.

"Does everything still work?"

"I think so." Ben responded.

"Good, now, remember if NHL players get injured doing that they still get paid. If you get hurt." The man started to laugh.

The stick always helped to get up from the ice, on his feet, Ben glided over to the bench.

A water tube stuck in his mouth-cold liquid coated the burning throat. The bottle was replaced inside the wall, fingered the top of the board with his glove.

"Haven't seen her before." A player remarked sitting on the bench. The way he needed to play in the second period filled his mind. An elbow nudged his own.

"You know her?" He craned his neck toward the bleachers. Sitting there was a figure dressed in a black sweat suit and flip-flops. He watched as the woman slipped a hair tie from her right wrist. Her long hair red hair was soon in a ponytail. Another elbow, and he took his eyes off of her.

"I know her." Ben said confidently.

The player smiled. "Nice, now, let's really play." Ben nodded, he felt relief flush his body.

During the next two periods, fatigue set in-it didn't matter. Every time he noticed Aine, their eyes locked and gave him strength. Ben found himself on the ice with thirty seconds left in the third period-the game tied. An opposing player controlled the puck, made a move towards him. The player flicked his wrist for a shot, Ben's stick hit the puck-careened over his shoulder past the goalies glove. The horn sounded, game over.

Hunched over, he looked down at the ice, felt his chest plate moving up and down with his heart. A stick blade came into view and felt it on his shin guard.

"Rookie you played well, see you next week."

"Thanks." He said as he stood up. "I'll be here."

Ben grabbed the water bottle from the bench and began the walk to the locker room-sweat rolled down his face. He rounded the corner of the ice, Aine smiled at him, gave a small wave with her fingers as he disappeared.

The locker room was busy with the sound of equipment being taken off, more laughing when the players recounted the plays of the game. He sat and felt his cheeks rise. This was good. Running was fine exercise, but this was different. The equipment came off one by one, and quick. Aine was outside.

The large bag was thrown on his shoulder as the legs began to move slowly through the door into the rink.

He found Aine in the same seat as when he left the ice-placed himself next to her.

"Hi," he said. "Thanks for coming, did you drive?"

Aine, motionless, her arms crossed around her waist, she looked onto the ice, and blinked. "How do you feel about me?"

The question stung his heart. *Do I really tell her she's beautiful. This is college, not high school, she's a woman. Do I use the word, like or go out? His mind raced, don't blow this. If she truly wants to be with me, no matter what I say should be fine.*

"I really enjoy being with you." His palms were either wet from the game or from stress. Enjoy? Was that a good word to use?

A smile calmed his mind, a hand traveled from around her body, touched his-hands flipped interlocked. She looked at him, the ponytail swayed to the side.

"So do I Ben…but."

"But?"

"I need a ride."

The trip back to the dorms seemed to last mere moments. The streetlights illuminated her silhouette. He imagined her fingers and hands to be softer, a split second his mind fired the reason-volleyball and lifting weights had to take their course. A ring on her finger dug into his, he had noticed it before, *is she with someone else and wore the ring for the first time tonight?* He felt ashamed.

Aine met his gaze as he parked the truck. "You played well, I enjoyed watching."

"Thank you, wasn't as good as you on the court. I did try." Ben noticed her eyes danced in the near darkness, and tried to wade into them.

"Nonsense, you did well." Aine looked out the window to the dorm.

"What?" Ben asked.

"Interest you in a walk?"

* * *

They headed down the stairs and outside. The dorm opened to the middle of campus.

"Where are we going?" Ben asked.

"Over there, past main hall."

Aine walked slowly as they talked. One of her strides equaled two of his.

Ben noticed where they were going, it was the same path that he had been running on in the last months. He continued to feel her hands, her long fingers clutched his entire hand. "You know I'm Irish too."

Aine gave a small laugh. "Are you really Irish, or do you have an Irish last name? There is a difference."

He smiled. "I'm Irish."

She looked down at him, pointed to their destination, a stone bench. Ben could hear the canal, not too far away. "Outstanding."

The bench was cold, to his exposed legs-the rest of his body, hot.

"Aine is your mother alive?"

He could see the question made her uncomfortable, yet she answered with a soft smile.

"Yes she is, she's a teacher. Little kids."

"I don't think I could ever be a teacher."

"That's what I want to do, I'm sure you would be amazing at it. I see you helping others."

They sat in silence for a moment. Ben's heart beat faster. He heard the canal in the distance as insistent chirping from summer's last cicadas calmed his mind. "Where in Ireland?"

"Somewhere south of Dublin." Aine gave a slight, awkward laugh. "You know, Amanda wants you."

Ben smiled. "I know. But the person I want is next to me."

Aine inhaled deeply and gazed up at the stars. "I don't have sex with just anyone. I hope that's not what you want."

"Aine, that's not what I want." Ben leaned over, their lips met. He took a long, nervous breath. "Wow," he said, their foreheads softly touching. "See each other?"

She placed her long, slender fingers on his cheek. "Yes."

Chapter Twenty

Aine exited the warm staircase, looked down the hallway-no one was around. While she traveled down to Ben's room, multiple doors were open. Students hunkered over notes, books or talked so soft only their thoughts were audible. *I should be studying* she thought, yet a hunger pang hit her stomach. *Popcorn would be nice-seeing Ben even better.* The next week would be a flicker of papers, tests and nerves, already she had went through two final weeks-*one night wouldn't make a difference.*

A muffled voice greeted her at his door- her brow bent, a hand pushed the half open door open-Ben had known she might come down. He smiled and she entered the room, he talked low and slow to the person on the other end of the phone. Aine opened a cabinet above the glass mirror, smiled as she saw microwavable popcorn bags. She thought she had eaten the last one a week ago, *Ben must have got more she mused.* A small smile crept into the side of her mouth. As she left the room, Aine pointed toward the dorm kitchen, the microwave was in there. Ben nodded, another response came-she closed the door.

The sound and smell of popcorn made her smile. Time seemed long and arduous from the press of a button to the final product. At times the smell would bring residents of the floor

out into the television room-tonight was not one of those. A voice came from behind her, she let out a small yelp, startled.

"I'm sorry." Ben said. "I thought you would hear me."

"Not over the popcorn." She noticed that Ben was flushed, "What's wrong?"

"My sister, going crazy as always, talk in my room?"

Aine placed her hand on his cheek, "Sorry."

The school beds were small-Ben had made his larger, which Aine liked when she came down to the room. She crossed her legs, to feel the most comfortable on it. The bag torn open.

"Love that smell," she said.

The twenty-inch television came to life, Ben fiddled with the channels and found ESPN's Sportscenter.

Ben placed himself next to Aine and grabbed a kernel and smiled.

"Nice popcorn." He turned his attention to the television. "The Broncos were so close today, they almost beat the Cowboys today."

"I don't really understand American Football." Aine pointed out. "Seems like a lot of rules." A handful of popcorn was placed in her hand, one at a time went into her mouth. "What was the argument about, if I can ask?"

Ben continued to watch the screen. "I really hope the Redskins don't win the Super Bowl again."

"Ben?"

"Sorry." He looked to her, bit his lip. "It was about, you and what I was going to do for winter break."

"What about me?"

Ben pointed toward the television. "Nice catch." He brought his attention back to her. "She says that you slept with her boyfriend last year, I don't know, she's crazy." He stopped. "Did you sleep with anyone last year, I mean no, right?"

He noticed her skin began to turn a slow burnt red.

"No…the last time I had sex was when I was fifteen. Your sister *is* delusional, if she thinks that."

"That's what I told her, and she wanted me to go to my aunt and uncles. I told her we were going to Big Sky."

"She said?" Another piece entered her mouth.

"How was I paying for it is what she asked. I said I was using some of the money and she freaked, I don't know and I don't care. Would have been using that money to get to Oregon anyways."

He heard a knock on the door, flashed a look at Aine. *God please don't be Amanda* he thought.

Before he could answer, the door opened, it was unlocked- Alice walked in.

"Who do you think you are?" A cold voice filled the room.

"What? I only said I didn't want to go out of town for Christmas. I'm staying here, that's all." Ben stated.

"This is the first Christmas without Mom and Dad. I already told our aunt and uncle that you were coming, Ben, is she worth disappointing your family?"

"Yes."

Alice walked over to his long desk and fiddled with a paperclip.

"You don't know what that word means. Just watch, she'll leave you like Devon left me."

Ben stood up. "Alice, calm down. You're making too much noise."

Derek's voice interrupted, filling the room. "Hey, it's quiet hours for finals. I can't."

"Look who it is," Alice said. "You are alive. Thanks for calling me in the last month." Ben shook his head and focused on Alice. "Don't do this," he said. "Mom and Dad are watching, and what they're seeing they wouldn't…"

Alice stepped toward Ben. He noticed the paper clip wrapped around her finger-it was too late. The slap was painful, but the sting and tear of the steel point was excruciating. Blood poured from his cheek. He saw Derek grab Alice and dragged her out of the room.

Remnants of the bag flew around, Aine, frozen with the sudden altercation struggled over to Ben. She examined his wound, a crimson river dripped down her fingers. "We need to go to the clinic."

***

Ben held a piece of gauze as he looked around the room. The light was bright-the crunch of white paper underneath him annoyed him. The last time I was in the hospital he thought. He sighed, memories of the worse night of his life, exploded in his mind. He shook off the thoughts, a short, elderly nurse made her way into the room.

"Let me take a look." She said with a short raspy voice. "Who did this to you?"

Ben grimaced as she probed the wound. "My sister."

"Really? I must ask, not the one the bought you in?"

"No, not her." He looked out the corner of his eye, heard a plastic bag rip open-a syringe was soon exposed. His palms, forehead and back became wet. "My sister and I have an interesting relationship."

"You might feel some discomfort."

Ben closed his eyes, took a deep breath. The room began to spin. The nurses voice brought him back.

"Are you okay, one last question. Did you hit her?"

The question stung as much as the needle. *She is my sister, no matter how crazy, I would never do that.* "No…I did not."

"You will need stitches. I will be back."

Orange fabric seats in the waiting room, were empty at this hour of the night. He took small steps, the only individual that waited was Aine. Hands on her face and she looked down, slowly moving her feet. Her hair out of a ponytail covered her face, she turned her head as the door behind him closed. A nurse wished him a good night. "Thanks, can't get any worse." He replied.

Aine, grimaced as she noticed the black strands that closed the wound.

"Jesus." She whispered.

"Sorry."

Aine looked confused and shook her head. "Sorry for what?"

"That you had to see that."

A long pause came, her green eyes penetrated his- her hands found his. Warmth took over his body every time she touched him his body gave a different response.

"Stay with me tonight?" she said.

***

The room-spanned the width of the dorm-the largest room Eastern had to offer. The same fluorescent light lit up half the room, the other he was guided to-complete darkness. A soft comforter he could feel underneath his arm-collapsed on the bed. Aine's face he barley made out, was close to his.

"You feel like talking?" she asked.

"I will always talk to you, even if I have stitches in my face...oh wait." He smiled as much as he could.

"While I was waiting for you, I realized there's a lot I don't know about you. Where did you grow up?"

"Around Missoula," Ben said.

"Such a different name."

"It's Salish, just think of two z's in the middle but say it like two s's."

Aine laughed. "I will try that, Salish? Who?"

"They are a Native American tribe, it's really different in the west, lakes, rivers, and mountains."

"I would like to go sometime."

Ben nodded "I will take you, this summer would be a good time" he said. "I have a question for you." Their fingers began to dance around each other. "Why did you leave Ireland?" Aine breathed deeply and grasped for the past. "I left because I wanted to go somewhere small. To be away, to be on my own."

Ben chuckled. "You can't get any smaller than this."

"It's different being far away from home."

"Do you talk to your mom?"

"Yes, every week. I have talked to her about you."

Ben stopped his fingers on her shoulder. "What do you say about me?"

"I tell her that I have met someone, he's good for me, I think she would like you."

"How long have we been seeing each other?" Ben asked.

"Since October or so, why do you ask?"

Ben wasn't sure if how or when to say it. A glacier of a subject thawed in his mind. "Do you like sex?"

Aine gave a low laugh. "Wow, you actually are a typical guy. Yes, I do. But the last and only time...was nothing special."

They lay still and watched each other for a few minutes. He felt her ring against his cheek and remembered that night from the hockey game.

"What type of ring is that?" he asked.

"It's a Claddagh Ring." She rolled her tongue as she pronounced the word. "Hold on." Aine flicked on another light, illuminated the bed.

"My mum gave it to me. The hands are for friendship, the crown is for loyalty, and the heart is for love. It's pointing out." She removed the ring slowly. "I decided not to wear it around you, just easier not to give the wrong impression." "It's pointing out since I wasn't with anyone, and now." She flipped the ring so that the heart pointed toward her and replaced it on her finger. "We are together, so the heart points toward mine."

He felt his body slowly slip into sleep, a word, barely audible, a word came from frothier lips, as he drifted off. "I love you."

Chapter Twenty-One

This year's formal dance would be held in the ballroom of one of the city's nicest hotels. Most people were staying the night there before and after the dance, but Ben preferred to get away from the crowd. He and Aine stayed in a rustic hotel. The outside looked like a lodge, and wooden logs formed an A-frame at the pinnacle of the roof. Multiple panes of glass warmed the building with natural light. They checked in and explored the hotel, finding ten large hot tubs and an Olympic-sized swimming pool. They wished they had brought bathing suits. When they'd seen everything, they brought in their luggage and formal attire from Ben's truck. Aine hadn't told Ben what she would be wearing, and Ben had assured her that the dress didn't matter. She would be beautiful beyond words. She shook her head every time he said that. Their hotel room was spacious, with a king bed which was to the left when entering, a large Jacuzzi tub, and a desk they wouldn't use.

Ben held the door for Aine, and she gasped. "Wow, you shouldn't have. I would have been fine just staying in the dorms." She opened the window drapes and looked out over the A-frame making up the inner courtyard. Below, hot tubs were nestled within a faux mountain scene built from logs and stones.

Ben stepped behind her and slid his hands under her shirt, massaging her lower back. "Anything for you. I'm glad you like it." She tilted her head over her left shoulder and bent down to find his lips. Aine turned around, and Ben's hands traveled to her stomach. She felt his warm touch travel up her stomach to feel her breasts, and slowly squeezed. A slight moan formed in her mouth. She looked into his eyes.

"Not yet, we have to at least make it to the dance." He continued to touch her, and she placed her fingers on his cheeks. "We have to get ready for the dance." She smiled and whispered, "Later."

Ben sighed and pulled away. "Okay."

"It'll take me a little while to get ready. You know I never dress up." She smiled and kissed his forehead.

A little while actually meant over an hour. She was ready by six, two and a half hours before the dance started. Aine emerged from the bathroom wearing a black, thigh-high dress. Her hair was in a tight braid, and her heels made her even taller than usual. Ben had always been struck by her natural beauty, in workout clothes and spandex.

"Well, what do you think?"

"What do you think I'm thinking?"

Ben stepped toward her, wearing a black suit with a green tie he'd hoped would match her eyes. "What do you think of me?" he asked. "Do I have to answer?" In heels, she had to bend even farther to meet him. They kissed, and their tongues met. He tugged at the hem of her dress, but this time she was ready. "Stop," she said. "Later." A long silence was broken by the sound of their moving lips. "I've wanted to ask," he said. "What perfume do you wear?"

"Chanel. Chanel No. 5."

"It smells very nice."

She grinned. "It's time to go, okay?" "Dinner. I'll pay." He always offered to pay, to be a gentleman, and she usually let him. He wondered if her family had money.

They arrived at the dance full of Italian food. Parking was difficult, but at least the February weather was cooperating, even though the temperature was in the single digits. Aine hurried inside. Her short dress didn't offer much warmth. While Aine waited for Ben to catch up, a teammate found her.

"Oh my god, you're tall," Amanda joked.

"Thanks, at least I'm not the size of an ant." Aine wasn't sure, herself, whether she meant to be playful or hurtful.

Amanda gave a sad half-smile. "I'm glad you and Ben are happy. Really, I am happy for both of you."

"We are. And thank you."

As Ben arrived, Amanda and her date went inside without staying to speak.

"What was Amanda up to?" Ben asked.

"Nothing, she's still irritated. But let's go in."

The front lobby was lined with couches, and a photo station was inside the ballroom door.

"What do you think? Want to take some?" "Are you crazy, pictures? Of course I do."

They stood in all the corny poses and smiled for the camera. The photographer told them to pick up the photos after the dance.

As they found the dance floor, the DJ played "3 a.m. Eternal" by KLF. The music was loud, and the bass was deep. Ben knew it was one of Aine's new favorite songs. She couldn't move as gracefully as she did on the volleyball court, but she loved to sing. As he listened to her sing along with the lyrics, he hoped they would be up past 3 a.m. tonight.

* * *

As the dance wound to an end the floor-nearly empty. The DJ played "I'd Die Without You" by PM Dawn. For those who were left, it was a perfect song to end the night. They danced face-to-face, lip-syncing the lyrics to each other. During one of the bass lines, Aine put her back against him. He could feel her ass tight against his hips. He placed his fingers on her back and moved in rhythm with the song. Ben could feel himself getting hotter. When the song ended, Aine smiled down at him. "What do you think?" "Oh yeah." From the beginning, they'd each promised the other a slow relationship. They didn't want to risk sex ruining their connection. But on the drive back to the hotel, Aine rested her head on his shoulder. Ben smelled Chanel No. 5 as her hands ran across his chest, down to his thigh. Her mouth moved to his neck.

Ben opened the door of the hotel room. He reached for a light switch, but Aine grabbed his hand. The hall light illuminated her face before she closed the door and fell into darkness. Her hand guided him into the room, and she began to undress him. Her lips and fingers ran over his body. His breath deepened as his back hit the bed.

He took her shoulders and held her still.

"What?" she said through the darkness.

"Are you sure?"

She leaned down and whispered into his ear. "*Leannan*, yes."

Her shape moved against him. He felt her skin, soft and muscular, and their bodies pressed against each other, from toes to legs to chests. Her fingers danced across his own then laced through them.

"Wow." Ben inhaled and stroked her skin, inches away.

Chapter Twenty-Two

Winter finally loosened its frozen grip. Spring arrived, and the sun felt warmer each day--relatively, of course. Highs were in the low fifties, perfect for shorts and pick-up softball games. University athletes got away with playing pick-up, even though intramural sports were strictly off-limits. Games were scheduled by notes slipped under dorm doors, as teams had been playing sporadically all month, when the weather allowed.

The field's backstop was right next to the major road that led to the airport, and the outfield stretched right up to the sandstone cliffs, which formed the leftfield wall. From center to right, a plastic snow fence marked the field's boundary.

Today's game was one of the last. Ben felt as though it were a championship game--the sixth floor versus the women's volleyball team. He had watched Aine and her team dominate every game, and she'd told him they hadn't lost a single game in two years. Pregame trash-talk was as intense as any major league game.

Ben and Aine were both pitchers, and they each had shutouts going through the first four innings of the six-inning game. In the top of the fifth, Ben's team got something going. He imagined the game being announced by Vin Scully, a legendary Los Angeles Dodgers announcer.

"There's two out. Derek, the junior RA, steps up the plate. He has had a difficult time today with the pitcher, Aine. Her size makes it seem that she is almost to the plate when the ball is released. The first pitch is outside. The next pitch-- that's lined to leftfield. The leftfielder mishandles the ball, and Derek's into second with a double.

"Kyle steps up to the plate, a strictly singles hitter. He looks at the first offering, then lines a single to right. Runners on first and third, two outs, and this is going to get interesting. Ben steps into the box with a smirk. Everyone knows that he and the pitcher have been together almost the entire year, and both would love to win this game. Aine is all business as she delivers the first pitch, low and outside. Aine takes a breath and winds up. Swung on-and hit high in the air to right. Does it have enough to get over the rocks? It does! Home run. High fives all around at home plate.

"The next batter grounds out to first. The score is three nothing going into bottom of the inning. Ben takes the mound, three outs away from breaking the volleyball team's winning streak. A senior passer steps to the plate. She swings at the first pitch, a fly ball to center field. Derek drifts underneath and makes the catch. Two outs away. A junior is next up. She, too, cuts at the first pitch--a single through the five-six hole. Amanda steps into the box and smiles at Ben. She *laces a liner into right. Runners are at second and third. A*

double play will end the game.

"Ben delivers the pitch, and it's off the second

baseman's glove. E four. Bases loaded, and look who is coming to

the plate, Aine, the team captain and Ben's love interest. This

is getting interesting. Ben's showing signs of fatigue as Aine

steps in the box. He's been very careful with her to this point.

With her six-foot frame, he has to continue to keep the ball

down. He takes a breath and delivers--catches the corner of the

plate, low and outside. Here comes the second--popped foul

behind the backstop. The count's one and one. Three more

pitches, and Aine has worked the count full. Kyle calls time

from first base to give his pitcher a pep talk. Two outs away

from the win, Ben settles his shoe on the rubber. Aine steps in.

This next pitch could end the game, and possibly the winning

streak for the women.

"Ben delivers from the stretch. Aine swings on a high

fastball and drives it to deep centerfield. The centerfielder

has a beat on it, all the way to the track, and--

"This one is gone! A walk-off grand slam for Aine. She

ends the game. Let's see that again with instant replay. Ben

knew as soon as the ball left his hand that he had made a

mistake. He tossed his glove as soon as it was hit. It looked

like Aine said something to him as she trotted around the bases.

That pitcher's going to have a lonely walk to the showers after
this defeat."

***

Ben wanted to clear his mind. The last two weeks had been
bumpy. Since the game he had only talked to Aine in passing.

He pressed his hand against a door and knocked. "Hey man,"
Kyle said, "Want to play some Tecmo Bowl?"

Ben never could beat him, but he always liked trying. The
first game started and ended--the score wasn't even close. Ben
winced.

"That hurt."

"Well not as much that softball game a couple of weeks
ago." Kyle said.

"Tell me about it." Ben still thought of that pitch,
the pitch that floated in at the letters. "Damn, we almost had
it."

Kyle nodded. "That we did. But it's okay, just a game. Have
you talked to Aine since?"

"No, I haven't."

"Should you?" Kyle said.

"Probably."

Kyle chuckled. "So why are you here with me?"

***

Ben flipped through his biology textbook as he stretched out on the foyers couch. The night before Kyle had asked why he was there with him. He didn't want to say that he had serious doubts about the relationship. He stomach was in a knot. The night of the dance-a feeling he had never had before. Aine's body was electric, no matter where he was with her. He took a breath, damn it, I fucked this up. A goddamn pitch was all it was. He rubbed his eyes and closed the book. A hand touched his shoulder, startling him. He spun around.

"Hi, Amanda."

"Hi. Biology?"

"It sucks. I don't know why this class is so hard."

"Because you're not a biology major. You need help?"

Ben thought for a moment "That would be great. Where?"

"How about your room?"

A lump formed in his throat. "Okay."

They walked up to Ben's room. Ben rested his head against his headboard; Amanda sat at the foot of the bed. She was a good teacher-quizzed him on notes from previous classes-a rhythmic tap came from the door. He looked at Amanda.

"Fuck." Ben exclaimed.

"What?"

"The door."

"And who cares?" Amanda wondered.

His expression turned sour. "I do."

Ben rolled off the bed and moved slowly toward the door.

"Aine."

She smiled, until she saw Amanda on his bed. Her eyes changed from smooth green to a violent tornado.

"Ben, what is going on?" Aine asked.

Before he could say anything, she turned and stomped down the hall.

"Don't go," he called after her.

Aine moved quickly down the stairs and bolted outside. She walked up the hill to the top of the plateau, Ben calling after her and trying to keep up. He caught her on top of the Rimrocks. Billings lay below, lighting the dark sky. Aine turned toward him, Ben felt in the presence of a giant, who could put him down with one swift stroke.

"What the fuck was that, Ben?"

"It was Amanda, why?"

"You don't see anything wrong with that?"

"Nothing was going to happen. She was just helping me with biology."

"I don't like it, Ben. I don't." She turned to face the city lights below, and Ben moved beside her.

"I don't understand."

"Are you blind? How many times do I have to tell you that she wants you?" Aine looked down at him. "We are fucking each other Ben."

"Well we haven't for awhile…what did I do wrong?"

"You didn't do anything wrong…I love you." She watched him. "If you really want me, I can't have that. No Amanda, no anyone else. I swear to god if I ever, ever see a woman in your room besides me, we will be over."

They sat on the sandstone outcroppings, their legs dangling in the darkness. A hundred feet lay between their toes and the valley floor. "I love you too." Ben remarked. Ever since they first made love-the glance that always would send him to another plain of existence, Aine's eyes flared, her cheeks moved upward, and her hair drifted across her face.

"Always."

Chapter Twenty-Three

Morning sun reflected off Aine's hair as Ben walked behind her. Classes-out for the summer, Ben smiled at the thought of training with her. The last two weeks had been difficult, training three days a week and skating after. They were silent when they entered the weight room; Aine connected the portable CD player into the weight room stereo. Ben grabbed the bar as

Aine placed herself on the bench. "2 legit 2 Quit", thundered in the room.

"Ready?" Ben asked.

She smiled. "The question is, are you ready?"

Aine lowered the bar, pressed up and down.

"Breath, Aine."

Ben placed his hands around the bar, slammed at the top of the bench.

Aine took her mouthpiece out. "That was good." More weight on the bench for Ben.

His hands felt tight around the bar; noticed Aine was not ready to spot him. "Hey where did you go?"

"I have a song for you."

He again was ready to bench. Aine looked down on him as the song began to play. A guitar riff began, Ben started his first

Set, then realized, he tried not to laugh as the bar hit his chest.

"Breath…Ben."

Ben rested the bench. The song at full volume. "I can't believe you selected "Meatloaf".

★★★

Near the end of summer, the campus showed signs of activity, signaling the beginning of school--and the end of Ben and Aine spending every day together. Ben understood that, for Aine, he would always come in third to school and volleyball. He did wonder what would happen when Aine graduated, and he was still here.

From the first game, it was apparent that Aine was correct in June-it would be a long season. Halfway through, the team stood one game above five hundred. Aine was having her best season yet. Her skills were unrivaled in the conference. Early October brought chilly weather and a weeklong break from games. Aine's coach gave them the weekend off from practice, and Ben arranged a mountain camping expedition. Students could check out equipment from the college's outfitting recreation center. Since the cost of non-returned items was added to students' tuitions, equipment was almost always returned. Ben and Aine checked out camping equipment, including protection from bears--bells on walking sticks, mace, and a lockable cooler--then headed to the campsite, four hours away. The drive took them along some of the most magnificent vistas the region had to offer. "Haven't we driven on this road before?" Aine asked.

"Yeah the lodge over Christmas break, the Lewis and Clark paintings, tried to ski, saw the white shit? This is the road."

"I don't understand your humor sometimes. It's snow, it's okay. So we're going to the lodge?"

"Oh no, not this time. We're going somewhere without people."

Aine rolled down her window, and Ben followed her lead. He turned on the radio as the wind tousled Aine's long, red hair, the sun reflecting off it with an autumnal sheen. The next song was perfect, as though the radio DJ played it just for them: U2's "With or Without You." Ben looked at Aine.

"So why don't you play for a bigger college? You could play for anyone you wanted."

"I like Eastern. It's small. Plus, at a bigger college, I wouldn't have met you."

"Still, you could play D1. Even Pac-10 or SEC."

"Keep your eyes on the road, Lover." Aine leaned over and slid her hand down to his crotch. She kissed him on the cheek and laughed. He remembered the first time she had ever called him Lover. He'd thought she was mocking him, but Aine meant what she said. They weren't married, and they weren't living together. But they were more than boyfriend and girlfriend. For her, they were soul mates, and the only word Aine knew to describe how she truly felt was Lover.

After three hours of traveling on two-lane roads, they stopped in the same town they had visited last December, where they'd stayed in the Red Lodge Ski Lodge and people-watched near the slopes. The town was crowded now that the snow had melted.

Ben thought there were two types of people: those who live in the snow and those who frolic in it.

Ben and Aine walked around the empty streets, window-shopping for trinkets and tourist clothes. Aine bought a postcard to send to her mom. Next summer, she was going to take Ben to Ireland so he could finally meet her. He had talked to her on the phone a couple of times--her voice sounded like Aines'. When they'd seen everything on Main Street, they returned to the Ford Ranger and headed up the pass to the campsite.

The pass was known as the Bear Tooth Highway because of the twenty-eight switchbacks cut into the side of a mountain. From an aerial view, the curves looked like a bear's paw. By the time they reached the top of the pass, they had risen to an altitude of over ten thousand feet. The ski town below was now a dot on the landscape. Ben stopped at an overlook.

Aine took a breath. "Wow! I have never seen anything like this. Truly amazing."

Through their smiles, they both began to choke up. The view was truly awe-inspiring.

A series of more than twenty mountains, each over twelve thousand feet rose from the floor of the valley to their left. "What are those on the peaks?" Aine said. "All of these mountains have them. Is it snow?"

"Those are glaciers." Ben replied.

"Are you serious? I have never seen one, let alone... Look how many there are." She jumped like she'd forgotten something. "I can't believe I'm not doing this!"

"Doing what?" Sometimes Aine's mind moved too quickly for him to follow.

"Taking pictures!" Aine pulled out her Canon SLR and clicked and focused. "It's not everyday you're on top of the world."

Aine had clicked off an entire role of film by the time they reached the campsite where they would spend the night. Ben had stayed at this site five years ago, with his parents and Alice. It was three in the afternoon, and the sun traveled across the sky to their right. They left the cooler full of food in the cab of the truck. They would walk back to eat dinner. They brought snacks in their packs, but even their crackers and granola would remain in the truck tonight, to keep from attracting bears.

The campsite was on a rocky outcropping, carved by glacier activity and surrounded by higher mountains. Around the edges, green meadows were dotted with flowers--a beautiful view, even in the fall.

"I'll help you with that," Aine said.

"Thanks, pitching the tent is the worst part of camping."

Aine hammered the stakes in the ground, each strike echoing through the mountains.

"Do you notice anything?" Aine asked.

"What?"

Aine drove the last stake into the hard earth, and Ben placed the dew cover on the tent's frame. He stood back. "Looks good. What do you think?"

Aine pointed the hammer at him. "Lover, how am I going to fit in this?"

He studied the dimensions of the tent compared to his five-nine and Aine's six-foot bodies.

"Shit, they told me it was a two-person tent."

"Well, I'm thinking the two people were from a Tolkien novel." "Or Smurfs?"

Aine shook her head.

"What?" Ben asked.

"Tolkien is classic, and you had to ruin it with Smurfs."

They both eyed the tent. There definitely wasn't enough space.

"Well we have padding. Below-zero sleeping bags, blankets, gloves, and hats. We'll be fine."

"Fine with what?" Aine tied her hair into a ponytail.

"Fantastic, as long as we don't become food."

"It will be fine," Ben said. "We could be tasty pigs in a blanket." The day turned to night.

Sitting on thick blankets and sleeping bags, they could barely feel the small rocks jutting from the ground. The night was dark, but the moon bright, reflected in the small lake below. The stars were brilliant, unencumbered by city lights.

"So do you like?" Ben thought he knew the answer, but he wanted to hear Aine say it.

"Are you kidding me, this is incredible. The meadow reminds me Ireland, except Ireland's a little greener." "I would love to see Ireland with you."

"Maybe someday."

They kissed under a sky that was theirs and theirs alone. It was the biggest and most open they had ever witnessed together.

"So tell me about the glaciers," Aine said.

"Well, this part of Montana and Wyoming were covered by them. Some stayed, some left. The ones that left dug out valleys and plains." He stopped.

"What?"

"See that glacier over there? Rocky Mountain locusts are trapped in the ice."

"Locusts?"

"They're extinct, now. But they used to inhabit this area."

They stared up at the stars. "What do you want, Aine?"

"I want a lot of things." She bit her lip. "I want a career. I want to have children."

Ben nodded. "I don't understand how you could want to teach elementary. I would never have the patience."

Aine laughed. "Partially because my mum is a teacher. Partially because I would be a giant to them."

Ben smiled. "Of course. You could give them shade, like you do for me." Aine punched Ben lightly on the shoulder.

"Bastard," she retorted. "So what do you want?"

"I want a lot of the same things. You know I want you."

Aine glanced sideways at him. "Ben, I don't want to be the reason, or even part of the reason you quit school."

He felt his face contort. "Why would you say that?"

"When I graduate, I don't know what will happen. I will probably go home."

Ben heard his sister's voice in his head. *Aine will leave.*

"We won't end then," Aine said and changed the subject before Ben could respond. "I would like a family. A girl…no boys. If I had a boy, I would just have to throw it back in."

"Why don't you like boys?"

"Because they smell, and they're just--boys. Have you thought anymore about what you might do after college?"

"Besides not teaching elementary?" He grinned. "No, not sure."

"You're really good at math. I think you should teach." "Did you hear me before? Me with a class of kids? I don't think so."

"Not primary, you could teach college."

Ben had never considered that.

"That actually doesn't sound half-bad. Everyone would have to call me *doctor*." "Could take a while to get a Ph.D." Aine gave him a long kiss. "Don't worry, I will wait for you." A shooting star streaked above them.

"Make a wish," she said. They made love under the stars. When morning arrived, they were nestled in sleeping bags with blankets piled on top. Gloves covered their fingers, and hats covered their ears. The sun rose to warm them.

Aine heard rustling and woke already wearing a smile.

"Don't move," Ben said.

"What?"

"It's not a bear or anything. Just sit there, and don't move your hair." Aine had removed her hat, and her hair fell across her left shoulder.

He found the Canon Rebel he'd given her. "Look over there, please." He clicked five shots, checking the light before each.

"What are you doing?"

"I think I got it. It was a "Last of the Mohicans" moment."

Aine thought back to the movie they had watched after fighting about Amanda. She smiled.

They packed up and headed back to the real world, not wasting any time before dropping off the film for development. A few days later, they had photos in their hands. Ben found the shots of Aine--the first was too dark, the next the same, but the last one had perfectly captured the moment. Aine's red hair absorbed the sunlight, and her face reflected the early morning glow. In the background, dark mountains were barely visible. "Are you happy now?" she asked.

"More than you could ever know."

Chapter Twenty-Four

Ben woke naked next to Aine, lying in her bed beneath a large window in her dorm room. The sun's rays reflected off the snowpack and reddened the landscape, and frost had formed on the

windows. With the dorm windows' poor insulation and the heat
from the register--and their bodies--water vapor had formed and
frozen on the glass. Ben rolled over, dressed, and went to his
room. He and Aine had been sleeping together since the dance,
almost a year ago. At first, he had felt weird sleeping naked,
but after the first few times she rolled over in her sleep and
he woke up with her on top of him, he had no problems with it.

He had been thinking about something since the camping
trip, and he needed to clear his head. The dorms were silent
while classes were out of session. After a year, college was no
longer foreign.

His room was oddly clean, as though no one lived there--
which was almost true. Aine's bed was so much larger; they spent
most nights in her room. Ben grabbed his hockey bag from his
closet and headed to the rink. Skating and being alone would
help him think.

At this time of morning, the ice rink was like an untouched
frozen lake. Ben pulled on his hockey skates and thought of Aine
and of his sister. How could he ever be with someone his sister
completely hated? Ben hadn't talked to Alice in over a year,
which bothered him. But not enough to call her.

He had always loved skating rinks-the smell of his bag and
the sound of skates cutting the ice. When Ben was alone on the

ice, the rip of his heavy hockey skates reverberated against the walls of the small rink. The scraping sound his skates made in turns reminded him of downhill races during the Winter Olympics. Ben worked out under the low ceiling and bright lights, completing crossovers to the left and right, up and down the rink. Finally, he halted center-ice with a hockey stop and saw Aine watching him from behind the glass.

Seeing her answered all his questions. He wouldn't worry about Alice. She couldn't stop him from being with Aine. Ben watched Aine's eyes glaze as she fought the lightheadedness from the smell of artificial ice. Ben skated over. He grabbed her hands, and Aine stepped onto the ice.

"Slow," he said, "you don't want to fall."

"I know. Shuffle my feet, right?" Ben skated backward, holding onto her hands. "Ben, we need to talk." Her fiery eyes turned soft, and they both stopped moving.

"Are you okay?" he asked.

"We need to talk about us. Not here, sometime tonight."

Ben's heart stopped. "We're okay?"

"Even though I don't show it," she said, "you are who I think about, maybe forever. I mean, I love you."

"Tonight after dinner, talk?"

She nodded, and Ben smiled. She had no idea that tonight he was going to show her how much he truly loved her.

When they reached the edge of the ice, Aine breathed a sigh of relief.

"What?" he asked.

"I didn't break anything." She laughed.

* * *

Ben disappeared for a couple of hours after lunch. He told Aine he was going to the library to research something.

When he returned to her room, he found her napping. He curled up next to her, fell asleep as well, only to be awoken by the phone four hours later.

Aine answered. Her face soured, but she didn't hang up.

"It's your sister." She pointed the corded receiver toward him.

"Shit."

He held the phone to his ear. "Alice?"

She skipped the pleasantries. "Ben, I don't want to get into it. I need help. I completed my last flight tonight."

"Congrats, Sis."

Aine rolled her eyes.

"I'm at the airport, and my battery is dead. I need a jump, and it's starting to really snow."

He ran through a list of excuses, but he knew he couldn't use them. She was still his sister.

"I'll be there in a few."

"Thanks, Ben. I will see you soon." Ben didn't have to explain himself to Aine. She knew he had to go.

"I'll be back soon," he said. "I love you. I want to talk more when I get back. Okay?"

Aine leaned over and gave him a kiss. "Don't be too long." She smiled and tucked her hair behind her ear.

Ben took the stairs and stopped in his room. He opened the desk drawer and removed a blue, velvet box. He tucked it in the left pocket of his blazer.

Outside the snow was already limiting vision. He'd have to drive slowly. The drive to the airport took fifteen minutes, triple the usual time. Ben found Alice's Jeep in the parking lot. She sat alone in the driver's seat, hood up. Ben parked his Ranger so that their front bumpers nearly touched.

The snow was beginning to build on vehicles, roads, and fields, and temperatures were plummeting. The day had begun in the low thirties, but at nine o'clock it was fifteen degrees. After a jump, Alice's battery clicked and turned over. She slid into her Jeep, leaving the door ajar to talk to Ben as he closed her hood and unclipped the jumper cables.

"What are you doing for Christmas?" Ben asked.

"I think I'm spending it with Aunt and Uncle. You?"

"Same. I'm going to bring Aine."

"Do you think that's wise, Ben? They haven't even met her."

"Isn't that the point of bringing her?"

Alice shook her head. "Ben, you have to graduate. You know that. That's still three years away. Don't screw up your life because of her." Ben rolled his eyes. "Fine," she said, tossing up her hands. "Do what you want. I'm graduating soon, anyway, and I'll be in the Air Force in May. Until then, I'll be with our aunt and uncle so you won't even have to know I exist. Thanks for the jump."

Alice slammed the door and pulled away, the tires crunching over new snow. Ben drew in a deep, cold breath and then expelled it, leaving a trail of white smoke as he climbed into his truck. Ben remembered winters when he was little, lining up outside the school building. He'd pretend he was smoking and then, when the class entered the building, would stamp out his imaginary cigarette on the floor. He turned the key, and the truck's engine hummed. His nervous breathing fogged the windshield.

He pulled out of the airport parking lot and started down Twentieth Street, winding from the top of the plateau to the shallow valley below. Ben stopped to turn right at the flashing red light strung across the roadway, but a semi trailer truck that had jackknifed coming off the plateau blocked his turn.

Lights from fire trucks and a city police car cut through the snow.

Ben could either keep straight and take an out-of-the-way route or he could make a U-turn and take Black Otter Trail--a two-lane, corkscrewing road cut out of the sandstone plateau. It wasn't the safest road, but guard rails lined its five miles, except at the very top, which was lined with Douglas Fir trees.

Ben turned around.

The snow was getting deeper, and Ben's studded snow tires hummed and gripped the roadway. He approached Black Otter Trail on his left. The edge of the airport was to his right, and straight ahead was darkness and miles of wheat fields.

He took the left and entered the pass, taking the first of three curves without a guardrail. The road was slick and heavy with snow. He slowed as he entered the second turn. The Ranger shuddered, and he let off the gas. When he felt his truck sliding he instinctively punched the brake. The truck responded and straightened out. The third curve was blind, with the side of the plateau on the right and a hundred-foot embankment on the left, lined with large pine trees and saplings. Ben cut the corner high, using the entire roadway.

A snowplow appeared through the gloomy white storm.

Ben mashed the brake and felt the truck skid. "Oh fuck!"

Chapter Twenty-Five

Alec was on call for her first twelve-hour shift. She was a twenty-five-year-old nurse who had just joined the rescue team. The day was slow--most people were staying off the roads during the snowstorm. But at eight, a highway patrol officer called in an accident. Emergency vehicles were on the scene and en- route. A pickup had collided with a sanding truck and rolled down an embankment. The driver needed help.

When Alec reached the roof of the hospital, where the emergency Bell 222 helicopter was stationed, snow obscured her vision. The two pilots had already untethered the helicopter rotors and where closing the doors to the cockpit. She jogged to the helicopter, opened the blue fuselage, and climbed inside. Alec was dressed in her winter gear, but she could feel the cold through her blue rescue jacket. A doctor followed her into the helicopter--unusual for him to come along. Alec had already plugged in her headset, and she gestured for the doctor to do the same. She was sure he didn't need to be told, but this was her first hop without a "guardian angel," and she wanted it to go smoothly.

The helicopter whined, the rotors turned, and the passengers heard the pilot and co-pilot communicating through their headsets.

"This is River West Life Flight 5832, requesting flight path to Black Otter Trail." The pilot spoke to the airport tower, which was on a plateau above the hospital.

"This is the tower. Roger that."

The co-pilot looked back at Alec and the doctor. "We have a twenty-one-year-old Caucasian male, approximately five-foot-nine and a hundred eighty-two pounds. Emergency vehicles are on the scene, and the highway has been blocked off. They do not believe the victim would make it to the hospital in current road conditions. The ambulance will bring him up to us for transport."

"This is the Medical Communications Flight Communications Center. You're on a primary frequency of 158.510." The pilot glanced at the co-pilot. Flight Comm monitored each flight to make sure the emergency room was ready, with personnel standing by, when the flight landed. The co-pilot was responsible for warning Flight Comm when they were ten and five minutes from the hospital.

"Roger."

"This is the tower. We have a FedEx heavy holding at one hundred twenty miles due south. Will approach when you are clear with victim."

The pilot, revved the first turbo engine, then the second came online. The instrument panel glowed a light red.

"Take off lights on. Lights on." The co-pilot checked and double-checked that everything was ready, updating the pilot as he did. With every second, someone was closing in on death.

The pilot pulled up on the control column, keeping the stick in neutral position. Alec felt the helicopter ascend. Snow clouded their view, and the co-pilot checked his instruments.

"We have positive rate of climb.

"Landing gear retracted.

"We have three whites."

Alec felt the rising altitude in her stomach.

"Tower, this is RW Life Flight, requesting to cut across the field at one hundred eighty degrees, then head downwind at a vector of ninety." Flying directly over the campus would have been easier, but the buildings were too high.

The Life Flight would have to go east for three miles to gain altitude before cutting back toward Black Otter Trail.

"That is an affirmative, RW Life Flight. Maintain at least five hundred feet in your final vector to the landing zone. Expect trees on your right and power lines on your left. Proceed with caution."

"Acknowledged, tower. We are on our way."

The hospital was close to campus and was the only large hospital within three hundred miles. The Bell 222 helicopter, affectionately named Airwolf was a familiar sight to Eastern students. By this time in December, freshmen didn't acknowledge Airwolf, and upperclassmen didn't even hear it. Aine was asleep.

The helicopter crossed over the airport and made a ninety-degree turn, due south. At ten miles from the landing zone, Alec saw city lights to their left.

The pilot told Alec and the doctor that at five miles downrange of the LZ they would make a one-eighty and fly over the power lines, bringing them in line with the road, trees to their right.

Alec felt the helicopter bank to the left and then level off as the pilot flawlessly executed the maneuver. Ambulance lights waited five hundred feet away, fifty yards from the turn onto Black Otter Trail. A fire engine and a city police car were stationed farther down to ensure a clear extraction.

As they descended, the doctor looked over to Alec. "Are you ready?"

She closed her eyes as adrenaline pumped through her veins. She had to control herself. A life was at stake. Alec opened her eyes.

"One hundred feet." The co-pilot gave verbal directions to the pilot. "Fifty feet. Twenty-five feet. Fifteen. Ten."

Alec felt the slow collision between the helicopter and the road. The engines began to spool down, and the rotors idled with just enough power to get them back in the air quickly. She opened the door to a blast of cold air--*shit it's cold*. The paramedic updated Alec as they hustled Ben to the helicopter.

"Ben's got compound fractures in both legs, possible collapsed left lung, head trauma, possibly other internal injuries." The doors closed, and the rotors hummed. As the helicopter geared up for flight, Alec checked the patient's vitals, already spiraling.

"Breaths are twenty-seven a minute. Heart rate is one nineteen." She continued to monitor the screens. "Blood pressure one thirty over a hundred, guys." The helicopter lifted off headed toward the airport.

"This is RW Life Flight. We are giving you the ten-minute check."

"Copy that."

"Something isn't right," Alec said. "Get there quickly."

The co-pilot looked back. "We are en route. ETA is nine minutes." Alec and the doctor nodded to each other. Vitals spiked. Alec's voice sounded through the headsets.

"His heart rate is going up, blood pressure. Shit, we're losing him. Come on, Ben. Come on!" Over the headset, she heard the five-minute call.

Alec's breathing was heavy in her headset. "Guys I don't think we can make the loop. We have to get down."

"Roger that. Flight operations, this is RW Life Flight. We are expediting our descent, code blue."

The pilot guided the helicopter directly over the tallest dorm.

"Two minutes." The heart rate monitor squealed.

"Ben, listen to me." Alec grabbed his hand. "Come on, stay with us, I have someone to go home to and I'm sure you do too." The doctor grabbed the paddles and motioned to Alec.

"Clear!" An electric shock raced through Ben's body. "Come on, come on."

"Twenty-five feet."

"Come on. Fight Ben. Fight!"

"Fifteen feet."

Another charge raced through his body. Alec felt the helicopter touch down, and the rotors began to slow. The medical machines now gave a positive signal. The doors opened, and Alec and the doctor raced Ben into the hospital.

Chapter Twenty-Six

He felt fingers caress his arm. A hand grasped his, and warm lips touched his forehead. His eyes opened slowly, painfully. His eyes slowly focused on a featureless figure to his right. In the next moments, Ben recognized the person was sitting next to his bed. He turned his head and lightly squeezed the unknown hand. He tried to smile with the breathing tube still down his throat. The blurry figure finally brightened and focused. "Hi, Ben. You're back with us." He tried to form his sister's name on his lips. "Shhh, Ben, it's okay. Relax. Our aunt and uncle will be so happy you're awake. I've been with you every day." Alice placed her hand on his head. "I'm glad you're alive."

He looked toward the ceiling, feeling his sister's hand and soaking in the sound of her voice.

During the next weeks he felt like an ancient mummy. His body groaned, cracked, and popped. Pain constantly attacked each organ, nerve, and extremity. But the worst pain wasn't from the broken bones or punctured organs, but from the simple words that had pierced his soul.

Alice peered into his room. "Hey, you. Ready for me to wheel you around?" Ben struggled to sit up. A nurse helped Ben into a wheelchair.

"Thank you, Melissa," he said dryly.

She watched him through curly, red bangs. "You will get out of here in the next few months, I promise."

He sighed. "Yeah, maybe someday." Alice took control of the wheelchair. Their nightly route twisted around the hospital, through glass breezeways and back to the room. As they entered one of the breezeways, Ben put up a hand, and Alice stopped the wheelchair beside a backless wooden bench. Ben watched the cars on the road below.

"It's March, right?" he asked.

She nodded, hunched over, her arms crossed at her waist. He took a long, deep breath. Alice eyed him. "Are you okay, Ben?"

He fought to find the right words. Ben looked outside and spoke away from his sister. "Why was I moved here?"

His sister was silent for a long moment. "I thought you would have a better chance here. Of surviving. I'm going to basic training in July." She paused. "I thought it would be better to have our aunt and uncle around, to help." Her head bent as though she was doubled over in pain.

"When is Aine coming?" Ben watched the cars' brake lights blur together as his eyes fogged over. "I really need to see her. Why hasn't she called, Alice? Why hasn't she?" "I gave her the number of the hospital." Ben couldn't imagine Aine not wanting to talk to him, but he was confused. Emotionally and physically broken.

Alice put a hand on his shoulder. "Ben, look at me. Please?"

He finally complied, unable to keep the pain from his eyes. She stuttered out, "Are you completely sure that she loved you?"

His eyebrows bent inward. "Yes, I believe that." He fought back tears. "With all my heart. Yes." Alice didn't stop. "Then why hasn't she called?"

He shook his head. "I don't know. Maybe." "Maybe what, Ben? If she loved you as much as you say, she would have called."

He watched his sister, his emotions raw like exposed nerves.

Alice smiled. "Okay, I promise that when you can walk, I will take you to her."

He nodded and closed his eyes, thinking of Aine's smile, her smell, her hair. He still believed they were soul mates. As Alice pushed him back to his room, he promised himself he would never forget her, no matter what.

***

"Are you ready for this?" the young physical therapist asked.

"I'm ready, I have things to do." He smiled at her, not fully understanding the type of pain rehabilitation would bring. He hadn't walked in months. Now his arms burned as he held the weight of his disused bones and muscles.

"You have to keep your back straight," the therapist said.

After a few feet, Ben felt like he had walked a half marathon. He tilted his head up, sweat seeping from his pores.

"I don't know if I can."

"Ben, you can and you will. Now again."

The pool exercises were his favorite form of torture. At first, his physical therapist guided him through the water. A few months ago he had been swimming laps in an Olympic-sized pool--now swimming fifty feet was a miracle. A month into his recovery, his body began to get used to the daily workouts.

* * *

The weeks turned into months. Finally, in mid-May, Ben left the hospital for the first time since December. His continued physical therapy constantly reminded him of the trauma--to his body, mind, and soul. Summer brought cool morning air, which gave way to warm days and rain-soaked nights. Ben sat carefully in the airplane seat, gazing out the window before looking back to Alice.

"I know you leave in a week, but thank you."

She smiled. "Are you ready to see her?"

He shook his head. "I'm worried, Alice. I've tried to call her, but--" He pinched his leg with his fingers. "She hasn't called back or answered my letters."

Alice looked away, scanning the aircraft. "I'm sure everything will turn out the way it was meant to be." She smiled as the aircraft shuddered, engines whirling. Ben noticed goose bumps on his sister's arms. "Are you cold? I can get my jacket from the overhead."

Alice smiled and put a hand on his knee. "It's okay. I love the sound of the engines. You should try flying, sometime. I know you would be good at it."

"I love to fly, really. But I think it would be stressful, knowing you could have a bad day and kill everyone on board."

She laughed lightly and looked out the window as the aircraft began to turn. The brakes were applied and released as the engines gained power. "You just don't have a bad day, then."

Ben leaned his head on the headrest and closed his eyes. His mending body felt the increase in pressure, making his joints ache. He breathed deeply and nodded off to sleep.

Three hours later, the jolt of landing woke Ben from his nap. They disembarked and tossed their small duffel bags in the back seat of the rental car. Alice climbed into the driver's seat with Ben beside her. The June afternoon was bright, and the pale blue sky was cloudless. Alice drove toward the college, taking the road that had been closed, and had forced Ben onto Black Otter Trail in December. The car glided down the plateau to the valley below. Alice took a right with the hospital to the left. After another right and a few more miles, she parked in front of Eastern's administrative building. Ben grimaced. "You

know we could have parked by the dorms."

She opened the door and glanced over the console at him.

"You and I need to walk."

Ben's walking had been improving ever since he'd given up

the wheelchair, but he still had a slight limp. The two dorms

were visible across campus, through the web of maple and

cottonwood trees. Alice stopped halfway to the dorms.

"I'm going to sit in the shade over there. Come get me

whenever. I don't want to get in the way." That was probably a

good decision. This would be hard enough with Aine and Alice at

each other's throats.

Ben looked up at the dorm building as he approached,

shielding his eyes from the mid-day sun. As he entered the

building, he saw a sign on the elevator: Out of order.

"Fuck."

A few months ago, these four flights of stairs would have

been nothing. Now they were like snow-covered mountains.

Focusing on one step at a time, he climbed slowly and steadily,

stopping to rest at each landing. Finally, he reached Aine's

floor. The silent hall smelled of freshly cleaned carpet. The

semester had ended several weeks ago, but Aine always stayed

during summers, rather than pay for plane tickets.

Ben ducked to the left to dodge the floor's great room, which was probably empty, but he would rather not chance it. He didn't want to get sucked into a conversation with a summer-school student. There was only one person he wanted to see. Ben stood in front of her door and frowned. The whiteboard Aine kept on her door was missing. He closed his eyes and knocked. What am I going to say? How am I going to act? How is she going to act? Does she still love me? The knock echoed through the hallway like the last firework on the Fourth of July. Ben took a deep breath and knocked again, his right shoulder aching from the vibration. He listened closely and heard no movement behind the door. Maybe she's practicing. He switched to his left arm and knocked for the third time, then the fourth. "Ben?" He tried to whirl around. Pain shot through his spine, and he collapsed his hands and knees. A familiar hand touched his back. "Ben? Is that you?"

He looked up. "Amanda."

She tied up her hair with the hair tie on her wrist.

"I'm going to help you up, okay?"

He nodded and let her help him upright. He ground his teeth, and Amanda grabbed his hand. "Don't worry," she said. "I won't try anything on you…yet."

He laughed as best he could. Amanda opened the door to her room--it smelled like apples. He hobbled in, and she eased him into a leather office chair.

"Thank you."

She sat across from him, on her lofted bed, legs dangling off the side.

"I can't believe it's you. I didn't think--"

He scowled. "What?"

She rested a knuckle against the corner of her eye. "I didn't think I would ever see you again. I didn't, think you were alive."

"Didn't Aine tell you?"

A tear jumped down her cheek. "Ben, Aine is gone. She left right after you were taken away from here."

"How, I mean, my sister told her. I tried to call, and I wrote." He closed his eyes. "Oh, fuck." His breathing began to build in his chest.

Amanda dropped down from the bed and placed her arms around him. "Aine loved you and will always love you. But, I don't think she knew what to do. I'm sorry."

She's really gone. It would have been better if he had died in that wreck.

"Do you have her address?" Silence cut through the air.

"No one does. She just left, didn't tell anyone. I cleaned her room."

Her embrace softened, and she walked slowly to the bookshelf against the wall. She wiped tears from her eyes, found a book and opened it. From between the pages, she plucked out two photos.

"I found these, when I cleaned her room."

The pictures were as vivid as any of his memories. He sucked in a breath, seeing how beautiful Aine was and how much they had, at one time, loved each other. Amanda dropped to her knees and covered the pictures with her hands. Her voice was barely recognizable.

"Look at me, Ben." Her red eyes matched his own. "I don't know what happened, but I still feel something for you." Ben tried to speak, but Amanda stopped him. "I will always love you, Ben, and I don't want to see you hurt anymore than you are now."

The envelope, hit his hand, it felt heavy-Ben slid the pictures inside, then tucked it into his pocket.

Amanda helped him to the elevator and to the front door. "Ben, could I call you?"

He smiled. "Amanda, you will always be with me."

★★★

Alice was sitting on a bench. As Ben passed her, he motioned with his hand for her to join him. When they reached the car, he leaned against the warm hood.

"What happened?" Alice asked. "She's gone. She left in January. You didn't know?"

She shook her head. "No. I didn't. Why would we come here if I did?"

He looked across campus, toward the hospital. "I don't understand why you hated her so much. I never did."

She placed a fist on the hood. "You remember Devon my boyfriend she slept with him?"

"Bullshit. There is no fucking way! She told me she had only slept with one person before me, and that was in high school."

"And you believe her over me? Your sister?" She glared at him. "Devon and I went to a movie, and I went to the bathroom." Alice took two quick breaths. "When I came out he was talking to her. Then he started disappearing. He had to be seeing her. But, of course you would believe her, instead of the person who took care of you. Obviously, she didn't love you. She ran away! She left you. She never wanted you anyway. So keep siding with her, and see where that gets you."

"Let's go. I want to leave tonight. I can't stay here."

The day ended, snuffing out his hope as the sun dropped over the mountains. Ben closed his eyes as the lights of the cabin flickered. He looked out the window, back toward Billings. Goodbye, Aine. I will never forget you.

He turned to Alice. "Hey." She was reading a magazine from an airport newsstand. "I'm going to enroll in community college in the fall and get my math degree. I want to teach college."

She watched him with a cool look in her eyes. "That is great. You will be successful, I know it. Do me a favor, please?"

He nodded. "What?"

She closed the magazine. "This is from experience, forget the past, it won't hurt as much." She pressed her lips together, opened the magazine, and continued to read. Outside the window, darkness enveloped the sky and the ground.

Ben's eyebrows peaked. "I don't think I can."

July 2012

A relaxed finger, flicked the tray table, release-back and fourth. Ben always humored landing in Missoula. He imagined the plane darting in and out of the mountains. A cat and mouse game, he hoped they would never be the victims of.

Lights on the plane illuminated the cabin. Restless passengers began to exit. Ben grabbed his carry-on out of the overhead compartment and wheeled it through the cabin. Into the short jet bridge, a woman's voice filtered into his ear. Ben glanced back.

"Excuse me, are you Dr. Meagher?"

In his mind he questioned why anyone would ever care who he was. Yet, he decided since someone asked him, it was the *Montana way* to acknowledge a person. The owner of the question, her short dark hair accompanied with streaks of blonde highlights caressed her rank on the shoulders. A perfect smile, made him smirk. Eyes-green as pure glacier water. She was beautiful. His body language didn't reveal what was in his mind.

"Ben, it' nice to meet.."

"Rachel…Noticed you on this flight before, and in the University of Montana alumni magazine.."

"The Montanan. Yes, I did an interview a couple of months ago." His feelings wanted him to end the conversation. His body told him otherwise. "Are you the pilot?"

Rachel's perfect teeth aligned, in a slow inviting smile. She probably lived with a perfect husband with perfect little Einstein children running around a perfect white picket fenced house. Things he did not possess, at times he tried. His professional life couldn't be better. Real-life with real

relationships didn't seem to be possible.

"Yes I am, been one for awhile. Congratulations on

becoming the department chairman of mathematics."

"How did? Oh, the magazine. Yes, thank you. My sister

and her family will be coming sometime to help me move into a

house...But, thank you for the flight."

He evaluated what he said and turned up the jet way.

"Dr. Meagher?" Her voice sounded scared and she

quickened her pace.

He stopped. "Please call me Ben."

"You have been on a lot on these flights. Would you

want to?" She paused, lowered her voice. "I could lose my job

for this…but drinks?"

Her eyes danced around, and watched him. Ben didn't know

who would listen or watch this conversation. It seemed the

threat of being fired was real.

"I'm sorry I…"

"Your married or with someone, I'm sorry."

Rachel began to make a turn. Exhaling silently Ben closed

his eyes.

"Wait, sounds like a good idea."

Ben pulled a small leather cardholder out of his jacket pocket. A pen, not far behind. "Here's my phone number, call me."

Chapter Twenty-Eight

It was a warm night for late June. Rachel did call back and not only once. They talked when Rachel landed in the western cities she flew into. Ben found himself along the Blackfoot River, large and meandering through canyons and the city of Missoula itself. Still rushing from the last of the snowmelt. The rhythm calmed him, while he told himself how to walk. A trait perhaps that had imprinted onto his psyche.

A paved trail guided them from the University to the heart of downtown. The sky opened with stars visible through the lights of Missoula a large city for Montana, yet an individual still could view stars from it.

"I always loved this walk when I went here."

Ben settled on her eyes. "When did you go here?"

"Graduated in 97', so I'm guessing we're around the same age?"

"You would be correct."

The pair stopped.

"So here we are." Rachel flashed her perfect smile.

"Have you ever been on the Carousel?" Ben asked.

"No, never, why?"

"Let's go."

The carousel found its home in the mid 1990's in the downtown area. Beautiful hand crafted painted horses adorned the ride. No one could ever walk away without a childish grin or smile. Some riders would try to collect rings that settled in a long tube in a certain area of it. The horses would start slow enough, but would gather speed with each pass.

Rachel fit one foot in the stirrup of the wooden horse and swung her other leg across. She noticed Ben tilt his head away.

"Hey, it's okay, you can look."

The horses began to spin. Laughter echoed off of the large wooden structure. Protecting it from the sun of the summers to the sting of winter.

Ben placed his finger around one ring and pulled it from the receptacle. The horses began to slow. In a moment the ride ended.

"So how many?" Rachel smirked.

Holding up three rings in his finger. "Okay I guess, you?"

Rachel came closer and held up six fingers, with a golden ring attached to an outstretched thumb. "I'm a pilot for a reason."

"And what's that?"

"Good reflexes."

***

A modest apartment, with upstairs and small rooms, greeted them after a night of walking and ice cream. Above all else Ben loved the night. The living room, stacked with white boxes, the move closer every day.

"Wow, nice boxes!"

Ben stared at her as she placed her hands on the tops of them. He gathered his thoughts as she disappeared onto the couch. He had to follow.

The only thing to look at besides the boxes was, a woman, who moment by moment, was growing on him. He was not alone in the thought.

"Thank you for a great night. I enjoyed being with you."

"It would be better without all of the damn boxes in the way."

"Yeah, when am I helping you move?"

He hadn't asked but liked the sound of her voice. "In three weeks or so. My..."

"Sister, yes I remember."

Ben exhaled, "My sister."

"You don't get along? She is helping you? Parents?"

Ben placed his hands together a feeling of loneliness came over him, for a moment, breathlessness. A hand was placed on his back.

"Hey, are you okay?"

"I have scars." He whispered.

The perfect smile came back.

"Don't we all?"

Chapter Twenty-Nine

July brought heat and low humidity. Everyday, an Open Sky, Ben believed. The world around him turned something he hadn't seen in years-colors, bright and bold. In the short month they had known each other Ben grew closer to his feelings. The Missoula Osprey, the minor-league baseball team in the area, was a perfect place for friends and family to gather. Lisa and Alan, the only people that he called friends were to meet them at the game. The first time they would meet Rachel.

In carrying the precious cargo of beer, Ben nodded to Rachel where their seats were located.

"How are the seats?" He asked.

"They are really nice, I've never been to a game." She placed her head on his shoulder and grabbed a beer from the carrier.

In a moment Alan's moderately thick Boston accent filled the air.

"Well there they are."

In standing Ben shook hands and gave Lisa a hug. Blonde hair intertwining in his fingers.

"This is Rachel. Lisa and Alan."

"Ben told me so much about you two, my pleasure."

He thought for a moment. They had never actually seen him with a woman, making him feel uneasy. This is right he told himself. This is what I want.

Flanked by Lisa and Alan, the night transcended a brilliant view. Reflecting the mountains the sun cast an orange hue on the few clouds in the sky. Stadium lights reflected off the batting helmets.

By the end of the first inning, everyone settled in and began conversations.

He recognized his friend's voice in his ear. "She seems great."

Thinking about what he said. Yes she is more than anything he dreamed for, now in the present. His mind brushed the past away. The umpire did the same to home plate. "She is, I'm lucky."

"That is good my friend. Work might seem easier to think about due to Rachel."

The game continued, cool air began to fill the air-alcohol soon needed replenishment. Lights from the stadium began to turn to life. A slight hum filled the night.

"Time for a ladies walk, gentlemen." Lisa announced.

For the Osprey the third baseman made a beautiful play for the first out of the sixth inning. She guided Rachel to the left field railing. Far enough away from prying eyes and ears.

"So."

"So.."

"Ben with anyone is interesting, since Alan and I met him. Just him, no one else."

Rachel looked puzzled. "How is that? I was thinking he would be seeing someone. The first time I met him, he had to be married."

The Osprey center-fielder made a spectacular over the shoulder catch, ending the top of the inning.

"No…definitely not married. To work yes, real life, he is a consummate bachelor."

"Lisa I need to ask you something. We just met…I realize that."

"Anything. You're with Ben, I will answer anything."

"I don't know how to say this, have you noticed his scars?"

Lisa waved a hand dismissing her. "Scars, small one's? People have those."

"His lower neck and legs. Lisa they are large…surgical. I never asked."

Looking across the diamond Lisa focused on the seats Ben and her husband occupied. The friend that she once thought she knew, now was a stranger. *Who are you truly, Ben?*

Chapter Thirty

Footsteps echoed through the shell of the house. Dark cherry wood floors adorned the living and dining room. Upstairs were carpeted and cork linked the laundry room.

"Wow, Ben this is huge."

He looked at the high ceilings; the living room was bathed in sun from the skylights.

"Is it nice though?"

"It's pretty amazing, you should be proud of yourself. But..."

"But?"

Rachel looked around, "Furniture, you need furniture."

"I have furniture...in my apartment."

"True." Placing her arms around his neck. "This house deserves real furniture."

The store was, as most furniture stores-quiet and soft. The smell of fresh leather permeated the skin.

Quickly hours passed. Different types of fabric and leather were chosen, felt and a nod of either yes or no. Ben noticed that Rachel had a knack for describing the spaces in the house to the salesman.

He touched the ridges of the stitching of the leather. It was never a choice of furniture that his parents placed in their house. They always had chosen fabric couches and chairs. The feeling of the fabric brought Ben back to the past, the time on it while eating popcorn while watching Family Ties and Night Court. Losing his virginity on it. His parents; going to see them should be a priority. Work lately was the obstacle, even during the summer. Ben made a mental note to visit.

Now there was Rachel-staying with him on as many off days as possible.

"Hey?"

"Sorry...was thinking how much this is going to cost."

She thumbed at the leather couch. "We should look at beds. Your double is a little too small."

A king bed was chosen. Why not, while looping his name on the sales and delivery receipt. Rachel had gone somewhere. The salesman, with an open hand greeted Ben to the back.

He approached Rachel, her body taunt.

"Are you okay?" Noticing she was focused on a piece of furniture. A crib.

"For many reasons I thought I would be single. Which was okay, but then I met you, it has been short for us I know. I'm falling in love with you."

"But?"

"But I don't know anything about you."

"Like what?"

Rachel placed a finger on his lower neck. The scar obscured by his polo.

"Your scars. What happened to you. I want...need to know."

"I think we should go."

"I'm not leaving until you tell me."

Ben placed himself on the floor next to the crib.

"When I was a senior in high school I was on a charter bus for basketball...and I was in the back of the bus with my girlfriend, a cheerleader." Ben blinked, his mind picturing the past. "The bus swerved for something. I was thrown through the window. I woke up in the hospital my sister told me, my girlfriend was dead...and that I had been close to death."

That night Rachel traced his scar as she laid her head on his chest.

"Thank you, again for telling me today."

Ben glanced at her soft hair. Imagining her smile. Water formed in his right eye.

Chapter Thirty-One

Boxes, twenty of them, were placed in a small moving van. The drive from the apartment meandered through large and small streets, all lined with cottonwoods and gas lamps. A high school and a church would become his new commute. A much shorter, historic drive-the church had been a Missoula landmark since the early 1900's. Silver brick made it a sight that few could ignore. Cottonwoods dominated the area around the church, planted at the same time of construction.

The van pulled into his driveway. A car parked alongside the large lawn that led to the house. Ben noticed the occupants of it, exiting the car as he was. He took a breath, mentally preparing for what was to come, keys found their way into his pocket. A woman approached, it was his sister, Alice. She approached with a dry smile; almost gray hair in a ponytail behind her. This could be a disaster.

"Alice."

"Hello brother, it has been awhile." In truth it had been awhile. Over her shoulder three others traveled from the car. One was Mark, her husband. A man, Ben admired, the notion of dealing with his sister on a daily basis would be difficult.

He was mild mannered, worked his way up the pharmaceutical food chain. Twin girls flanked him. Ben couldn't remember their ages, twelve possibly, it had been awhile.

"What did you guys do yesterday?"

"We went to see Mom and Dad and picked some flowers for them."

"That sounds like a nice day." He placed his hand out to shake Mark's. "How's work?"

"It's work, I like it."

"Work?"

Mark made a motion with his head toward the house.

"Yes, the house, thank you. It is nice. And the twins, I haven't seen you in…a couple of years." They didn't seem like they wanted to be there. *Typical almost teenagers.*

"What do you want us to do, Ben?" Mark asked.

"Well I have boxes in the van, that will need to be brought into the garage."

"Do you have any furniture brother?"

The question or statement from Alice made his facial muscles expand. "Oh…I do."

He could have opened the door to the garage and made a simple entrance. The full view of the house was on his mind, the front door would be more, advantageous. The wood floor and the leather furniture matched perfectly-couches to the right with small table in front. A fireplace to the left completed with two love seats encircling.

Alice placed a finger on the dining room table, ran it a short distance.

"It's new but you need to clean. Mark would you take the twins to Target and get some supplies. I wouldn't think he would have any."

He gazed at her, "Your right, no I don't."

"Sure we will go, ladies?"

The twins were no longer visible, muffled sounds echoed from the upstairs.

"Wow, nice bed!"

"Ladies come down here."

His sister smirked, "We need to talk."

Ben sat the last of the boxes on the garage floor, all in perfect rows.

"Who is she?"

"Someone, she will be here in a couple of hours or so."

He noticed Alice rolled her eyes, "It's more than a someone."

Ben touched the door that led from the garage into the house, traveling through the heart of the house into the kitchen.

"Her name is Rachel, and she makes me feel great."

"That's obvious there hasn't been very many, since..."

"Amanda I know, Alice. I know this is why we haven't talked very often. It wasn't my fault that you two were friends."

"You know the truth of why we don't talk like normal siblings."

"Yes I know I screwed over Amanda. For the millionth time, I know, I apologized."

"Please Ben, she loved you and just." Alice tapped a finger on the dining room chair as Ben sat down. "Did you tell her about the wreck?"

"I told her about it, my scars…everything."

"And she was okay with it?"

He nodded. The doorbell rang, startling his heart.

"That must be Lisa and Alan. Her flight doesn't land for awhile."

"Flight? Ben, where does she live and what does she do?"

As he traveled to the door, projecting his voice off the wall. "You should ask her. Both of you have something in common."

Chapter Thirty-Two

Chairs were lined in a circle on the redwood stained deck. Stretched into the backyard, a pine fence encircled it. The sky open with whiffs of clouds, the sun beginning its dance with the Rocky Mountains. They had cleaned for the last hours. It was time to discuss life and any other topics that came to mind. Mark and Alan, were discussing higher education and the politics associated with it. He loathed the political *"game"* that Alan mentioned. If the *"game"* was doing his job well, appearing at conferences that he could not care about or going to work when he felt like shit, then he played it well. Lisa and Alice discussed the house and Missoula weather. The twins read *Pet Cemetery* and *Misery,* he knew he had read while their age. Ben excused himself and ventured upstairs, there was still unpacking to do.

A white box hit the mattress with a thud, it was heavy, what does she have in here. The thump of a door closing whispered into the upstairs.

Rachel, rested square boxes on the table. The evening sky, casted a red hue that enveloped her. Ben could smell tomatoes, bread, cheese and meat. As he approached he heard her voice.

"Hopefully I know who's behind me."

He ran his hand down the small of her back. She turned and placed her arms around his neck, their lips met.

"How was work? I could have made something for dinner."

"The flight from Seattle was delayed and we had to play tick-tac-toe with some thunderstorms in the area. Is everyone here?"

Ben sighed. "Yes, they are, you ready?" He had told her about his sister. How they had gone years without talking in the past-life differences is how he described it.

At her side, embraces were given from Lisa and Alan, a handshake from Mark. The sister and the girlfriend wasted no time with questions and answers.

"Alice, I'm Rachel it is so nice to finally meet you."

"It is. I didn't know about you until some hours ago. My brother is keeping secrets from me. He is good at that...forgive me I have high hopes for my little brother, what is your occupation?"

"Of course I don't have a brother but if I did I would feel the same. I'm a pilot for Alaskan Airlines."

Ben noticed his sisters' eyes; from slits they became wide open. Her cheek bones once tight, now soft. Alice glanced at him.

"He told me you and I had something in common. Now I realize why. I'm a pilot for Delta." Rocking back and forth in her seat. "Excellent. I think I smell pizza."

Chapter Thirty-Three

Snow was lightly falling on the cobblestone walkways of the University. October was possible winter, this year snow had found November. Days before Thanksgiving it started for real. Ben noticed the M on Mount Sentinel, was barely visible.

"Hey stranger."

He would always recognize Lisa's voice, mixture of east coast, English and western U.S. She must have seen Alan for something, rarely walked onto campus for nonbusiness engagements.

"What are you up to?"

"Met Alan for lunch, you up for talking? Haven't seen you around, Rachel keeping you busy?"

He nodded. "Yes, but let's walk."

Students and staff scurried, it was lunch as well, as final preparations for the holiday ahead. Finals loomed afterward.

"So what are you doing for Thanksgiving?" Her pink
fuzzy hat began to cling to the snow, filtering the small and
large flakes.

"We are meeting at Big Sky, to just relax." Big Sky, a
large ski area south of Bozeman, filled with small, medium and
large cabins. A ski area, where skiing, relaxing in hot tubs,
and people watching, were in ample supply.

"Very nice, are you driving?"

"No I'm flying, she will meet me at the airport in
Bozeman."

Lisa smiled. "I will never understand your reluctance for
driving."

Ben noticed, in her tone, that she was searching for a
hidden answer. "I just don't like it, never have."

In front of the math building they stopped. Snow now dusted
the walkways; soft footprints were seen, then disappeared.

"What is it Lisa?"

"Ben..." Her speech slowed, and calmly said, "Rachel
wants to marry you...I see it when I am with both of you...but,
she doesn't know anything about you...who you really are."

"What are you getting at?"

A long breath came out of Lisa's nostrils, the air around
the pair colder by each fallen flake of snow. "Your scares, the
story you told her isn't true. I searched for any news about the

wreck and couldn't find any. So you need to tell yourself to stop lying to Rachel, to everyone including you...what would your parents think?"

"Both of you have a great Thanksgiving." Ben turned, and traveled through the doors. He noticed a reflection of her pink hat walk away. *What did she know,* he sat on his desk chair and checked his phone for messages. There was one.

"Thinking of you, talk to you tonight." It was Rachel.

***

Snowflakes enveloped the gray steel wings as the small jet pulled into the Bozeman International Airport. It was small and quiet, even more than the airport he had just left. Flight time was a smooth one-hour, quicker than the four-hour drive from the west. Bozeman, settled a larger valley than Missoula, the gateway to Eastern Montana and the first National Park in the United States-Yellowstone. Temperatures in the winter, colder than Western Montana with more snow. The white precipitation that fell from the heavens guided celebrities, tourists and residents to a ski area forty-five miles south, Big Sky. The drive between Bozeman and the ski area connected along a stretch of two-lane road, vehicles negotiated with care. The road meandered through meadows and rivers, all overlooked by large mountain peaks. His palms were clammy at the thought of the road and driving it-calmness took over his body when he remembered Rachel would drive it. He brushed his hands on his jeans as the cabin door opened. Thoughts of the one and only time he had traveled to Big Sky, a lifetime ago.

Raspberry, he told himself as their lips unlocked.

"How was the flight?"

"It was quick, good, ugh Bozeman."

Rachel, once having her arms around his neck placed both on opposite shoulders. "Stop it, Bozeman is a good school."

He always loved her smile. "I just noticed you didn't say the name of the institution you so mentioned."

"Correct, sometimes you can't bring yourself to say certain words."

As they traveled to the baggage claim, he thought of the remark Rachel had given him. The schools name was Montana State University, it had one sister college that shared its name. Sometimes dark, painful crevasses of memories needed to be frozen in time.

Radio reception in the canyon leading to Big Sky was weak at best. Rachel had thought about this, pressing play on her phone. U2 could be heard, *With or Without You,* Ben thought. He bit his lip.

"Are you okay?"

Ben noticed a glance as they exited a corner. "I'm okay, I hate this road."

"How many times have you traveled here?"

Transfixed on the road, snow encroached on it. The sky was open, a brilliant sun reflected off of it. He again, thought of the distant past, the possible future with Rachel. "Once, about ten years ago."

"With one of your many girlfriends I presume."

He smirked, "It was with a very on and off again relationship."

The car crossed a small bridge and began to climb.

"You haven't told me about that one."

"Her name was Amanda, and...we had known each other since college."

"Oregon, right?"

"Yeah." He dug his thumbnail into the door handle, felt it dent the leather. "We broke up for good not long after, she met someone better than me I guess...had kids." He felt his voice trail off, "It was my fault."

A finger touched his leg. "It's okay, you haven't spoken about her, just wondering why...I mean we are living together right? I still don't know who you completely are."

He remembered the last turn, "I don't know what you want from me."

"I'm not going to fight with you about this now. I love you, just want to know everything about you."

"I've told you, there isn't that much to tell."

The car slowed into a parking spot. He met her gaze, eyes a glowing blue.

"Let me know you...the real you...please."

Cabins, apartments, rooms and houses were all available to any guest of the resort. Each had their own decor and architecture. Some looked as if out of the alps, others were modern, with a touch of country. Work had been long days and nights. Rachel made the reservations with his credit card, a first for him-control to someone else. Other relationships had come and gone, some lasted more than a month, others ended as fast as a firework. The door opened, a distressed wood hallway connected the granite tile kitchen, with leather couches in the living room. A loft completed the room. In truth, it was bigger than the apartment he left months ago. They were living together, a conversation the she had plunged themselves into one night after love making, drinking and even more drinking. Ben told himself from the day they met, not to lose control and to let Rachel know who he truly was. The surroundings made him feel at ease yet on edge with what conversation could happen next. He thought of Lisa's warning, she will ask you to marry...A smell

came over the loft into his nose, Rachel was in the kitchen
brewing coffee. He wanted to say what he felt and wished. He had
told her that he had fallen in love with her, anyone around him
would see and know that. She however, had questioned his
statements with love, with a quip.

"You only love that of me, you don't truly love me."

Coming from someone else this would have sounded crude, the
opposite of love. Yet, for Ben, this was as close to the
relationship truth, anyone in the recent past had pursued.

"What are you thinking about?" Steam raised from a cup
in her hand as she looked at him, a notion of her seeing right
through him, crossed his mind.

"It is cold in here, I can see your coffee."

Rachel approached him with the same smile that was perfect.
"I'm sorry for the car, I know that you will tell me when you
want to...and for it being cold. There are things we can
do...start the fire...and later on..."

He felt his muscles in his face move to a smile. No self-
respecting man could turn down a beautiful and smart woman as
she was, no matter the conflict in his mind and heart. "I will
get the fire started, and the rest, you know me."

"Do I?" She bit her lip, the words flowed out.

"It's okay, I'm not mad, you deserve…everything."

Chapter Thirty-Four

Skiing for Ben, during high school was out of reach. At times financially, it would have been possible. Sports were the main obstacle. He weighed either blowing his knee during recreational time or doing the same in a game. The threat seemed to be fantasy, until his sophomore year girlfriend destroyed both of her knees on the slopes, never to play basketball and run track again. He had never forgotten the look of pain on her face when he spent time with her at the hospital, and later physical therapy. Skiing is just one of many winter sports that any visitor could enjoy at Big Sky. Today for both of them, snowshoeing.

"You up for this?" Asked Rachel as she placed her goggles over her eyes, her bright pink coat would be visible to him even if she would get too far away.

He thought he was in decent shape, but running once a week left his mind as they crisscrossed the first hill. Poles dug into the snow, the snowshoes lightly flicked the powder around them, Rachel was ahead as they stopped on the hill. The sky open, with the winter sun visible.

Rachel turned to Ben showing him the way with her pole. "We're going up the next hill, and then there is a flat trail that looks pretty cool, leads back to the lodge."

He could feel himself getting warmer from the inside of his lungs to his eyes. He thought, obviously I need to run more than what I do.

"Let's do it." Steam came from his mouth, leaving a constant trail as they crested the second hill and made it to a smooth powder covered trail sparkling in the sun, lined with pine trees. Rachel looked back and slowed the pace. The air was silent, the only auditory stimulation, the crunch of snow, the rhythmic exhaling and inhaling of them. To his surprise Rachel suddenly stopped.

"What is it?" Ben asked.

"We need to talk, here...among the trees, away from everything and everyone. Okay?"

Ben gathered his breath; he could feel the perspiration on his skin.

"Okay...but about what?"

A pause developed as Ben watched the same steam rising from her mouth and nose.

"Your not a stupid person, Ben...I want to talk about us."

"Rachel, we are fine."

"I'm glad you feel that way. Since I don't, what do we do besides fucking each other..."

Ben opened his mouth and saw that she wasn't done.

"Wait...I need to say this, do we go out like a normal couple, go to movies? No, we don't. Do we talk about normal things? No, we don't?"

"Normal like what? We both work?"

"I don't know, every time I bring up anything that has to deal with us being together forever, as in marriage, you slip off somewhere else, the only way I can bring you back is to stop talking. So that isn't normal, my god if you didn't want to be with me, you shouldn't have let me move in. Am I a charity case too you? Did you feel sorry for me in some way? I could give a shit about us working, everyone works! It's something that everyone in a relationship has to balance, it's priorities. Before I met you...I just felt that I would be alone for the rest of my life. That my career would take over, and one day I would wake up and be ninety years old. It would hit me that my life was about to be over and I had never shared it with anyone. Why? Because of a career, and that's it. This is my time, I truly believe that you and I should be together, maybe forever. But…are you cheating on me?"

He looked away, and the sun warmed the surroundings, snow lightly began to fall off the laden branches, now too heavy to carry. His goggles began to condensate on the inside, raised them off of his eyes, and exposed a terrain in color, not the amber tint of the plastic film.

"You're not a charity case, believe me, I do want to be with you."

"Forever?"

The question seemed so vague, what did she mean. Forever? Eternity? His heart sank.

"I don't know."

"Then you know where to find me if you want to talk, or maybe not. To be honest, Ben, I talked to Lisa, whatever happened to you, I want to know."

A tranquil moment under a large, opened Montana sky, left Ben, alone and scared.

Ben shoved a pole in the snow, the pink coat drifted away. "Rachel."

****

He sat on a bench by a lift and began to study the people that went down and then back up the mountain. Clouds began to filter throughout the sky, once a brilliant blue had turned into a deep gray, snow a certainty. Weather here, could turn in an instant. As small flakes fell, thoughts as many as the crystals that made them, filtered through his mind. It was simple, if he would talk to Lisa or Alice they would all agree with Rachel. If you're truly in love with someone why would you not let them know every tiny minuscule aspect of yourself. Why would you hold onto the past, Lisa he thought would say? He had never told Lisa or Alan about his past, betrayal to his closet friends entered his heart. A deep long puff of steam came out amongst the snow. His relationship with his sister was passive aggressive. She knew about his past, who he truly was. He felt he was a different person and had been, before his sophomore year in college. That was so many years ago, he had only guessed at her motivations, someone knew the real truth, of what had happened to him. If they were still alive, he did not know-he had always wondered if he should look for the answer, or quite possibly there will never be an answer for the question he so wanted the answer to.

The snow began to fall harder as Ben traveled back to the lodge where they were staying. He decided to wipe his memory clean and see if Rachel was who he wanted. He needed to do this now! This could be the last time!

Chapter Thirty-Five

Ben traveled the distance to the room and opened the door. What was expected was sound, only the slow hum of the refrigerator could be heard. He looked up to the loft and noticed a faint rustle of the large duvet cover that kept both of them warm last night. Rachel laid on the bed, noticeably silent. He pushed his hand on the cover and Rachel moved her head to see him.

"Are you okay?" Ben asked.

"Do you think I would be okay?"

Her perfect smile was no longer what he needed to concentrate on.

"I know this is a lot to ask...but please trust me."

"Ben I'm trying to do that, every day, minute, second. I am trying to do that...what we have I thought wasn't fake."

He focused on her face, they way it moved, her eyes, hair and mouth all interconnected.

"It's not fake, don't think that."

"So after dinner, I am asking you, please, tell me everything…I need to know." Her voiced dropped from the volume he had always been accustomed to, a low soft, poignant voice of strength filled the air. "I won't go any farther if I don't know the person I make love to."

He bowed his head, "I understand...I won't disappoint you."

***

Dinner was located in one of the many restaurants the resort had to offer. The interior was glass with chandeliers red carpet lined the floors.

"I think we will have the Cabernet." Ben nodded to the waitress across the dining room as he made eye contact with another diner.

"This is a pretty nice place." Rachel, trying to bring Ben back to the present. "Hello, Ben?"

He turned, "Yes, it is, I think it's new, read somewhere."

Rachel paused, "You recognized someone?"

"No, no one, just surprised how many people are here, they day after Thanksgiving and everything."

The night went on, dinner was a pair of steaks, each ordered to the taste of each. Butter for Rachel, salted crab with sauce for Ben. Conversation was back to them talking about what could happen next. The thought of him asking a question entered his mind. They had discussed it in the months that past.

"When do you want to get married?"

Rachel looked across the table, silent, the smile returned to her. "Are you going to ask?"

"Sometime...I just don't know what you will say."

She laughed, a laugh that made his heart at ease whenever he heard it. "If you have to think about that, then the answer could be no."

"I guess..." A person, not the waitress came up to the table.

The unknown person was shorter than each of them, darker skin, black eyes with a little bit of gray in his hair.

"Excuse me, but I couldn't help it are you Ben? Right?
I can't think of your last name." The voice, soft,
educated.

Ben nodded. "Yes I am."

"You went to Eastern Montana College in the 90's
right?"

"No I didn't. I went to a small college in Oregon."

His eyes narrowed, "You look so much like a person I knew
for awhile, I swear it was you, the person I'm thinking about
was here with me, when I met my wife. I'm sorry, you two have a
wonderful evening."

The visitor turned, began to leave as he came back to the
table.

"Ben."

"Yes."

"Do you know a woman with a name of Aine?"

Ben could feel his throat tighten, "I'm sorry I don't how
to you pronounce her name?"

"It's not important, your not who I thought you were,
have a great night."

He looked at Rachel as the visitor left. Her eyes were
focused on the table he returned to.

"What is it?" Ben asked, following her eyes to where she looked. The man returned to his table. A blonde woman was sitting with him. They began to discuss a topic, and both of them shook their heads. He glanced at Rachel, eyes moist. A tear, streaked down her right cheek. "What's wrong?" He asked

"You just can't tell the truth can you?"

"I am telling the truth."

"No you're not, he knew you, the woman he's sitting with knew you. I can't do this."

He placed his hands on the table, "Please, no they didn't."

She pushed back her chair and looked at him. "Bullshit, I'm done."

"Rachel wait."

***

Dinner was over, Ben stared at the full plate, ice in the glass had melted long ago. He had let the waiter know to take Rachel's plate-box it up and send it to the room.

"Is there anything I can do for you sir?" The waiter softly asked.

"No, here is my card, thank you for everything."

"Of course." The waiter disappeared.

Ben looked around, the dining room now barren of customers. Staff began to place the linens, unused silverware and glasses away, which exposed dark wooden structures of the tables.

"Thank you." He expressed to the waiter as the paper copy of tonight's failure appeared before his eyes. A quick scribble-Ben strode out into the hallway-decided not to go back to the room, and take a much-needed walk to ease his mind and body.

He left the small building, which, included the restaurant and entered the main lodge. A collection of visitors sat in wooden chairs, granite slabs under feet, wooden walls and a fireplace. Not wanting to talk or be around people, Ben decided to continue on his way, traveled up a staircase, another long wooden hallway waited him. A quick thought raced through his mind, he should go back to check on Rachel, yet he wanted some more time to think.

The end of the walk greeted Ben with a large window. Frost was gathered on the outside, obstructing some views of the lights that lit the ski runs during the night. He turned to the right and began down a small wooden staircase that he noticed led into a room. It had two chairs, a fireplace on the last embers, the only light that was visible. Ben sat on the chair, it moaned. The fire flickered, and highlighted a log next to it. He got up once more, placed the log onto the commanding embers. It lit-the room became brighter. He hadn't noticed the rug now under foot. A brilliant pattern of reds, beiges and greens traveled the room, a long river of color. In the orange light, he studied the pattern, pressed his lips together and looked toward the walls. There were slabs of rocks, unlike the lodge itself which he noticed was adorned with wood-everywhere it seemed. His eyes, strained to the mantle of the fireplace, until this moment-obscured by darkness. What they saw, or what he thought they saw, he moved to study. His finger traced the pattern, one after another-what the mind deciphered from his fingers, were steel, cold and in a perfect U shape. "Horseshoes" Ben whispered to himself. He looked back at where he was once seated, noticed the rug wasn't a pattern, it was a depiction. "Oh shit." He thought of himself. The pattern turned into a map, a map of an expedition by Lewis and Clark that traversed half of the continent in the early 1800's, including Montana. As he studied the room he looked for something, no longer there, "Where are the paintings?" He told himself as he sat down and looked into the fire. The tops of the flames danced around the wood, much like hair does on a windy day. In the trance, the fire entered his mind. He jumped, when a hand was placed on his shoulder.

"I'm sorry sir, the reading room closes at midnight, sir? Are you okay?"

"Yes I'm sorry, I will be going." He exited the chair, looked at the owner of the command. "Can I ask you something?"

"Yes anything."

"Where are the paintings?"

"Your referring to the C. M. Russell paintings?"

"Yes."

"They are down the hallway, yet again, the fireroom is closed."

"Is there anyway I could see them?"

Ben looked at the distance from the fireplace and thought it was 50 feet away, a thud of a light switch was heard in the darkness. A hallway big enough for three grown adults, was lightly illuminated. Lights over a series of ten paintings, lined the hall.

"Wow...I mean the room...this wasn't here...like this."

"When was the last time you were here?"

Ben felt a knot in his throat, "December, 1993…was coming back, sometime."

"Such specific dates..."

His breath soft, "That's what happens when your life changes, I guess."

"I'm sorry to hear that, this room was remodeled around three, fours years ago. The paintings were moved from in there, to here. Farther down the hallway is a small library with their journals, I can give you a couple of minutes if you would like. I would like to go home though."

He nodded, "A couple of minutes."

It looked like the paintings were hung with great care. Lights shown above them, their colors glowed, reflecting off the pine walls. His mouth moved as each painting was passed, "York", "Indians Discovering Lewis and Clark", each pass brought more of the paintings alive, "Captain Lewis Meeting the Shoshones". They were each of the same size, his eyes followed the line, there was a larger one. Out of the darkness arose a large, antique wood framed masterpiece.

Ben had seen this print before. A much larger version, he remembered, was in his high school hall. As he passed it every day came the hopes and fears of what had transpired before, and what was to become in the future. His mouth moved again, "Lewis and Clark Meeting the Flathead Indians at Ross's Hole." A valley arose towards him, a white horse in the middle of the painting guided to a meeting that would change Montana forever. How glorious it would have been to live then. No phones, no Internet, no cars, just life. He studied the picture, the noses of the horses, the Native Americans, the children, and the snowcapped mountains in the background. The paintings were in a much different setting, the hallway did not exist. The fireroom was there and so were the paintings. Today the room was warm,

just as it was the only time that he had traveled to Big Sky
with someone else. A someone, that made the room warm, no matter
the temperature. I have to tell Rachel, I can't live like this
anymore.

Chapter Thirty-Six

The journey back to the cabin was cold. He placed the key
into the door and turned the knob and darkness greeted him. He
stepped in, a crackle of the fireplace echoed. It was low,
another log on it, fire spit around the new entry, igniting the
sap. Ben traveled up the stairs and sat on the corner of the
bed. The covers were pulled over a lump in the bed.

"Rachel, I'm sorry." Ben placed both hands over his eyes,
as they made their way down. He turned; one hand went on the
lump. The hue of the new fire made his mind and eyes re-adjust
to the setting. The lump wasn't a human; it was made of textiles
and fabric-not flesh and bone. Ben made his way to the bathroom,
a light flickered, toiletries that were once there were no
longer. He felt his cheeks become flushed, his body began to
shake.

"No, Rachel no, God damn it!"

The cold encircled him as he located where the car was
parked.

"Shit!"

He stood in the empty parking spot, looking at the sky. The galaxy ring made its faint imprint across the large expanse of sky. Shimmering of suns from across space came into his optic nerve.

His voice made plums of steam, *"I've lost her."* He kept telling himself as he traveled to the room.

He stared at the fire, yet felt cold. So much had gone right in the months that had passed. She was it, he told himself, Rachel was the last time he would be this close to love.

"Maybe she'll come back in the morning." His head placed on the corner of the couch, his eyes closed.

He awoke to a smoldering fire, cold air bit his eyes and nose.

"Rachel." He called, "She's not here." He told himself. "How am I getting home?"

He reached for his phone and dialed the number.

"Alan, could you do me a huge favor, please."

Alan's car came into view, he noticed the head of Lisa in the front seat. Ben placed his hand around the suitcase, the wheels bounced on the rocks used for foot traction and the snow. He placed it in the back and got into the back seat.

"You okay?" Alan asked into the mirror.

"No, not really, thank you for getting me, I would just like to go home."

"And Rachel?" Lisa asked.

Ben took a breath; his mind still hadn't caught up to what had happened. "Later, okay?"

Ninety-five miles west of Bozeman, Ben continued to look out of the window. Lisa's voice brought him into the present.

"Pull over Alan, here, pull over."

"What?" Alan questioned.

"I told you to pull over, here PULL over."

Alan did as his wife instructed, as the car stopped, Lisa glanced at Ben, we need to talk.

The outside air, much colder than the comfort of the car stung his face.

"Who are Ben, we need to know?"

"Lisa what is this?" Alan protested.

Ben looked into her eyes, unlike last week, her hair fluttered in the wind, strands sticking to her lipstick.

"I don't know who you are Ben. We trusted you, as a friend…I trusted you. Rachel has left you, that for sure is over, for some reason you could never tell her who you are. So you have to ask yourself, are you going to lose me as friend today too?"

"Lisa." Ben muttered. Rachel must have texted or called her, no response from his frivolous pleas.

"I have come to realize that I don't know who one of my friends is, someone who I have talked about my life with. Don't you get it?"

"Please…Lisa."

"No Ben, I need to know, I need to know who you are. Who actually knows you? Alice? Who?"

He looked at her; the wind felt numb against his eyes, anything that could come out would be frozen in an instant. "Let's get back into the car."

"No, who are you, last time I will ever ask?"

A long breath came out of his mouth, his face turned warm, the sting of water freezing on his cheeks bit at his nerves. "Okay, my parents, their dead, because of me, and that I have lost someone I loved."

"We all have lost Ben, all of us."

"No…not like this, I have tried for the last twenty years to forget my parents, my sister and a love, that was taken from me. I can't forget, I'm sorry Lisa, I can't forget."

"Why didn't you tell us this before?"

"I wanted to forget, erase everything that has happened to me in certain times in my life. I battle everyday with the past."

Lisa placed her hand on his shoulder, "I'm sorry about Rachel, let me help you."

* * *

The door opened, Ben traveled up to the bedroom, his finger traced the empty draws. The glimmer of hope that she would be at home, was gone. All of her clothes had disappeared. He made his way down to the first floor-looked at the perfect furniture. Ben placed a hand inside of his pant pocket for a cell phone. He found the card of the furniture salesman in a kitchen drawer, a cell phone number scribbled on the back-he dialed.

"Dan this is Ben, Ben Meager, yes the furniture is amazing…however." Ben felt his voice stumble, "I have a very strange request for you."

August 2017

When the sun's morning rays licked the Rocky Mountains, Ben was already at work. He slid his hands over the well-worn oak desk, and gazed at an algorithm he had worked on for several months. The Science and Forestry departments had applied for a grant from NASA, and Ben's task was to complete the algorithm and make absolutely certain that it would work. He worked in a notebook filled with mathematical computations, one page after another, with hundreds of hours of work poured onto them. Finally satisfied, Ben slipped the notebook into an envelope and sealed it. He would hand deliver it across campus.

He placed the long envelope on his desk and noticed a face peering around the wooden doorframe. Ben smiled. "It isn't every day the dean of students hangs around my door. How long have you been out there?"

Alan covered the distance from the door, adjusting his three-piece suit and removing his ever-present fedora, which gave way to wispy blond hair and black-rimmed glasses, slipping down his nose. He sat down in his favorite pine wooden chair and grinned at Ben. "How was your weekend?"

"It was fine, worked on this algorithm, worked out, went to dry cleaners, about it…nothing special…it was a weekend."

Alan rocked in the old chair. It slowly creaked beneath him. "I see." Alan adjusted his tie slightly and pushed his glasses up higher.

Ben's face held as he mentally thought of the times, Alan had appeared in his office unannounced. "Alan what is it? Why are you here?"

"I'm sure that you have heard that the university has a new partnership with a college in Cork, Ireland."

"No, should I have?"

"Well you should have, it is very important to the universities outreach programs. Which brings money to us. Also there is a symposium next weekend on teaching there."

"What does this have to do with me?"

Alan laughed. "The history department chairman, was going, yet, has changed his mind. I have come to request that you will go in his place."

Ben gazed at his friend. "You've got to be joking."

"I'm afraid not. The trip will be there and back again, just enough time for you to attend, show your face and come back."

"I'm not doing it."

Alan looked at the floor. "My friend, this is not up for negotiation. Think of it as a quick vacation."

Ben closed his eyes; he couldn't believe what was being asked of him. He chuckled at the thought of himself, people would actually listen to him talk about teaching? His eyes opened, a secretary that he had for the last five years came into focus.

"Dr. Meagher, I have a letter for you, it was just dropped off."

He thanked her, glanced at the note and peered at Alan.

"Okay, I'll do it." Ben opened the envelope, his cheeks lowered.

Alan rose from the chair and made his way to the door.

"Excellent, I shall tell the president you will be attending."

Alan looked back at his friend. "What is it, Ben? Are you okay?"

Ben rubbed his hand across a cheek and noticed he didn't shave today. He ran his fingers through his hair. He needed a haircut. He was disgusted with who he had become. His thoughts trailed to the past for a moment, before he forced himself back to the present. "Yeah, I'm okay. Just stressed about this NASA project. It's important for the University."

"Yes it is, but...is there anything else...my friend?"

Ben pawed at the crisp folds of the letter, brought it into the air. "It's from Rachel."

Alan's smile, dropped. "I'm sorry Ben, I hope all is well."

"Can I ask you a question?"

"Of course anything."

"Does Lisa still talk to her?"

Alan backpedaled to the door. "No she does not, the last time was when...well you can remember." With a soft smile, he left the office.

***

The day was long, classes, papers and students took it into the night. The kitchen light illuminated what Ben could see of the bottom floor and headed up stairs. A letter bag was flung onto the bed. He took a breath, the trip was two days away, he still needed to make a presentation on how he taught, and make it interesting. A travel toothbrush, placed into the bag, the doorbell came alive. Ben looked at the time, eight-thirty. *Someone selling something.* The doorbell continued its chant. Both hands were placed on the top of his head, "okay." He breathed.

The outside light came on, as the door opened. *He wanted to tell whoever it was.* A smile-always perfect, glanced back at him. A smile that was somehow not the same, however it belonged to the person he had told himself, at one time he had loved. Hair, longer than he remembered.

"Rachel." He pursed his lips.

"Hi Ben, did you get my note?"

"Yes I did, I just didn't know if you would want to come over."

"I wouldn't have left the note if not. I was half expecting a wife, or girlfriend answering the door."

"That has happened since, you."

Rachel's smiled dropped slowly. "Can I come in?"

"Yeah...I'm sorry that I didn't invite you in."

Rachel began to walk to the light in the kitchen, her steps echoed in the house.

"Could I get you anything? To drink I mean?" Ben asked.

Rachel stood next to the table, looked out the windows toward the back yard. "Water please."

Ben retrieved a glass, and slid it into her hand. His hand touched an adornment that was not part of her the last time they had met.

"Rachel?"

She took a sip of water. "Ben I am getting married, I'm pregnant..."

Ben studied her, stunned, only one thing he could say, "Congratulations, I am happy for you. That is what you always wanted."

Her left hand went up to her eye. "You don't remember me do you?"

"Rachel I don't understand."

Again Rachel asked him. "You don't remember me do you…I guess senior boys, don't remember sophomore girls too much. Especially fleeting."

"I still don't understand."

"Ben…can you remember someone named Laurie, she liked to play video games?"

He studied her face, her hair. Chills raced down his spine. The past appeared in front of him. She was shorter than before-hair appeared longer, her teeth, younger yet still perfect. *In his mind*-Rachel transformed into a high school aged girl. The same girl he watched play an arcade game, watched cheer at the State Championship games, and comforted by after the final game. *Oh fuck*, he closed his eyes, "How, why, I sent you a letter?"

"There were three Rachel's in my class, so I said what the hell and went with my middle name."

"Why didn't you tell me, I would have…"

"You would have what? Fallen truly in love with me if you would have remembered me. I wanted that from you, you and I. I had wondered where you were, and then I saw you with that girl. I wanted to see you and be with you. Were you cheating on me? Was that it? Who was she? This should be my house with you, this should be yours...I need to know."

"I wasn't cheating on you, I swear." Ben whispered.

"Who was she? I know you were thinking of someone, tell me Ben."

"Someone a very long time ago."

"Longer than me? Amanda? You can remember her but not me? Seriously?

"I didn't even know your first name."

"Do you know how long I sat up in OUR bedroom and cried. How long it took me to pack my shit up. Was I being so selfish, that I should be with someone that can't find who they are. How I drove by this house when I was in town and wondered what you were doing. Wondered who you were with?"

Ben closed his eyes. "I'm sorry."

"Fuck, it should have been you and I, no one else…I need to go, I'm sorry."

Ben traveled behind her as the door opened. Rachel turned to confront him.

"What did you do with the furniture?"

He looked around into the darkness. "I donated it after you left."

Rachel's eyes went soft, her finger placed on his chest. "You will die alone, and if that's what you want than all the better. I decided that I wouldn't die alone…please, you deserve to be with someone Ben, please figure it out. If someone comes along, don't lose her like you lost me."

Ben slid his palm down the door as it closed, feeling the curves and the cold. Fuck it he told himself, and found his way into the garage, and looked at a line of white boxes. All the boxes that remained, he still hadn't completely unpacked. One of the boxes he had hid from Alice and Rachel. In it were pictures of her; the woman Rachel had accused him of being with. Ben decided that a printed photograph wasn't how he wanted to see her. He trudged up the long, isolated stairs and fought for restless sleep.

Chapter Thirty-Eight

During the flight, Ben had time to shape and convince himself what he was about to present was authentic and meaningful. Teaching, in any matter to him was hard. It took years to acclimate from student, the taker of knowledge to the teacher, the bringer of it. His early years of teaching at a college setting, proved difficult. Some of the students were his age or older, bringing into conflict at times; who was the student and who the teacher. He hoped what he would say to the fellow educators attending, would make them think and not dismiss in moments. Too many times, he had seen educators roll their eyes at knowledge they either didn't understand, or more to the point, didn't want to change their minds to think differently.

***

He stood facing a small marble desk. The hotel looked small from the outside, yet inside it was warm and invited him to stay more than two days. Two days were all that he told Alan he wanted. A quick get away from the university, in which work was still to be done and completed, grant work filled his mind.

"Sir? Can I help you?"

A woman no older than thirty, he surmised, was asking him a question. He stood with a garment bag over his shoulder and his bag in the left hand. His hand began to tighten, his breath slowed.

"Yes I have a room for the next two nights, Ben Meagher, actually it could be under Doctor."

"Yes, Dr. Meagher, I see you're coming from Montana, I've seen beautiful pictures of that place."

"Thank you, yes it is beautiful, but the summers are the best time."

"If you could just sign this." The clerk slid his hotel information across the desk. "Do you live around mountains?"

Ben scribbled his name, and smirked, every time he signed his name it looked different. A doctor's signature he thought, today's was one of the best. "Yes I do, but not as green as here."

The clerk looked at him. "Well, we have one of the best breakfasts in town, I encourage you to stay and have it, the university that you will be at, is just a short walk down the street."

"Thank you." Ben started to turn, yet the clerk beckoned him back for one more piece of conversations.

"Dr?"

"Please, it's Ben."

"Enjoy your evening."

"You as well." Ben found his way up to the third floor. The room was small, one bed, a window, the usual hotel furniture. He was tired, yet the time change was eight at night, however his body was twelve hours behind. Ben traveled outside, a walk seemed in order.

The streets were at times lined with people, others devoid. Signs, instructed him which direction for the university. He passed pubs, hotels, a river, and a bridge. Lights became more vibrant, the sun traveled to other parts of the world. Ben noticed the pavement ended, a small worn dirt path led him to the left, underneath a rock lined arch, large enough to fit two bikes side by side. The path continued, streetlights dotted the path, meandered and ended on a small hill.

He gazed on a massive stone structure. It could have been out of the middle ages. Approaching it, a plaque proved as much, as it read, "*the first university building*." He felt his cheeks form a smile; it was the oldest building he had seen. Ben felt for his phone, snapped a picture and sent it to Alan.

Chapter Thirty-Nine

There were more educators here than he thought. He took a breath, in a way it helped that the crowd was obscured in the darkness of the hall. The movements and low whispers he strained to hear, and he wondered, if they were talking about him or the day. Across the university, other sessions had involved academics from around the globe. He shouldn't be worried he told himself; he will quite possibly never see any of these people again.

In a moment, it was his time. Behind a projection screen, illuminated his name, title and institution. With a brief thought of, *here we go*. Ben started.

"Good afternoon, as the screen says, I'm Dr. Meagher or Ben as I like, from the University of Montana-Missoula. I am the mathematics department chairman."

A trick he taught himself in college was to have his mind wander as he spoke to an audience. At first, it didn't work-yet with practice he taught his mind to speak, and let his other mind travel to different times and places. Thoughts of the flight back, life, Montana, joined his mind. Maybe tonight he would order a pint from a pub he noticed while on his walk last night. In a moment his mind traveled to his parents, he often wondered if they would be proud of what his life had become. What had his life become? There was no doubt he was inspired at

work, his personal life-Alan and Lisa would call it a failure,
he thought. It was years after Rachel, that he felt Lisa could
trust him. He held the past near to himself; the one that knew
the complete truth was his sister. Pity he thought was for the
weak. This view had cost all of his relationships-nearly Lisa
and Alan.

"Mathematics just isn't a subject, you can show your
students, science, history, art and many other real world
examples using the power of math. Not only is solving equations,
it is also solving where we have come from and where we are
going...in closing I would to thank all of you and this
university. I have always wanted to travel to Ireland since
college, in the day I have been here; I have been welcomed in so
many ways. Again thank you. I will be out in the foyer for any
that would like to talk about math or anything else."

He shook hands with the next presenter as he left the room-
clutched the water bottle given to him before his session. He
noticed he had forgot to take a drink. Nervous energy he
thought, as the water inside of the bottle trembled.

A crowd of a dozen started to encircle Ben in the foyer.
Handshakes and businesses cards were exchanged. He smiled at
each one, and so began the give and take of knowledge from
colleagues.

An enchanted smell invaded his nose. His mind began to isolate it. As he talked to a professor from England, he felt his eyes widen. *Chanel No. 5* He told himself.

"Come again Ben?"

He began to scan the crowd; a quick red strand of hair, highlighted behind a black suited gentleman caught his eye. In a second the thought was gone, the smell lingered. Men were the only people visible. If his thoughts were true, most men's colognes didn't smell like Chanel.

"I'm sorry, I thought I...never mind it...excuse me, I need to head to the restroom for a moment...excuse me."

"Certainly, I actually had to hit the loo before your talk."

"Thank you, it was nice speaking with you. Don't hesitate to contact me." Ben shook his hand.

After he excused himself, Ben found himself outside, scanning the same hill from the night before. A lump in his throat formed; again, he scanned and closed his eyes.

***

The airline seat was as soft as it could be; Ben was comforted with a wing seat. The plane began to back away from the gate, he thumbed through his satchel for anything to take his mind off of the trip. The first, was a stapled pamphlet from the conference, he began to take each page one by one. Usually he hadn't looked at the swag that was given to presenters, *pretentious* he called it. Each page was flipped, he had met some of these people, looked at their biographies, placed a check mark next to the ones he could contact. His page was in the middle of the book and he flipped quickly passed it. The jet had reached the runway for take off. He continued to scan. The pilot let the cabin know that takeoff was imminent. The engines whirled; a high pitch squeal rang through them as they came to power. Another flip, the plane trembled down the runway. Ben flipped again, and stopped. His body tingled, the scars inwardly started to burn. A woman looked back at him, much the same age as he. His mouth moved slowly, forming the letters that made of the name. A name he had only dreamed of, he repeated it, looked out the window, the planes wings began to lift. Ben pressed his hand on the glass, for the first time in twenty-two years he spoke her name, *Aine*.

Chapter Forty

The short trip home felt like hours. Ben had to take the pictures of Aine out of the boxes. He had to bring her into the light. Ben knew his mind could never bring her to life. Even images captured on glossy paper were more beautiful than those his mind could produce.

Finally, after decades of searching, he had found her
again. But why, why, did she leave so long ago?

Ben hiked down the long, empty hallway to the garage.
Opening the door, he saw the boxes against the far wall. Like
most of the house, the garage sat empty, except ten boxes,
stacked in a precise five-on-five order, labeled Misc 1, Misc 2,
and so forth. After being promoted to department chairman and
moving from his apartment, Alice and her family had helped him
move in. It hadn't taken long. The apartment, like the house,
had been devoid of furniture.

Ben sorted through the boxes, knowing Aine was there
somewhere. The first box he cracked open was filled with
newspaper clippings from his elementary through high school
years, honor roll, announcements, and sports scores. Memories
skipped through his mind, but not the memories he looked for.
The second box held stuffed animals from his youth. His
favorite; an A&W Bear given to him by his parents and Alice,
while he recuperated in the hospital from a childhood illness.
This frustrating search continued until the tenth and final box.
She seemed to have vanished, again. Ben slowly pawed through the
box, lifting a Time magazine detailing the assassination of John
Fitzgerald Kennedy and uncovered a small, unremarkable shoebox--
blue with a white- and red-striped lid. He thought again of the
past; a tricky thing. Most times, he knew, it is better left

untouched, like an extinct species. With an archeologist's touch, he placed the shoebox on the cool concrete slab and removed the lid.

The sun's rays though the garage door windows illuminated the past. He plucked out pictures of his first eighteen months of college. He thumbed through photos of orientation, the first few days of his freshmen year, friends and acquaintances, their names lost to time. He flipped through them slowly, as if reliving each one, and then he found the two photos he needed. Ben hadn't seen these photos since moving in, and he didn't know why he had kept them. Maybe he wanted to torture himself. He just couldn't let go. The first photo depicted the sunrise. A woman's outline dominated the left side of the picture. Large, black mountains filled the background. Ben could see the faint reflection of the sunrise on Aine's face--draping her features in warmth. The second photo saw her resting her head and hands on a stone structure, covered with snow. Her irises were a solid emerald green. Ben closed his eyes and heard a soft, Gaelic voice. Leannan. He strained to hear the word again. Early in their relationship she had called him by his first name, but she soon found another name for him, Lover.

Chapter Forty-One

Ben sat on the cool, gray garage floor. His phone vibrated, and he noticed he had missed ten phone calls in the last three minutes--Alan. He moved into the kitchen and shuffled through his bottles of wine, neatly stacked in rows at the edge of the counter. He pulled out a merlot and placed it on the long dining-room table before calling Alan.

"Hey, what's up?"

"Not much. We were just wondering if you were sick."

Ben paused, deciding whether to tell him the truth. "I just was tired. I took a nap, and now I'm feeling better."

"Would you like to come over or go out?"

"Nah, I'm okay. I'm just going to have some wine and probably call it a night."

"I understand. We need to get together soon. Have a great rest of your weekend."

"You, too. Say hi to Lisa for me."

Ben ended the call and realized he had forgotten the pictures. He went back to the garage, holding the glass and the bottle of merlot, and brought the photos inside. He passed through the downstairs--the living room had only one chair, and the dining room seats were rarely-used and uncomfortable. Ben slowly climbed the stairs, being careful not to spill on the carpet. He placed the bottle and glass on his nightstand, flopped onto the bed, and propped his back against the headrest. The TV flickered on, and Ben searched for something to watch. He finally found something to transport him to the past, a replay of a women's volleyball game on the Big Ten Network. The game reminded him of the first time he had seen Aine.

Chapter Forty-Two

Ben had drifted off. The wine glass toppled onto the bed, the picture teetered on his thigh. He awoke slowly, noticing the large puddle of red wine. He'd have to wash the sheets, possibly purchase a new set. He grabbed his cell phone, and dialed Alice. He tried to keep his voice even.

"Wow," Alice said as soon as the line opened, "what has it been? Like two years?"

"Yeah, I've been busy."

"Ben, you're not the only person who works. Have you been up to cemetery to see Mom and Dad lately?"

"I sent flowers for Valentine's Day, but I haven't talked to them for a while."

"Could you go see them, please?" She breathed into the phone. "So why did you call?"

"Are you sitting down?"

"Why? What's--"

"I saw her," Ben said.

"Saw who? Rachel? Are you seeing someone? How long?"

"I saw her." Ben picked up the photo from his nightstand, lightly brushing it with his finger. He began to shake. "I saw her. I saw Aine." The phone went silent.

"Alice, are you there? Did I lose you?"

Alice cleared her voice and said softly, "Where?"

"Coming back from Ireland..."

"You went to Ireland? Why?"

"For work, I presented who to teach math...anyway...I thought I smelled her perfume, and then I saw her picture on the flight back. She was a presenter."

"Ben, how can you be sure? That's crazy."

"It's her, I know it sounds crazy, but I'm positive. It's Aine, I have a picture of her next to me."

"Hold on for me, Ben."

The line went silent again. He thought he heard keyboard strokes. "Ben." Alice's voice was soft, but cold and clear. "I don't know how you have a picture of her besides what was at this conference. You promised me you didn't have any, after Rachel. Which I would have to say was another huge screw up on your part. Don't even get into the conversation about Amanda."

"Alice."

"I'm going to get you a round trip ticket to come see me this weekend. You don't have anything planned?"

"No, I don't." Ben rolled his eyes.

"Good. Your flight leaves Missoula at 6:35 a.m., arrives in Portland at 10:30 a.m. The flight is on Alaska Airlines 1430. I'll see you Saturday morning." The call ended. Ben took a deep breath, knowing this would be a long week.

***

Monday morning began as it had last week. Alan walked into Ben's office and sat down.

"I see you're in the same position you were last week. Have you taken a shower?"

"I take two a day," Ben said. "And we saw each other on Saturday. Did I smell bad then?"

"No, you didn't." Alan laughed. "But you were preoccupied with something, and it had nothing to do with work."

Ben thought about lying, he had done that before, he couldn't do that to his friend again. "You're right, it wasn't about work. I saw someone."

A wide smile crossed his friend's face. "You need to tell us all about her. Come over this weekend?" "I can't. I'm going to see Alice."

Alan's eyes lit up. "This lady must be very interested in you to talk to her. How long's it been, five years?"

Ben put his hand on his chin. "Remember her and her family coming down, when you and Lisa were helping Rachel.... move into the house? That's the last time I saw them. That last time on the phone, two years."

"Can I ask why?"

"It was about Rachel and how I treat people in my relationships."

"Hmm, the past can be difficult to deal with."

Ben squinted his eyes. "Why are you here today?"

Alan smoothed his tie. "I am here on behalf of the Chancellor. If the university gets the NASA grant, you my friend will be asked to abandon this position for one that's more-- lucrative, shall I say."

Ben's stomach churned. "Alan, I didn't start teaching for money."

"You forget I taught, too. Save me the change lives for the better speech. Think about it."

Ben nodded.

"By the way, I need a lift to the airport Saturday morning."

★★★

Ben had never understood why getting to the airport early was so important. If the flight left at six in the morning, the counter didn't open until five-thirty, leaving just enough time to get your ticket and go through security--a slow and meticulous process at a small airport like this. He had flown all over the United States, and the security at this postage-sized airport was the most obnoxiously serious he had seen. The small-town feel of the airport meant that being nice always earned a smile. But sometimes I just don't feel like being nice, Ben thought. He passed through security and traversed two flights of stairs before arriving at the gate. He saw his plane through the glass, and the attendant announced the plane was about to board. He found his seat, strapped himself in, and proceeded to ignore the flight attendants--that was the name of the game. The plane sped down the runway, and the pilot gunned the engines, climbing fast to clear the mountains. Ben always wondered if this was how it felt to fly a space shuttle. In mere minutes the plane had banked around the mountains and climbed to the cruising altitude of thirty-two-thousand feet. Ben closed the window shade. As he fell asleep, he mused about the past.

Chapter Forty-Three

The plane touched down and jolted Ben awake. The flight had been smooth as glass. Landing was just as nice. The plane's back landing gear gently touched the surface of the runway, and the airbrake deployed. The plane slowed enough to turn left toward the terminal.

Ben followed the other passengers off the plane and met humid air. He was craning his neck to look for his sister when he felt his phone vibrate.

meet me outside terminal 1

He scanned the crowd. A Dodge truck directly ahead of him moved, and a white and black 2015 Corvette ZR1 flew into the vacated spot. The two front windows were rolled down, and Ben half smiled as he recognized his sister in the driver's seat.

Alice waved to Ben, and he dropped into the low car. Alice looked the same as the last time he'd seen her, except her white hair. She eyed him through her John Lennon-esque sunglasses. "I know, I'm getting old." Alice smiled and ran through the gears. She hit the interstate at over a hundred miles per hour. Ben noticed the radar detector on the dash. He closed his eyes and clutched the door, only relaxing a little when Alice set the car on cruise.

An hour later, they reached Alice's house, stuck in the rural area of the metropolis. The house was a Victorian replica; worth at least he thought a million plus. Large maple trees rose on either side of the paved driveway, which split toward the four-car garage and the front door. Ben had known the house was large, but he had never seen it. Alice and her family had moved here four years earlier, two years before Ben had moved into his, with Rachel. He'd always thought Alice was trying to one-up him.

Mark now was on the payrolls of the world's largest pharmaceutical companies-they could afford to travel on weekends and during summers. Their twin seventeen-year-old girls, Melissa and Tiffany, always had the latest clothes. Ben hoped he'd see them today. He hoped they'd remember him.

The house itself a silent, showroom for the life they had built. Pictures adorned the walls from the front door to the kitchen--photos of their family's travels, Alice's time in the military, the girls' birth and childhood. Ben noticed there were pictures absent-of him. He rolled his eyes, no surprise he thought.

Early afternoon-he was exhausted from getting up early, the drive to the airport, and the flight. Ben decided he needed a break.

"Hey Sis, I think I'm going to lie down."

"I thought you would say that. The guest bedrooms ready for you. We're having lasagna tonight."

"Mom and Dads' favorite." He pursed his lips. "When are Mark and the twins coming home?"

"They're at the beach, and will be home before dinner. I'll wake you up when they get here."

The guest room, one among the house's five bedrooms--he traveled through the state-of-the-art kitchen, a small dinner area, a sitting room, a living room, a movie room, and a formal dining room. He wondered if they used the dining room on holidays. He had never been invited. Ben curled up in the strange bed and took a much-needed nap

Chapter Forty-Four

The sound of opening and closing doors awoke Ben. Voices began to echo through the house-filtered to his ears, more than one voice. The stairs began to come alive with muffled sounds of footsteps up and down. Ben exhaled, this could be interesting, the last time he had seen them was with Rachel. He moved out of the bed, spread the comforter with his hand, and the ripples soon disappeared into a smooth lake of textile. He knew Alice would check. Ben stepped into the hall restroom-splashed water on his face and noticed more gray hair in the mirror. Damn, I'm getting old he thought, a birthday was coming up, too soon he told himself-what do I have to show for my age besides, grey hair? A career, a house and then what? He blocked out the thoughts-and went to find his sister.

Stainless steel dominated the kitchen, it looked to large for any house-felt larger than his living room. Alice was busy placing long lasagna noodles in an oven pan.

"Hi, sis." His voice echoed off the walls as he approached her.

Alice jumped. "You scared me."

"Sorry."

"It's okay, glad you're up. Mark is in the garage, the twins are upstairs on their phones or doing something. God only knows."

Ben stuck his finger into the thick red sauce. "Very good...I'm going to say hi to Mark."

"He would like that, been a while since you talked."

Ben found Mark inside the open Corvette, he lightly brushed the dash and the seats in perfect slow circles. It was her car, yet Ben knew who's job it was to keep it perfect. He rolled out of the car and wiped off his hands with the yellow towel he had just used to clean the machine, and tossed it onto a yellow collection of at least ten Ben thought.

"Good to see you. It's been too long." Mark extended his hand and smiled.

A short chuckle came from Ben. "Yes it has. How are you?"

"Good. Tired. The twins are giving me a run for it, no doubt. Your sister and I have both been doing some traveling. I've been to India and England this year." Mark placed the edge of his palm on the corner of his eye. "Heard you were in Ireland?"

"There was a conference that I spoke at, it was a very
quick trip."

"Beer?" Mark asked as he motioned to Ben to sit on
one the two bar stoles across from the Corvette. As Ben made his
way to the stool, Mark traveled to a workbench that extended
half the length of the garage. He pressed on a wide cupboard and
a refrigerator was revealed.

"312 from Chicago, I hope you like it."

Ben took a quick swig, he couldn't remember the last time
he had a beer, with anyone. The taste of the wheat, flashed in
his mind. The summer sun beat down on his combine.

What else besides work?" Mark queried.

Ben shrugged as he took another taste, this time it held in
his mouth-swallowed. "Just work."

"You're still thinking about her, aren't you?" Mark
gave a small grin.

Ben looked at the yellow and black label of the beer,
brushed off a drop of condensation and answered. "Rachel was my
fault, completely all mine. I have to live with that." He took a
breath, another wheat taste entered his body and mind. "She
appeared, a couple of weeks ago, actually."

Mark stumbled for words. "And?"

Ben nodded. "...She wanted to let me know that...she was
married and was pregnant. I still think about her at times." A

long pause consumed the two as they wiped the bottles slightly

back. "So what can you tell me about this car?"

"Oh, it's not a car. It's a machine." Mark laughed and

began to use his fingers to point out the cars features. "Ben,

you should visit more often."

He took a breath. "Why doesn't my sister come to Missoula

to see Mom and Dad?"

"I think she doesn't want to see them, if that makes

sense...she has always had a difficult time talking about what

happened."

The beer was almost gone as Ben pondered what Mark had

said, a voice broke into his mind.

"Hey you two, are you ready to eat?" Alice called from just

inside the house. "We're eating in the small dining room. The

table is ready."

* * *

Ben could tell their family hadn't eaten together in a long

time. The teenaged twins tried to bring their phones to the

table, but Alice put her foot down.

"Teenagers," she said.

Melissa and Tiffany reminded Ben of Alice at that age. He

shuddered. He didn't think he could have survived two of her.

"I'm glad we didn't have cell phones when I was a teenager," he said.

Tiffany spoke up in her fiery tone. "That would have been lame, no texting."

"I know," Ben said, "you actually had to talk to people. Tragic."

Alice grinned. "And I remember Dad telling you to get off the phone."

"Who were you talking to?" Melissa asked.

Ben stuck his fork through the lasagna. He remembered the day Alice was talking about, and he remembered his sister and parents regulating his phone time.

"Friends." He popped a piece of lasagna in his mouth.

"My friends," Alice retorted.

"You dated Mom's friends?" Tiffany had abandoned her lasagna.

Alice lifted her eyebrows. "I wouldn't say *dated*."

Ben felt a smile across his face, he glanced at Mark as he rolled his eyes.

"Ladies, they grew up in a very small town, and your uncle, I mean I don't rate guys but if I would, he would be around the top of the numbers."

The table erupted in laughter. Ben could never tell Mark, that at that moment, the moment of laughter was the closest he had felt to having a family since the death of his parents. He looked around the table, for a moment all that was lost was forgiven, all that was lost was in the past.

Dinner, and outstanding conversations transpired that he hadn't had with Alice for decade's. He volunteered for the lesser of the two evils and cleared the table, while Alice and Mark made short work of the dishes. As Ben entered the kitchen, Alice was placing the last dish in the dishwasher.

"Mark, start the fire in the den please?"

What the hell does this house not have!

"Wine?" Alice asked.

"Red."

Chapter Forty-Five

The den was softly lit; dark leather furniture surrounded the fireplace. Ben placed his drink on a low marble table as he sat down. The leather felt soft, much like the furniture he once had. A chair was all that was left of a reminder of Rachel, his failure. He still wondered what Alice was up to-from an early age to the days in college-she always had a plan.

Ben admired the fire. "I like the room."

"Thank you."

He scanned the room, no Mark.

"Mark went upstairs to read...we need to talk, I mean we haven't talked for a very long time...since."

A lump formed in Ben's throat. "Rachel, I know."

"Ben, what happened with her, she was beautiful, had a career...she loved you, you know."

It was just like his sister, to bring up the pain of the past, no matter how long ago. He was surprised she hadn't needed him for something he had done to her the moment he came from the womb. He stared at the fire. "It was my fault, I just...I just couldn't tell her, and then she was gone."

"I saw her two days ago." Alice said.

"And."

"She said that she saw you some weeks ago."

Ben nodded, placed his hand through his hair. "Yes, she did."

"Why didn't you tell me."

"BECAUSE...because...it was between her and me. She is married and having a kid, what did you want me to do? Call you and say, hey Alice guess who came to see me tonight. Oh, the person that I completely screwed over. The person that I should be married to, the person I should be having kids with. Oh, yeah that's right. It's that person, it's Rachel. If I would have never met Aine, maybe I could be married now. But, no I'm not, I don't

have a perfect life, house, everything like you Alice. I don't,
I only have my career and that's it. And then, here's the kicker
on my trip from Ireland I swear to god I fucking saw her. I saw
her hair and smelled her. Then, I say to myself no, no it
couldn't be her. Who would ever want to see me, on the plane I
get out this program or whatever the fuck it was from the
conference, and she is staring back at me. It was her, I need to
find her Alice, for my mental health I need to talk to her. I've
thought about a ghost for twenty-two years. What do I have to
show for it…nothing."

"Well."

"Well what?" Ben asked. He noticed Alice had placed
her wine on the table and had traveled to a desk in the far
corner of the room. A click, preceded a drawer being moved. The
fire crackled, Ben turned to a log that moved, it guided his
attention until he heard another sound-a letter slid across a
table. It was dark in the room, yet the fire seemed to highlight
what he needed to see. He looked down at the letter, picked it
up with his hands. The smell of Chanel came into his senses. The
dress came difficult to see though the mist in his eyes.

"How, ALICE, how did you get this?"

"Ben, she's the one that left you."

"I don't understand, how have you had this for this long?
My god it was mailed in." Ben examined the letter, the corners

were crisp, the writing dark. "February 23, 1995, how long were you going to keep this from me?"

"At first I didn't want to keep it through the years, I thought you would forget her. Then, you met Rachel, and I prayed you wouldn't fuck it up, Ben, I prayed, I asked Mom and Dad."

He pointed the letter at her. "Don't, that is *bullshit* and you know it." Ben noted the letter was heavier than just paper, he would wait to open it at home. A thought crossed his mind. "Where's the ring?"

"I don't know what you're talking about," she said.

"Alice?"

A tear formed in Alice's eye and made a line down her cheek. "I really don't know. I wish you would have talked to me before you forged my name."

Ben took leave of Alice, paused at the doorway. "Take me to the airport tomorrow?"

Chapter Forty-Six

Alan, leaned his back on the cool airport wall, and waited. He looked over the three counters that handled the flights out of Missoula. Today, a long line of individuals waited at the Allegiant counter. Alan smiled, maybe Lisa would like to take a vacation sometime soon, one of their destinations, cheaper than Delta, no "frills" however, Vegas maybe? He smiled, the last time they were on Allegiant he wondered if he needed to swipe

his credit card for landing gear, and again for speed breaks. A

silent laugh crept into his chest, Ben appeared down the stairs-

headed out the doors to him.

"So how was the sister?"

"Thanks, Alan. Nice seeing you, too."

Alan placed a hand on Ben's shoulder. "What is it?"

"Alice...I will let you know."

"Promise?"

There was an edge to his question, in knowing why, he let

his best friend know. "Always."

★★★

As Ben stepped inside, the silence of the empty house was

more noticeable than ever. The clang of the bag that hit the

floor echoed through the house. He put on a pot of coffee and

set the letter on the dining room table, Aine's loopy and

elegant cursive was so different from his students' chicken

scratch. Ben grabbed a butter knife and slowly cut it open. He

would usually rip into a letter, this one, elegant and old

guided an archeological touch. Inside a letter opened with three

pictures that fell to the table below. He moved to the chair in

the living room and carefully looked at the pictures, her

handwriting made the scars burn. He couldn't keep from asking

himself, why did she leave?

Chapter Forty-Seven

Ben woke to brutal knock at the door. He looked around the living room, the sun casted its low rays onto the floor. How could this be he thought, as he looked through the peephole, he knew how. Alan looking back at him.

"Didn't I see you in that ensemble yesterday?"

"Yesterday? Damn it, Alan, what time is it?"

"It's nine a.m."

"Nine a.m.? As in Monday, shit." Alan let himself in and walked past Ben. "Damn!"

"What, Alan? You know I never miss work."

"No, you have one chair. I bet Lisa you had two."

Ben closed the door. "Well, thanks for thinking better of me than Lisa does."

Alan walked into the kitchen and started the Keurig. "This is the first day you've ever missed."

"Whoa, I'm not missing today."

Alan removed the mug from the coffeemaker and started another cup. "Creamer?" he asked.

"No, I like my coffee black."

"Ah, right. Anyway, you're staying home today. Clean or something." Alan ran a finger across the spotless granite countertop. "Well, I'm not sure what you could clean, actually. Since you have no furniture. However, do something. I already emailed your students that classes are cancelled, and I'll tell the Chancellor your sister gave you food poisoning."

"She, what?"

"Can I take this mug?" Alan didn't wait for a response before carrying the coffee out the door.

Ben watched him go, shook his head. He sat in the living room and opened his laptop, hearing it hum as it started up. He clicked open his calendar and scanned the dates, looking for the perfect day to leave. A month and a half from today. The NASA grant, along with Ben's promotion, would be decided in the middle of July. Ben wiped the thought from his mind, focused on a flight, a car, and a hotel room in Ireland, near Aine's address. At least, that had been Aine's address, twenty years ago.

He opened Google Maps and searched for the address, bringing up an image of a two-story house. It was quaint, with white siding, red shutters, and a porch with a bay window. He thought of the house they had seen after watching "Legends of the Fall."

***

As they headed back to the dorm, the snowfall grew heavier.

"Before we go back," Aine said, "let's go look at Christmas lights."

"Okay, that sounds awesome."

Ben's Ranger plowed through the snow, falling thicker by the minute. They looked at the lit-up houses.

"Stop. Ben, stop."

"What's wrong?"

"Nothing, just stop."

He pulled the pickup to a stop next to a single story house, with a basketball hoop hung over the garage, and a Christmas tree shining behind a bay window.

"What do you think? That's going to be our house."

Ben smiled. "Someday, it will be."

* * *

Ben looked around his empty house. He would never know how Aine would have felt about this house.

He could use the address to search for a phone number. But he brushed the thought from his mind. He didn't know what he would say. He had drunk dialed her once, in college, the night before a game day, after partying with Kyle. He'd thought it would be funny, but she hadn't been amused. The next morning she came to his room and said that if he ever did anything like that again, it was over.

Stressing over missing work, staring at his computer screen, and thinking of Aine were beginning to give him a headache. He had to talk to someone about this. He texted Alan.

Hey, mind if I come over tonight?

Alan replied immediately. *Of course, you can always come over, we will be waiting for you after work, get some rest.*

* * *

The April air was cold. Clouds gathered in the air, bringing dampness- rain threatened. With Alan's salary, Ben wondered why he and Lisa didn't live in a mansion, or at least a house bigger than Ben's. The real beauty of their house was its location, riverfront property. Ben entered the house through the garage and walked down the hallway to the kitchen. The walls were filled with pictures documenting Alan and Lisa's ten years of marriage. They had traveled the world together-Lisa bustled in the kitchen, gave him a hug and a kiss on the cheek.

"It's so nice to see you. It's been awhile. Sit down."

"Beer, water, juice, or soda?"

"Actually, I'll have a beer."

She looked at him puzzled. "That's interesting, what's the occasion? I think I might have something that you like." Lisa poured a glass of Ben's favorite, Dragon's Breath from Bayern, a local brewery. It was a dark beer, but it tasted light.

"Dragon's Breath?" The name of the beer seemed to fit the moment. After five years, it still seemed that they had something to say to each other.

"Yes." She retorted as the church key popped the top of the beer.

"Thank you, where's Alan?"

"He's outside cooking and keeping the shepherds away from the food." Ben laughed. "What's he making?"

"Burgers and brats."

"Nice."

The door closed, Alan was holding a plate of food that smelled delicious. The meat on the plate sizzled and popped.

"With that, we are ready." Alan placed the plate on the counter.

"So tell me about the NASA grant," Lisa asked as Ben placed part of the burger in his mouth. "I know I have great timing."

"As always, ahh, it's about glaciers, how much they gain or recede in any year or season. The technology is pretty impressive, the software is first rate, but to some I guess it could be boring, I believe in it. Glacier I believe is one of the last best places, along with Banff and Jasper."

Alan pondered. "I think you could get a date by just saying that."

Some of the Dragon's Breath had went down as Alan had used his one liner. A bubble, expanded in his throat. A cough expelled it. "Yes, I guess you are right, but."

"Could you do the dishes, Ben and I are going to go for a walk." Lisa asked.

"Of course." Alan replied.

* * *

The outside deck was half as wide as the house, with a view of the Rocky Mountains and the Blackfoot River. Ben and Lisa walked along the riverbank, past houses, lumberyards, and a minor-league baseball field.

"How's the Children's Theatre, Lisa?" Ben tossed a stick into the river.

"It's good. We are doing some amazing things. I would like to do more."

"Do you miss what you had before?"

"You mean my career before I met Alan? I miss being part of major productions. I miss working in Boston and London. But when I met Alan, everything changed. He is, I can't say it in words, just a feeling. My position now, is more fulfilling to my soul. It's something that someone has to experience to know."

The walk back to the house seemed shorter. Lisa grabbed a flat, worn rock and threw it into the river, making ripples.

"Ben, what's on your mind?" Ben watched the river, wished it could bring the past back.

"I have been looking for someone for twenty years, and in the last month I think I saw her and learned Alice had the key, all these years."

"Alice?"

"She gave me a letter with her address on it."

"This is the one that you lied to me about?"

"Lisa…"

For a moment she looked away. "You did lie to me, you lied to Alan. You don't know how much that hurts. To think you know someone…yet you find out, that the person you think you know and love, is a fake. Someone that can't stand up to their own past, someone that will have no future if they continue."

"I know you will never forgive me and for that I will be always sorry. I must try to meet her, again."

Lisa studied Ben, his face, posture. "You have to be careful. You can't just show up in someone's life."

"I have to finally know, for myself."

She smiled. "Ben, do me a favor. If this doesn't work out, move on. Rachel loved you…life is too short."

Chapter Forty-Eight

Weather turned from spring to summer. Trees wore thick leaves, the grass was green, the snow in the mountains began to disappear. Papers littered his desk, Ben looked over the various summer school assignments-began marking incorrect answers. The mind concentrated on correct math, his heart thought about Aine. A pen left a red gash when interrupted.

"You are pushing them quite hard this term." Alan quizzed.

Ben continued to grade. "I guess, we have a lot to do before..."

"You leave? Maybe you should have left earlier."

"Maybe but...damn it, this was such an easy question, how are they missing this?"

He heard the chair creak as Alan placed himself. "Can I have a word?"

In the years he had known Alan, not many times would he ask. Ben stopped his assault on the truth of mathematics and looked toward him. "Yes, I'm sorry, I just wanted to get these done. I have a lot on my mind."

"I know, I needed to tell you that we will know next week if the award for the grant is given to us."

Ben took a breath, and looked down at the red marks on the papers. "Damn, I'm going to be gone Alan. I can't cancel the trip, damn it."

"I know what you should do." Alan mentioned with a clear voice. "Go to Ireland, my friend, I will get ahold of you when I need to."

A small smile crept into the side of his mouth. "Thank you, tell Lisa thank you."

Many times before, Alan had gotten up and left his office. This was the first time Ben looked out the window, his thoughts as jumbled as the broken sidewalk below-a repair from the snow and ice of the winter.

The thought of Ireland scared him more than anything, the unknown. What if Aine didn't live there anymore? What if she was with someone else? The questions made his stomach churn. He hadn't seen her in twenty years, and he couldn't understand why she had left him, when he'd needed her most. He thought, too, of what Lisa had said, he should move on with his life. Seeing Aine would give him the closure he needed. No matter what, he would finally be free.

The marks continued on the papers, the pencil broke, arched a significant make shift letter on the paper. He stared-took out his phone and texted a number. "Are you in Missoula soon?" The number returned within a minute, his hand began to tremble with the response, his brain echoed his stomach, this could be a bad idea. "Yes, why?"

Ben continued, "Could we meet somewhere?"

The number retorted "Mackenzie River Pizza, in two days ok? 5 p.m.?"

Ben shook his head, "Yes, I will see you soon."

***

The streetlights illuminated the inside of his car, as he approached Mackenzie River. He told himself in the last two days he didn't know why he, asked for this meeting. Was it some way to torture himself or the other person? Soon he would know. The door to the restaurant opened, the smell of pepperoni and dough highlighted his senses. The floor was pure Western Montana flare, giant slabs of shale placed in irregular patterns guided patrons to wooden seats and tables. Pictures of the valley's history dotted, grey walls.

"Table for two." Ben spoke to the hostess.

"Dr. Meagher, I know." She retorted. "I had you for trig last year, your table is over there." She pointed to the corner of the restaurant, obstructed by a small wall.

"Of course, thank you." Ben took a breath and began to travel to where the hostess had pointed. A step around the wall and she was already there, her short curly dark hair, draped around her shoulders. Her eyes fixated out the window, he sat to her right.

"Nice to see you, Rachel." Ben spoke slowly and softly.

"Hi." She paused. "I didn't know if I was going to make it, what am I doing here. I have been asking myself that Ben. In some ways I don't give a shit why you want to talk to me. You had that chance, yet another part of me is curious, be straight with me, tell me now why I shouldn't get up and leave."

He looked at her, placed his phone on the table. "This is why, I need to tell you why." The phone came alive, the clear screen filled with one picture, then another and a third. "I want to tell you why I am myself, why I couldn't be who you wanted me to be." He began to cycle the pictures, one a formal dance, another a softball game and the last a picture taken at sunrise.

"That was you...who is that?"

Chapter Forty-Nine

The engines began to drown and seemed to come to a stop, the wing dipped, puffs of clouds encircled them. The plane began to descend, skirted some clouds; the engines gained speed for a moment, and returned to a slow soft hum. Ben checked his watch, 1 p.m. He looked out the window and noticed green fields that were separated into squares, the color of the earth, he remembered.

A small compact car pulled into the parking lot of where he was to stay. It was a small lot for an even smaller inn. The grey crushed rock of the lot reminded him of Montana. As he approached the red door to the entrance, he noticed a stone bridge that connected the small road he once was on, to the village.

He opened the door to his room, *quaint*. A small room awaited him, it was a place to rest. He fought the feeling of sleep. On the dresser, his fingers found a card for a local coffee house; *I don't look my best, it's time to see.*

Tables and chairs crisscrossed the inside of the shop; deep yellow covered the walls and the lighting was soft and low. The smell of the coffee and the decor relaxed his mind. He looked at the many different types of coffee on the menu.

"Can I help you?" A young woman behind the counter asked.

"I will have a solo macchiato, please."
The cup arrived quickly and hot.

"Here is your solo macchiato, thank you and have a great day."

"Thank you." He took a sip, it was as good as any he had ever tasted. "This is outstanding."

She smiled. "I'm glad." A moment passed, he thought she was going to ask another question and then it came. "If you don't mind, are you from the States?"

"Actually no I'm from Canada." She again smiled. "You got me, I don't sound Canadian?"

"No you don't, but…where are you from?"

"Montana."

"The mountains there look amazing."

Ben took another sip. "They are."

The woman grabbed a towel-began whipping the counter. "What brings you here, this isn't exactly a large place on the map."

He paused, *should I tell her*? "I'm looking for…and old friend."

"I see, does this person know you're coming?"

"No they do not, wanted it to be a surprise."

She paused. "So either it will be good or bad, hopefully good, if not…I know some older single friends."

Ben took a sip and coughed at her conclusion, and cleared his throat. "Thank you very much for the coffee."

"I hope you find what you are looking for."

* * *

The phones global positioning system told him to take a left, and a stretch of road that was sloped and straight presented itself. *Over the hill*, he told himself. At the top, the scenery opened, a deep horizontal hedgerow complemented him on the right, and to his left a stonewall, with accents of green grass that clung to the edges, a field with sheep behind.

Ben took a breath as hedgerows ended, the GPS announced he was at the address, he opened the gate that led to a small, two-story house with a porch and a bay window. He placed his hand on the door, and knocked. His breath still, the house *felt* silent. Seeing the porch furniture, he decided to sit and wait.

A brilliant day lay in front of him; the wind blew slightly, a tree filled with leaves moved. The multicolored stones of the fence, the field behind. *Whatever was going to happen was meant to be.*

From the hedge to the left, someone came into view, opened the gate and stopped. Ben slowly walked down the stairs from the patio. His heart pounded, his breath stopped. *Is this her?*

Ben stammered to say the name. "Aine?"

The figure, wearing a sun hat, stayed silent, and moved in a half circle around him and disappeared around the house.

***

He flung the suitcase, on the inn bed. It opened to the force placed on it, contents spilled out. He felt his face turn red. *"Fuck!"* He yelled. *"Goddamn it!"* Clothes were rolled and thrown in, no placement, just to get in the suitcase. I'm such a fucking idiot, what did I think was going to happen. That she would actually just say, wow, you're back, sure let's go out. Maybe have sex. Yeah, that sounds great, I'm sorry you're dead, so screw you. Not a hi, not anything, I'm not fucking dead Aine, I'm right here, right in front of you. I know it's hard since you're tall and I'm not." Ben placed himself on the floor next to the bed. What have I done, I'm old, I don't have a family like normal people, I will never have kids. Being married probably will never happen. Fuck, why can't I..I know why, I can't get over someone that I only had known for almost two years, who fucking falls in love with someone that fast and can never forget them? What has that got me? No where!

Ben placed his hand on the long counter. An older gentleman was on the phone, he touched his small rim glasses as he looked at a computer screen.

"Checkout time is now. I'm sorry you are so dissatisfied with your stay, I must apologize, yet if there is nothing else I can do for you Checkout time is now." The receiver was placed down. His attention now was to Ben.

"What can I do for you?"

Ben looked at him for a moment, "I need to checkout tomorrow."

"Name?"

"Ben Meagher."

The man typed his name into the computer and adjusted his glasses; his finger guided his eyes across the screen. "I have you for a weeks stay, you are leaving only after one?"

"Yes, work has called and I need to go back to Montana and soon as possible."

He grumbled, "Work must be important, it's a long flight back to the states."

"It is, on both accounts."

"You have anything else there?" The man asked.

"Work."

"I see, I see, well I will print out your card in a moment."

While he toiled, Ben took a breath and decided to ask a question. "That phone call, someone was unhappy?"

"Hmm, yes they wanted another room, yet we don't have any, so they will be checking out now."

"There are some people you just can't make happy", concluded Ben.

"Yes well, now let's see." The man looked over Ben's shoulder; "I will be with you in a moment." A frown crossed his face as the card was produced by the printer. "Sometimes names smudge, not knowing who the card is or belongs to so." The card was placed upside down in front of Ben, the clerks hands trembled slightly as he placed the appropriate answers to the questions, room number, where guest was from and others. The top space-left open, the guest name. He peered above his glasses, "I'm sorry I forgot your name, you told me who you were, age I guess."

As Ben began to answer the question, another voice, this one smoother and darker than his would ever be. "It's Ben Meagher." He craned his neck. Behind him, dressed in a black t-shirt with black sweat pants, and sandals was Aine. Her hair covered both shoulders. Only on certain instances had Ben seen her out of her hair style of choice-pony tails. She continued, "someone I knew in college, someone I once loved and." Her voice began to slow and moisture consumed her left eye. "And someone who died, for me, a lifetime ago."

"Aine?" Ben questioned.

"Can we talk please?"

★★★

Day turned into night. As they left the Inn, Aine pointed over to a dark structure, illuminated by a single light.

"Over there, is a stone table."

The table was cold to the touch, Ben had noticed it in the morning, a dark grey palate. It was from a quarry he thought. The edges were rough, yet the table and bench were smooth and worn. Her face became dark and light, as the solitary light changed her face as she moved. They stared at each other for a moment. Ben was the first to speak.

"I think we should start this off differently than the first time we met each other?"

"And how was that?" Aine asked.

The thought of the first time he had seen her glided across his mind. "Don't think I will pick the volleyball, maybe the balcony, or Petro Hall." He became concerned when an auditory response faded, as the wind did early in the evening. "Aine?"

"Sorry, just thinking, all those years ago the first time I saw you, which wasn't on the balcony or the court, the court was fun."

He could see a half smile appear in the light, then disappeared.

"It's just hard Ben, so hard."

Ben looked into the open sky, where flickers of stars dotted it. "I understand, I have thought of why you left, so many times in the last twenty years."

A long exhale came from the other side of the table. "Me, leaving…you?" "I can't do this Ben, I can't, I have tried so hard to forget." Aine, gathered herself to stand.

Oh shit he thought. "Okay, hold on." Ben placed his hand in the middle of the table. "Please…what do you do Aine?"

"Don't you know?" She questioned.

His body began to tingle, the red hair, the perfume. "It *was* you, you *were* there."

"Yes, I was there." She smiled "So you know what I do, I teach, small children, the same children you said you could never teach, or that you wouldn't want to teach."

"I don't remember saying something like that." He smiled at her.

"Ben, you did something with a small tent, and magnificent mountains. But that is in the past. I do know that you teach, and by all accounts very good at what you do. I should be going."

"No wait." Ben protested.

"I'm sorry I thought this would be easy, yet it's not, I do have one question for you."

"Anything." He whispered.

"How could you find my address, it's not listed, and the pamphlet only gave my name."

He exhaled, "one letter."

Her voice slowly filled the space, as she sat down. "A… letter?"

"Stay here please."

Ben found pace in his walk back to the room. The letter was neatly packed in the suitcase. He traveled back to where Aine had been…still was.

The letter, placed in the middle of the table. Aine leaned over, her hands cupped around her mouth. A glint of metal attracted his eye, a cross from her necklace dangled.

"You've had this for twenty years and have never came to see me? This is cruel Ben."

He shook his head; his right hand touched the letter with an archaeologist touch. "No, if I would have known where you lived."

"So why didn't you come?" He heard a sniffle across the table.

Ben grew frustrated at the thought. "Because I didn't know where you lived."

"How?" "I sent you letters every day, for one year I…"

"What? Aine, I only got this one letter from Alice, a month ago."

The light showed the reaction of Aine towards Ben. Not that of a scorned lover, that of someone that never had a chance of seeing someone, so many years ago, she loved. A short shriek was audible. "Oh dear Jesus, I mailed you so many times, and you never returned any them. I thought you were dead. I didn't talk to anyone at Eastern after I left."

"Why?" Ben asked. "Alice took me to Billings after I was able to walk…I saw Amanda."

Aine's eyes pierced the night. "So many things happened Ben, so many things, would you like to talk tomorrow?" "I'm not sure, I can do this tonight."

He nodded. "Okay."

Chapter Fifty

Ben rolled over, a sound, hallow, soft came from somewhere in the room. He peered at the clock, *seven* he muttered. He placed his head in the pillow, maybe whatever the sound was, it had to end. The sound stopped, then continued. The sheets unwrapped as they hit the floor. Ben reached for clothing, a shirt and shorts. The sound continued, through the fog of sleep he noticed what the sound was-the door. The latch pulled, the door revealed the sound.

"Hi." He stammered.

"Hello."

He thought of the words he could say, and wanted to, his mind was in overdrive, and vocal chords wouldn't produce.

"Were you sleeping?" Aine asked.

Finally, something spilled out of his mouth. "The time change isn't exactly the greatest."

"Yes I, well we can talk about that later, I do remember though." A moment seemed to enter into minutes. "Would you like to go for a walk?"

Ben looked into her eyes, dark and green. Her hair in a thick braid, hanging over her left shoulder.

"Ben, are you okay?"

Her voice put him into the past and brought him into the present. He felt his eyes blink. "Yes, that sounds great, I'm sorry I was just thinking."

Aine nodded her head, and flashed a smile. "I will wait for you, I'm sure you don't want to go out in those clothes."

Ben looked at his ensemble, an orange t-shirt with a red pair of shorts. He smirked, "Absolutely not, I didn't know I even packed these."

"I'm sure you didn't."

The door closed, a deep breath consumed his lungs. Oh my god, she's the same person, I swear, but am I, he thought-careful to pick clothes that matched, brushed his teeth, sunglasses were the article to be placed on top of his head, and headed outside, the sun was warm on his skin, the air crisp and cool.

"It's kind of like Montana."

"Greener, no mountains, but in a way."

Their walk took them into town, cobblestone streets, and small-multicolored buildings. He tried to relax his thoughts, thinking that every person they met noticed them. A tall woman leading a shorter man he thought, or were they so different that everyone noticed. Ben brought himself to talk.

"This is nice." He closed his eyes, here we go again, like twenty years ago he thought. He could feel her look down at him.

"It is, I love living here, it's my home, and don't you feel the same way about Montana?"

He could hear their feet on the stones, the sun warming his skin. "It's really the only place I have lived, besides Oregon."

Aine slowed her pace and stopped. "Oregon?"

"My aunt and uncle, I worked for them on their farm, after the wreck, after you, then I went to school." He looked into her eyes, some thought traveled through her mind, what, he did not know.

"I would like to show you something."

★★★

His hands wrapped around a large construction grade chain link fence. A black crater of earth was in front of them, the green of the grass offset the scene.

"This is where I teach." Aine pointed through the fence. "Well did."

"What happened?" he asked.

"It happened at night, no one was here, so we will be getting a new school next year."

"That's great."

"I guess, I mean a new building doesn't come very often. But this is where I did my schooling, and where my mom taught."

"So a lot of memories, I can understand."

"Understand."

"What?" He asked. Ben noticed a small smirk come across her face.

"Nothing."

Ben wondered if he should let it go, or press. His body became calm, a feeling that gave his vocal cords strength-he felt this only when conversing with academics or teaching.

"Tell me, please."

"You really want to know?"

"Yes."

She turned to him. "Then we need to sit down somewhere."

* * *

The coffee shop was the place Aine picked. Ben sat outside as she ordered. Aine returned with two coffees and was on the phone.

"I will see you later." Aine placed the coffee next to Ben, the phone conversation ended.

"You could have talked on the phone." He stated.

"That would be rude, it was work anyway, we are in a church, and it needs attention."

"I see."

"That's where I was when you waited for me."

Ben smiled. "Do you always dress like that when you teach?"

"I'm no longer in college and."

"What is it?"

Time to answer took two slow sips of coffee. "And I don't play volleyball but understand."

"Yes, anything."

"I don't understand why you never came looking for me, and I don't understand why you never wrote me back. I don't understand what you are doing here, please make me understand."

He noticed her face became red, her freckles hid underneath the color. Her eyes were now a light green, soft and wanting an answer.

"I didn't come looking for you, since I didn't know where you went. I woke up in Oregon, with Alice next to me. I swear to you I never got any of your letters until now, and that is one letter. I don't know what happened to the rest."

"Amanda told me she handed them to you in Oregon."

The name she used hit his heart as the hot coffee stung the inside of his throat. He thought for a moment. "Amanda knew?" His scars began to burn. "You talked to Amanda?" He began to panic, then Aine knows Amanda and I had sex, this is the talk about how it will never be the same and it's over even before it begins, no matter how I feel about her. He had another thought, *how does she feel about me?*

"I wrote her at times, but then that stopped. I do know Ben, I know about you and her."

He felt mist in his eyes. "I'm sorry, I swear I never got them."

"If what you are saying what is the truth, then there isn't anything to be sorry about. It hurt me, more than anything at that moment. I hated you; it was a very long time ago. What is time Ben?"

"I don't know."

She leaned toward him; her hand came across the table. He felt not in control of his body, as his fingers began to touch her nails, a warm electric sensation began to rush through his body.

"Time is something that is in the past, I have hated and loved you ever since we met."

"Hated?" He asked.

"That I could never say goodbye to you."

He felt his body tighten. "Is that what we are doing now… saying goodbye?"

Her fingers tightened around his. "There are many things about the past that I like, there are some that we will need to forget for our sanity. We need to speak of everything at some point, but not here. Tomorrow let's go somewhere."

Chapter Fifty-One

The green, rolling, countryside passed by Ben's passenger side window, it was odd seated in the passenger side. Albeit, he was in the same position with Alice only months ago, the car was much slower, more mechanical. A thought rolled through his mind, he had never been with Aine while she was the driver. His hand still gripped the plastic of the door as he looked over to her, hair down, covering the side off her face.

"You okay?" She asked.

"It's going, driving isn't my thing anymore."

"Since, the wreck?" She asked.

The hum of the engine enveloped the cabin, an electronic sound came from the speakers startling Ben. He looked at Aine, which used her thumb-pressed a button on the steering wheel to silence it.

She looked at him "Work."

"I was beginning to think that it was a boyfriend or someone." A soft laugh came from his mouth as he looked out the window. The hills became smaller, a green plain enveloped them, he could feel the car weight shift forward, they were going downhill and out the windshield, a dark blue green mass appeared.

"Wow, it's amazing I've never seen an ocean like that."

"Ben can I ask you something, and no it's not a boyfriend."

He continued to study where they were headed. "You can always ask me anything."

"What did you think about when you were asleep?"

In his mind he heard a loud metallic crunch, tree limbs ripped and silence. Warmness of blood flowed down his neck, his legs burned, somewhere a thought entered, *I am going to die.* Coldness, loneliness, a light consumed the emptiness. A Montana Highway Patrol officer flashlight illuminated his eyes, he felt weightlessness and then…darkness.

"Ben?"

Warm sweat dibbled on his forehead and hands. "Sorry, I."

"I'm sorry I shouldn't have asked, we are almost there."

"It's okay."

The warmness of her apology swelled inside of him, he had to tell her, he had to tell himself.

***

The car, guided to a spot that overlooked the ocean. Aine's door opened, Ben looked from his seat- a gesture with her hand told him what was needed.

"Come on, this way."

In exiting the car, the temperature was cooler than where they began the morning. The smell of the ocean permeated the air, the wind bit his ears. Aine followed a path down from the car, stopped and sat on a rock outcrop that overlooked the blue and green water. He followed-noticed to his right there were higher hills, black rocks expressed out of the land-the left he could see a town with sail boats in dock. The ocean churned and crashed against the rocks below. Two hundred feet he thought. Pebbles on the rock matted against his hand as he placed them on the black and red rock, he sat, two hand lengths apart.

"Thank you for bringing me here, this is amazing!"

Red hair flittered in the wind, tamed by a hair tie. "I should have put one of these on in the car." She looked at him and smiled. "It was no trouble."

"That question, I need to answer." He noticed she no longer looked at him-turned her gaze toward the horizon. "When I was asleep, what did I think about? It was more of a dream, not real but *real*, if that makes any sense. I dreamed of *you*, of what I was going to tell *you* when I woke up. I dreamed of seeing you everyday, your smile, watching you play volleyball, or coming with you to Ireland, of us traveling and meeting your mom."

A sound made him stop, Aine had picked up her hand a placed it in the corner of her eye.

"I came here as often as I could after I left Montana, it made me feel as if we were on that mountain. Sometimes my mom would drive me…since I just couldn't. It brought peace to my mind. I looked out over the ocean and wished you were with me." She took a breath and placed her hand back down, closer to his. "Why haven't you married, have you been married, are you with someone?"

The ocean seemed more violent as she asked the questions. He could imagine the hiss of the foam far down below. "I have dated, I've been with people, but I just couldn't, I couldn't…I think of you."

"Why have you put your life on hold because of me, I'm not anyone special."

He touched her hand and the same spark, enveloped his body.

"I never got to say goodbye, I never knew what we would be."

Aine turned to him, the wind had moved some strands of hair out of the pony tail. It whipped her face, and stuck on her soft eyes. "We only were together for a short time, why me?"

His mind paused, "If someone was just a girl, that I knew in college, then why did I think of you for twenty-years. I just couldn't forget you, I will never forget you."

Chapter Fifty-Two

Ben opened his car door, and looked at Aine, "I'm leaving in a couple of days, tomorrow?"

"I will need to go to work, but later yes," she replied.

A light flickered in the room, Ben reminded himself that he turned his phone off before the car ride. A press of a button brought it to life. His back felt the smooth sheets of the bed. Text messages from Alan appeared on the screen, he told the phone, yes I'm still alive Alan." His eyes closed.

***

Aine closed the door of her bedroom--big enough for a queen bed. The floors were deep, red wood, and an armoire was positioned opposite the bed. Two nightstands bordered the window behind the sleigh headboard.

She undressed and put on her green silk nightgown-grabbed a bottle of lotion from the nightstand and rubbed lavender-scented lotion over her long legs, then reached for her black paddle brush. She ran the brush through her long, red hair, streaked with gray. She brushed and brushed—

The brush fell to the floor. She covered her eyes and wailed. In the next few minutes, she wept more than she had in years.

"God why?" she whispered into her hands. "Please. Why now? Why couldn't you have brought him sooner? Why did he wait so long? Am I a second thought?"

Aine tried to wipe the tears away, but they continued to pour. She crossed the room to her closet and found a black photo box, adorned with a white five-leaf clover. She cradled the box and crossed her legs on the bed, emptying the contents--letters, ordered from first to last. She hadn't looked at them since December nineteenth; the same day she unearthed them each year. Aine took in each word she had written twenty-two years ago.

* * *

December 23, 1994

Heigh,

I have decided to write you a letter every day. I'm sitting next to you right now. I know writing letters could be stupid, but I really need to talk, and since I can't talk to you, I'll write.

For the last three days I have been wondering whether you thought of me, when it happened. I've been wondering if you are thinking of me now, if you can hear me.

It's late, and I am crying and laughing at the same time.

I am lost.

Lover come back to me,

Aine

★★★

December 24, 1994

Heigh,

I held your hand for three hours tonight. I get here when your sister leaves. I can't be here with her.

I don't think you know how much you mean to me. I wish I could tell you. Alec says hi and Merry Christmas. She's a cute girl. I hope you didn't flirt with her in the helicopter. I wouldn't want to see your legs broken again.

I'm kidding, but you know that. Alec said you were a fighter and that we will have a long life together. Please stay with me. I am going to midnight mass soon. It's snowing again.

I miss you so very much,

Aine

P.S. Lover, the doctor asked for blood. We match, I gave.

***

December 26, 1994

Heigh!

I want you to know I love you! I burned a phone card and talked to Mum again, which helps. The doctor talked to me today. I feel so helpless watching you.

I think we should go to church more. When you wake up.

I'll see you tomorrow,

Aine

P.S. Lover I just kissed your forehead

***

January 19, 1995

I'm more lost than ever. I can't do it anymore, I can't. I am halfway home. I have cried every day for a month.

Almost a week after your accident, I went to see you, and the room was empty. You left me. When I walked in, at eight as usual, the room was dark, but I could tell you weren't there. The rose I'd brought you fell to the floor. I thought you had ... left me forever. I felt a hand on my shoulder, and Alec turned on a small light and closed the door. She told me something she had no right to tell me. Since I'm not anything to you. Not according to the law. Alec told me about power of attorney and moving closer to family. I do not know where that

is, and I couldn't ask Alec to tell me. She could lose
everything.

I went back to my room and packed my things.

I am going to send letters to your dorm address, and when
you get them come find me. Please, find me. I can't do this
alone.

Aine.

Chapter Fifty-Three

Startled, Aine placed the letter down and looked up.
Downstairs a door closed, then feet were pressing on the stairs-
a slow breath came from her mouth. Her door opened slowly, a
dark haired woman walked into the room.

"Mum, are you okay? You haven't returned any of my
texts or phone calls?"

"I'm sorry I was working."

"Mum, you weren't working today, I was worried and was
coming home from Dublin anyways, so tell me what is going on,
and what are these?"

Aine smiled, her daughter was very perceptive in any
situation. Sports were never her passion, yet music, she could
sing like an angel, Aine had always thought, and not because she
was hers', more influential people agreed.

"I'm okay, Ash."

"Mum, no you're not. Tell me, please? I know I'm only twenty-two, but I do know some things."

Aine smiled, thinking of herself at twenty-two. There are things a mother and a daughter would rather not know about each other.

"I'm sure you do, Ashling." Aine only used her full name when she wanted to get a point across. "Okay, my daughter, I have met someone." Aine felt as she had whispered it.

"Mum, who is he? He's not rubbish, is he?"

Aine put her hands over her mouth and closed her eyes. She shook her head.

Ashling sat close to her mother and held her.

Aine's head was spinning. For the fourth time in her life, she didn't know what to do; this would be difficult for all three of them.

Chapter Fifty-Four

A long five hours of work passed for Aine-she gathered the enrollment for the year that would soon start, answered questions for incoming parents-something she loved to do. Today was a different day, the last days had involved more than herself, it-she felt was beginning to spin out of control. The hours passed slowly, and then it was over.

***

Aine decided not to change her clothes, the dress she wore, was perfect she thought. Her hair-seemed to be all over, in every direction. A knock on the door, could be heard from down below as Aine placed one stroke of the brush after another. The sound of footsteps trailed from the stairs into her room.

"Mum, some man is here to see you?"

Punctual, as always, Aine thought. She studied herself in her bathroom mirror.

"Let me do that, Mum."

Aine sighed and handed her the brush.

"Who is he, Mum? I've never seen you with men."

Aine felt her hair tug her scalp tightly.

"He's a friend from the past. Who was special to me."

"How far in the past?" Ashling asked.

Aine closed her eyes.

"Far."

Aine felt Ashling's slow hands form each knot perfectly, not a strand out of place.

Chapter Fifty-Five

Ben sat in a plastic chair on the porch, while he perused his email. One from Alan caught his eye, the Missoulian wanted to interview him about the NASA project. Obviously, someone had tipped them off; Ben figured it was the chancellor. The news not made public, until he went back to work, sometime in the next days. Days, he thought that's all I have left, here, with her. The thought hit his heart, a sound of a door opening, made him put the phone away. He smiled as Aine stepped outside in black sandals and a black and white dress--the neck cut low, and hair fell in one long braid down the middle of her back.

"Hi, you look."

"Thank you, I think we should go for a walk."

The pair turned right past the gate. Ben had noticed the path, but he'd thought it ended after a few feet. When they crested the hill, he could see the meandering path approach the horizon. With the breeze at their backs, Aine and Ben followed the crushed tan rock lined by oak trees. The grove created a canopy, allowing only streams of sunlight. The wind was calm, Aine and Ben were quiet. She slowed her walk, shortening her long strides.

"When I was a little girl," she said, "I came here as often as I could. I love the feel of the trees."

The sound of their footsteps reverberated off the oaks and escaped through the canopy.

"It feels very warm," Ben said.

"You sound like my father."

"Is that a good thing? If I remember you never talked about him."

"Of course it is. He was a great man." She sighed. "I was always a daddy's girl. I didn't know what to do after he-- It was sudden, and I blame myself for his death."

Ben shook his head. "I don't understand."

Her voice turned cold as the oak grove in winter. "I was somewhere, doing something I shouldn't have, he looked for me, and died trying to find me."

"I'm sorry Aine, I truly am."

She looked down the path. "I know. I will never forget."

They reached a stone bench, and Aine motioned for him to sit next to her. He smelled the familiar Chanel No. 5, after all these years. Her eyes were greener than even the Irish Countryside. The sun glimmered off her face, her freckles highlighted. The stone bench was cold, yet warm.

"Aine what do you remember of the wreck?"

He noticed her smile soon disappeared as she turned her gaze toward him. "I, someone was pounding on my door at 3a.m., Derek was the one, he said you were in an accident and that I should come to the hospital. When I got there so was Alice, and I wasn't allowed to see you, you were in surgery." Her eyes became red. "And all I thought about was another person in my life that I loved was going to die because of me, Ben that's why

I left Ireland, I picked Eastern since it was small and I needed to get away. Then I found you, and I didn't know what to do. A nurse at the hospital tried to help me, her name was Alec."

"Alec who?" Ben questioned.

"She saved your life twice in the helicopter, she became a friend while I saw you during the nights, she would stay with me, even though she didn't have to...then you were gone."

Ben's mind was on fire, he never knew what happened after the wreck, only what Alice had told him.

"Ben what were you doing on Black Otter, why didn't you go another way?"

That's it he thought, if he would have just went another way, this conversation would be in another world.

"I wanted to get back to you...I...needed." The hairs on the back of his head began to stand on end, and the scars began their fiery cycle. "I wanted to ask you...I had a ring." A warm smile involved Aine's face, tears began to form on each eye.

"Jesus...I didn't know."

"How could you?" Ben remarked.

Aine wiped the tears from her cheeks, the wind began to pick up-dried her face. "Ben do you have scars?"

At that moment, they, his scars that stretched his skin for half of his life stopped burning. "I do…they hurt everyday."

Their hands touched-interlocked. Ben closed his eyes, the feeling calmed him, his heart slowed. A thought came into his mind.

"Aine, that woman I saw at your door. Who is she."

Aine's red braid raised, as her head dropped, her free hand touched her eye, wind moved the canopy of oaks.

"She, she is Ashling, my angel."

Ben looked into her eyes, her dark green eyes now red and soft.

"Our daughter, Ben."

A moment passed, the words that appeared underneath the canopy, Ben didn't know what to say. A word appears in his mind and vocal chords "Ours?"

"That is what I needed to tell you when we were on the ice." Aine's voice became as ridged as a dagger. "Alice called…I lost you. I left school because I lost you, and I was pregnant. Please tell me what else I could have done?"

"I, have a daughter?"

"Yesterday when I told you I would go to the ocean and think, that is why, it calmed me, yes we do and she is beautiful and caring."

He felt his muscles form a smile. "I don't know what to say, my god, I never thought I would ever have a child, a daughter…Aine, does she know?"

Chapter Fifty-Six

Aine and Ben parted ways. She thought of how much she had loved him in the past and what these years without him had been like. Aine had succeeded, but always wondered what their life would have been like.

After leaving the States, she promised herself, love would never happen again. She would work hard and be the best mother to Ashling she could be. Aine felt she had kept those promises. Without her mother pushing and helping her, she might never have finished college. Now, Aine had to show her own daughter the love and care her mother had shown her.

These past days had been pleasant. Ben had been the question mark hovering over her life. But, she could never leave this place. Ireland was her home. She could never leave Ashling or her career, all the young children she taught. Her head spun. Ben had finally come back to her, but she couldn't follow him. Would he? In her entire life, Aine had felt her life spinning out of control three times. The first was when her father unexpectedly passed away-how her father died gnawed at her soul. It spurred how she played on the court, how her life was lived.

With only her mother's teaching income, making ends meet became difficult.

The second time was when Ben was taken from her. She couldn't control her emotions, for the first and only time in her life, Aine quit. She shook her head, what could I have done differently?

As she crested the hill, Aine thought of her mother when she told her she was pregnant. A perpetual educator, she had been adamant that Aine find a way to earn her degree. She graduated two and a half years later, attending class during pregnancy and only taking two weeks off to have Ashling. Aine followed in her mother's footsteps and became a schoolteacher--second grade. Her mother taught fifth. Then, when Ashling was eight, her mother passed away from cancer. Through her loneliness, Aine faced the truth. Ashling was hers and hers alone. Her little girl needed her, and Aine needed her daughter.

Growing up in a loving household, Ashling never saw her mother with men. She never knew her father, but she always felt he must be a warm, loving person--a feeling she couldn't explain. Ashling herself was as loving and caring as she imagined Ben would be. Aine always said she had the voice of an angel, and she wasn't surprised in the slightest when Ashling decided to study music at the university.

Ash decided to follow in the footsteps of her mother and grandmother and become a music teacher, Aine had frowned at the idea. Aine had fought hard to become good at her job and earn a decent wage. She told Ashling the first years of teaching would be difficult, with long hours and low pay. Ashling said that was okay. She wanted to teach because she loved music and wanted to pass on that love, to her students.

After Ashling was born, Aine had tried to continue her volleyball career, but the flood of memories on the court had been oppressive. Ashling did not inherit her mother's love of sports, and Aine soon resigned herself to the fact that her daughter's passion would be played on a stage, not on a court.

From the driveway, Aine saw the dining room lights shining through the bay window. The day, a cauldron of feelings, the dreams of the past and present finally came together. Now the thought was what Ben would do? How can this work? Would he move here? She couldn't leave her job and Ash. The faces of primary school students warmed her soul, no she thought, leaving was out of the question. Tomorrow she would see Ben again.

Her fingers touched the cold, brass handle, the door pushed open, heart skipped, stomach knotted. Eyes watched Ashling at the table, all one hundred and eighty letters spread across. One of the large wooden dining room chairs glided across the floor, Ashling would need to know the truth, it will be

difficult telling the truth to make up for a lie. A nervous
calmness came over her body-much like before a feeling before
she played in a game-the time was now.

"Mum, what is going on? Who is this person, that you have
been with and what are these?"

"Ashling, Please."

"Please? *What*, Mum? These letters, all of them, my god
how many are there? I stopped counting and reading...his name
was Ben..."

"There are over 180 I believe, there are some things I
need…I *want* to tell you." Aine looked into her eyes,
connections becoming fact.

"That's *his* name isn't it, the man from today?"

"Yes it is."

"Mum, what, *who*?"

"Someone I fell in love with, a very long time
ago...in college."

"Is that it? Is that all he is, just someone from a very
long time ago?" Ashling began to tremble, her dark hair
encircled her face.

"Ash, when I knew I was pregnant with you, I left
college, volleyball. I left him, and he left me."

"Mum? Mum!" "Don't tell me he's my *dad*. This is crazy! All
of my life I thought my dad was dead, I have told everyone that

story, and now it's not real…I can't do this, I'm going to meet him, not tonight, but I'm going to meet him, and not with you either, you lied to me." She began to lift herself out of the chair.

Aine felt fire inside of her lungs, she too rose out of the chair. "You don't know what I went through, *to* me he did."

***

Ben woke to a knock on the door, glanced at the clock 7a.m. The room spun, not from a binge of alcohol, yet the thought of what happened yesterday. He was a father of a daughter, who is now a woman? It felt as someone had placed empty memories into his mind. He walked sluggishly across the room, dressed in boxers and a soft red shirt. As he opened the door, the security chain went taut, and he peered through the crack. An empty memory was soon filled with one. His heart quickened, what should I do? he thought. Does she know? What should I call her? Take a deep breath.

"Hi." Ben flinched, what else could I have said? He thought, and then noticed her hair was straight, no ponytail or braid like her mother wore.

Ashling's eyes were red and puffy, but she still had her mother's perfect smile.

"Would you like to get coffee? There's a shop not far from here." Ashling squinted in the bright morning sunlight. She wasn't as tall as her mother, but she had the same firm tone.

Had Aine sent her? If not how did she find him.

"Sure, that sounds great, but I need to take a shower.

I'll be quick, I promise."

"Coffee? I've been waiting twenty-two years…dad." Ashling said.

Ben thought the tone she used was cold, yet how would he

react?

* * *

Seating was outdoor only, on uncomfortable plastic chairs.

Ashling recommended the Americano, and they each ordered a slice

of orange cardamom cake. The morning was clear, and the sparse

clientele gave Ashling space to question him.

"What do you do?" she asked.

"I'm a math professor at a university, so basically."

Ben sliced through the soft cake with his fork. "I tell students

how to be students, and I tell adults how to be adults." He took

a bite and shook his head "Wow, this is good."

"How does that work? I'm a student."

"Well, students are easy. They tend to listen. The

adults are a pain."

They both laughed. "So you go to the university?"

Ashling flipped her hair across her back. "Yeah I love it.

I study music."

"What do you want to do with your degree?" He sipped his coffee.

"I want to teach." Ben coughed on his drink and smiled.

"What?" Ashling said.

"Nothing. Just, teaching isn't easy. The first year is horrible, plain and simple. But eventually it becomes, well, gratifying."

"You sound like my mother."

He took another bite of cake. "Well, if it weren't for your mother, I never would have become a professor."

"Do you have children?" Ashling was obviously Aine's daughter. She said what was on her mind.

"No, I don't." His voice trailed off. "No girlfriend, wife. Only friends."

"Were you in love with my mother?"

Ben watched her, trying to gauge her intentions. "Ash, can I call you that?" Her bright smile glowed in the sunlight. "Let's put it this way. You are so lucky to have her as your mother. There's not another person like her on the planet, not one. The time I had with her was a blessing."

Ashling sighed. "I've never seen my mother with anyone. I've also never seen her this happy. Please don't hurt her." She paused. "Are you going to leave?" Ben froze. How could he stay? But listening to Ash, he thought how he would never want to hurt Aine, and the question became, "How can I go?"

"When I lost your mother, a part of me died, a part that I really liked." Ashling's eyes widened, and she swallowed the last of her coffee.

"I want you to stay."

He looked into Ashling's eyes, the deep emotions kept there. "I wish I could."

"I have an idea...let's go see Mum," Ashling said.

Chapter Fifty-Seven

Ben entered the house, one small step at a time. He was amazed at how much the house felt like home. He thought about his own house-much larger, but it always felt cold, even in summer.

Ash led him to the kitchen where he found Aine chopping vegetables. She wore sweatpants and a tank top, with her hair in a tight braid wrapped around her head.

Watching her move, he thought they could skip dinner, and he would forget he'd been hungry.

"What?" Aine said.

"Did I say anything?" Ben walked into the kitchen. "No, but you were thinking something." She gave a half smile.

"There's a bag of potatoes on the table. Peel them for me, please?"

"I will only if you"

Aine moved closer.

"Give me a tour of the house afterward. It seems

nice," Ben said.

Ben peeled the potatoes slowly, they were more difficult to

prepare than mashed potatoes from a box. When he'd finally

finished, Ben asked if he could lie down for a few minutes. Aine

left Ash reading a book on the sofa and showed Ben to her

bedroom.

She led him upstairs and opened the door.

"Wow, nice bed," he said.

The sleigh bed was made of oak, and the footboard and

headboard were adorned with intricate carvings of trees, leaves,

and rivers. Aine held his hand as they both sat on the bed,

looking into each other's eyes.

"You fly back soon, don't you? I see that Ash found

you."

He wished that she hadn't said that. The perfect moment

fell to the knowledge that he would lose her and his daughter

all over again.

"She's perfect. I do, in a couple days." He put a hand on

her cheek. Ben wished they could be together forever, a thought

closely followed by the memory of Alan's news. "Don't go," she

said. "Stay. We can work things out. I know it will be hard for

you, but."

"I wish I could."

"What? You want to see if this will work, right? Don't
you like it here?"

He felt her soft skin against his palm.

"With everything I am, I want to, but it seems my
career is taking me in a different direction." He
paused. "We can always visit each other."

"Ben." Aine put her hand over his, against her cheek. "I
want to be with you everyday, not just some days."

She pursed her lips when he didn't respond.

"Shit, I didn't put the dinner in the oven. I'll be
back."

Ben released a long breath when she left. He didn't know
what to do, how could he leave, how could he go.

                           * * *

"Good, you didn't go anywhere." Aine placed herself next to
him.

"I didn't know I had a choice?" He looked into her eyes, he
wanted to touch her lips. In a moment an electric shook jolted
his lips, he closed his eyes. It felt as a dream-those dreams he
had in Oregon. They had calmed in the last years, yet the real
thing could never compare to what his mind could conjure. Lips
unlocked, eyes opened.

"We were always good at this," Aine said.

Ben placed his head on a pillow, looking at Aine next to him.

"I've always dreamed of this," he said.

His hand found hers, and a slow warmth covered his body. He closed his eyes and brushed her hand lightly with his thumb. He fought sleep as long as he could, until finally surrendering to Aine's warmth and the peaceful home.

When he woke, the room was darker, and the bed was empty. He heard clinking plates and smelled food. He walked downstairs and entered the kitchen as Ashling was setting out wine glasses.

"Would you like some, Ben?" Ashling asked.

"Yes. Red, please."

Aine only made this meal on special occasions. The recipe was handed down from her mum--meat, carrots, and peas layered with mashed potatoes, all topped with a red-wine rue. The dish cooked slowly for five hours until the flavors were perfectly mingled.

They talked through dinner--about the day, Ireland, Ashling's dreams. Ben had no doubt she would achieve them all. The dinner plates were cleared, and they sat at the empty table, enjoying the wine.

Aine sat silently.

"Is everything okay?" Ben asked.

Aine cupped her wine glass with both hands. "Ben I need to show you something."

Ben frowned. "I don't understand. I told you I never got the letter or the ones you wrote."

"Excuse me," she said. "I will be back."

Ben heard her footsteps upstairs. When she returned, she placed a box in front of him. She returned to her seat and bit her lip.

"Open it, please?"

He lifted the lid and was greeted by folded papers, filed neatly. Her perfume clung to the pages. He lifted one gently and unfolded it, whispering, "Aine, what are these?"

She took a sip of wine. "When you were in the hospital, I promised I would write you everyday, and then."

"Aine." He stumbled over his words. "Aine, why didn't you send these?"

She composed herself, only to break down again.

"I did. With God as my witness, I did."

"Then how are they here?" Ben asked.

"These are the originals. I rewrote each letter and sent it to your address at Eastern. I sent you over a hundred and eighty letters. I thought you would come to me or write me back. But after a year, I gave up hope."

Ben was in shock. Finally he pulled himself together long enough to ask the one question he needed an answer to.

"Alice said you left."

Aine thought for a moment. Finally, she grabbed Ashling's hand.

"Ben, why did Alice hate me so much?"

Aine deserved closure. Ben cleared his throat and stared at the wine glass half-full of merlot. "A-L-I-C-E. I haven't been honest with you, Aine."

"Ben?"

"I never told you the truth about my parents, about how they died." Ben clinched his teeth, he had never been truthful to Rachel, to Lisa and Alan, until that day on the pass. Now was the time to tell the truth to not only someone, but to Aine.

"You told me they died in a car accident."

Ben focused on the merlot, trying to dispel the horror of that night. "Yes, they did. But what I didn't tell you was that there were four people in the car that night, driving home from my basketball game. I was on the team bus an hour behind them. Four people. My father, my mother, Alice--and her boyfriend from high school to college." Ben bit his tongue. "My father and mother died instantly. Alice and her boyfriend, Devon, made it to the hospital. Eventually word got back to the bus, and a highway patrol officer took me to Alice. I..." His words stumbled as he gained the strength to finish." I was the one who told her she had lost a father, a mother, and a boyfriend she loved. Because of me. *They* died because of me. I cost a love in her life."

Aine grabbed Ben's hand and led him up to her room. The past was darker than the night could ever be.

Chapter Fifty-Eight

Ben awoke to a view he had only dreamed of. Aine's propped up her head with her hand. She had taken down her braids before bed. Last night had released years of feelings. They had been separated in the beginning of the digital age. Finding each other, without a clue or starting place, was next to impossible. Ben tried to put the feelings of failure behind him.

"Hi, this is a nice view," he said.

Aine gave him her full attention. The sun sliced through the clouds outside the window and reflected off her hair and her green eyes. Ben could only stare.

"It is." She nodded in agreement. "Stay with us, Ben."

Ben looked into her eyes, thinking how much things had changed since the first time she asked.

"I wish I could, but ... I don't know how to be a dad. I don't know how to live with someone."

"You can learn. And you could always teach here, at our universities." Aine put her hand on his chest. "You will be a great father to her. She needs you."

"Aine, she's a grown woman. She doesn't need anyone. And it's not just teaching at a university. The University of Montana is my life."

Aine's face began to turn red.

"What has that university given you?" She paused, her arguments running in separate directions. "It doesn't matter how old she is. She still needs a dad."

"Yeah, a dad she knows." Ben saw the hurt in her eyes.

"That's not fair."

They stared at each other.

"What happens if I move here and it doesn't work out, Aine. What then?"

Her eyes were turning a dark turbulent green.

"Don't you think we owe it to ourselves to try? If you wanted to die alone, you should have stayed in Montana."

"I just needed to see you, to find answers. I didn't know if you would be married or involved with someone."

Aine sat up, removing her hand from his chest.

"I never asked to fall in love with you, you know. I never asked to be a mother. Never the less, they both happened, and I believe, especially now, that we are destined to be together. So tell me again, why haven't you ever married?"

"When I would go on a date or meet someone, I always thought of you. I couldn't forget." Ben placed his hand on her lower back, applying soft pressure with his fingertips.

Aine closed her eyes.

"I have always loved you, and I will always love you. Stay with us."

"Aine," Ben whispered.

"Live with us, Ben."

"I want to be with you forever. I truly do, but there are things I have to work out for myself."

"Ben." Aine sighed. "I can't lose you again, but--" She turned to face him. "I can never leave here. I know it's hard for you, me asking you to move here. I'm asking you to sacrifice your job and the life you've made, but there will always be something. So the question is, what's more important to you, Ash or a job?"

"Aine, I am getting a promotion."

Aine's green eyes faded.

"I've already lost you," she said. "For the final time."

Her words cut Ben, but she was right. Ben had less to lose and more to gain.

After breakfast, the three of them walked the oak path one more time before Ben had to leave for Dublin. He snapped a close-up picture of Aine and Ash, and his heart hurt. In finding them, he felt he had found himself. He remembered hiking, skating, and watching movies with Aine, things he had loved and no longer did. He had been a different person with her, and he had liked that person more than he had liked the career-centered loner he had become.

Saying goodbye to Aine and Ash was harder than saying goodbye to his parents at their funeral.

* * *

The house was cold and silent. Aine noticed the box of letters on the table. She pulled up a chair and slowly touched each letter. She felt Ash behind her. Her daughter rested her hands on Aine's shoulders, and they both wept.

Day turned to night. Aine watched the sky through the window when Ben's plane was scheduled to take off, placing her hand on the glass and closing her eyes, whispering a prayer that no one besides herself could hear.

* * *

Some of the plane's passengers were angry at delays. Some were excited, sad, or lost--like Ben. As the plane left the runway, he put a hand on the window, wishing he could touch her one last time. *I can't believe I have a daughter.*

The flight would take twenty-two hours. He thought he could spend all of them staring at the photo he had taken of Aine and Ashling. Somewhere over the Atlantic, he took out the leather-bound notebook he had used to record his search for Aine. He turned to a blank page. His pen softly touched the paper, forming letters into words. He mouthed sentences as he wrote.

He finished the short letter and frowned. It wasn't right. He turned the page and began again, feeling as though he was writing a paper to be published. The stakes for this letter was higher than any academic paper he had written. Finally, after about twenty drafts, he was somewhat satisfied. He looked out the window, wondering if he could have the courage to start a new life, without a career.

Could he venture into the unknown for a life with Aine and Ashling? It was possible that life wouldn't work. But how could it not? They had continued to love each other through decades apart. He shook his head, hearing Aine's voice. Was his career worth being alone forever? Teaching was all he had known. His

sparse dates had amounted at most to meaningless sex. One woman
had even accused him of thinking of someone else.

In Ireland, he no longer thought of anyone else. The person
he wanted to be with was there. They had walked softly, getting
to know each other again after a lifetime apart, but Aine had
made it clear that happiness for her meant being with him and
growing old together in Ireland. Ben had been born in Montana.
He'd lived and worked there, and leaving it behind would be
difficult. His parents were buried thirty miles south of his
Montana home. He would hate to leave Alan and Lisa, but then
again, they would remain friends no matter what he chose. Then
there was Alice. He had never known how much she truly hated
Aine. If he decided to be with Aine, he wouldn't tell his
sister. Alice had hidden Aine from him. She didn't deserve to
know.

The pilot alerted the cabin that landing was proceeding as
planned, but passengers may notice poor air quality. Small
whiffs of smoke appeared as they approached Missoula. As they
closed in on the airport, they could see the source of the smoke
through their windows. Winter had brought some snow, but not
enough to keep the summer fires away. A month-long drought made
conditions worse. In the week Ben had been absent, the Montana
views had changed drastically. Huge clouds of smoke rose from

the mountainside. As they closed in on the airport, Ben could make out helicopters and a DC-10 fire-retardant jumbo jet trying desperately to extinguish the fires.

When the plane touched down, Ben migrated toward the baggage claim, where Lisa and Alan waited for him. They looked like a normal married couple--Ben smiled. What is normal? Is that part of my destiny? Did all of this happen for a reason? He replayed scenarios in his mind. He had found the courage to face his past. Now he needed help facing the future.

Chapter Fifty-Nine

Baggage claim was small, but busy. Passenger's toted suitcases, duffel bags, fly fishing rods, and tents. Ben hugged Lisa and gave Alan a tired handshake.

"How was your trip?" Lisa asked.

"It was good and not good. Maybe I shouldn't have gone. Life would be a lot simpler right now."

Alan interjected. "You mean boring?"

"Yeah, boring. But I wouldn't have a migraine right now. When did the fires start?"

"A couple days ago. Humidity should go up tonight, so the fire crews should get control of them." Alan looked Ben over. "You seem tired. Dinner tomorrow night?"

"Yeah, that sounds fine." He grabbed his luggage off the baggage belt and headed outside. Ben choked on the smoke and the taste of pine trees. The Western Rocky Mountains blocked the sun, and the sky was turning a dark orange. During the drive, they passed green buses filled with firefighters. As Alan's BMW pulled up to the house, Ben gawked at his lawn.

"Shit, the nitrogen in the air is growing the shit out of the grass. I should mow it." As he spoke, he wondered if he would be around to care about the tall grass. "Good night guys, I'll see you tomorrow."

Lisa lowered her window as he hauled his suitcase toward the front door. "Have a good night," she yelled. "Get some rest." Ben looked back and waved. They didn't leave until he was inside.

Ben's house was much larger than Aine's, but it felt like a cave in winter. The inside was dark and sterile. The only voice he heard was his own, reverberating off the picture less walls. By the time he showered and lay down, it was ten at night, but it felt like early morning. He snatched his phone from the nightstand and texted Aine, not caring how much the message would cost.

Hi, I'm home, without you :(

To his surprise, he received a response within five minutes.

I'm here in bed, thinking about you :(

He smiled and fought the urge to text her all night. He needed to sleep. He sent one more message.

The flights were good, text you tomorrow

Please decide soon

His mind was spinning as he fell asleep.

By the time Ben woke it was nearly noon. The first of August and the start of classes was approaching, which meant he had to go through his department checklist. He'd gather the faculty to see if anyone had quit, which never happened. Then he'd go to the chancellor and lay out the math department's plan for spending their yearly budget--a formality he hated. It never changed the amount the department received. Today, though, mowing the lawn was first on his to do list. He checked his phone and found messages from Aine.

Are you awake?

Still asleep?

He typed out a response.

Just woke up, going to mow lawn

He pressed send and immediately began typing another.

How are you? How is our daughter?

His thumb hovered over the send button. He read the words and thought, *What am I doing here?* He shook his head, sent the message, and went to the garage for the mower. Growing up, he had mowed neighbors' lawns for extra cash, which was probably why he hated the chore as an adult. As a middle school student, he would think of cartoons while he was mowing. As a high school student, he'd think of girls and sex. Today, all he could think of was Aine and Ashling, a world away.

In the evening, he met Alan and Lisa at MacKenzie River Pizza, a local favorite. The restaurant smelled of dough and pepperoni. Ben's favorite pizza used buffalo wing sauce in place of tomato and was topped with mozzarella, celery, and blue cheese, all on sourdough crust. He began salivating as they sat down.

After two rounds of beers, Lisa finally asked, "So?"

Ben took his phone from his pocket and slid it across the table.

"Who are these two?" Lisa swiped through his photos. "Seriously, who are they?"

"The one to the left is Aine," he said. The waitress appeared, Ben asked for two more rounds. "She was in my calculus class," he said after she'd left. When she returned, she brought three beers for each of them. Ben thought he might fall asleep before the pizza arrived.

"So, Aine." He told them their story, how they had started seeing each other in college and fell in love. "I was in a car accident," he said, "and I lost her." He told them how he had searched for her all these years and that his sister had hidden the key to finding her. Alan looked shocked, and Lisa's eyes glistened.

"She's your daughter, isn't she?" Lisa whispered.

Ben nodded. "Ashling."

"And how did that work?" Lisa asked.

"What do you mean?"

"You just walked into her life. What had Aine told her?"

"That her father died. It was difficult at first, but Ashling is great. We have a lot of catching up to do, but I think ... I think she thought of me as family."

"Ben, I'm not being mean, but if that's the case, what are you doing here?" Alan nodded along with his wife.

"I have work, my career. I am being promoted."

"You have a family." Lisa put her hands on the table and leaned over, speaking in a harsh whisper. "You have a daughter, someone who loves you. I wouldn't give a fuck about my job if I had that."

He bit his lip. "I don't know what to do. Quit my job and go to her? Ask her to move here?"

"She won't move here. What would she do? Ask her daughter, *your* daughter, to quit school? Or leave her? And I'm guessing she has a career and a life of her own. You have to go to her. Leave your job. Take a sabbatical or something." Ben had never heard Lisa this passionate. "Alan, tell him, please. Ben, you have been alone for as long as I've known you. Don't lose her."

The pizza didn't taste as good as it usually did. They said their goodbyes in the parking lot.

★★★

Alan let Lisa out to water the yard before he pulled the BMW in the garage. He was sitting on the couch when Lisa opened and slammed the front door.

"Jesus what is it?" Alan asked.

"Do you remember when we got together?" Lisa asked.

"Yes, of course. How could I forget?"

"Where was I living?"

"Boston and London."

Lisa blocked the television. "And?"

"And what?"

"And what did I give up for us to be together?"

"Your career, and--your husband."

"Damn it, he is just like us. He has to make the decision. My decision was the hardest I've ever had to make, but

I wouldn't trade my life with you for anything." A smile consumed her face. "Fuck it, where's my passport and the credit card, I'm not going to stand here and watch him lose her, like how he lost Rachel."

Alan sprung up from the couch. He remembered meeting Lisa for the first time. He had literally bumped into her while walking the Freedom Trail in Boston, which connected all American Revolution sites in the area. He had been enamored with the way she looked, spoke, and moved. Lisa was only in the area for a few weeks, and she had a husband at home in London. But even after she left the States, they texted and made phone calls. Alan was finishing his doctorate at Boston University, and whenever she was on the east coast, he would go to her. After two years, Lisa divorced her husband and moved to be with Alan. They visited Missoula together and fell in love with the mountains, the winters, and the community. Alan secured a position at the University and they were married soon after.

He watched her fire burn as she packed for Ireland, and he knew he would have done the same for her.

Chapter Sixty

Ben's morning routine had included exercise since rehab, all of those years ago. His treadmill was used more than any other piece of furniture in his house, with the bed being a close second. The middle of August brought cooler mornings and hotter afternoons. August also brought the ever-present thought of work. Classes would resume in three weeks, but the university's football season was beginning earlier than usual. The first game was two days away and would be nationally televised on ESPN. Kicking off the college football season, the game was all but guaranteed to sell out. The stadium was snuggled below 5,258-foot Mount Sentinel, making the screams and cheers of the twenty-five thousand spectators seem to double.

Seven hundred feet up the mountain's face, a large, concrete M was visible from anywhere in the valley. Today Ben had decided to run through campus and up to the letter, braving the twelve switchbacks in the mile-long run. The university bookstore sold a shirt that read *I Ran the Switchbacks*. Most chose to walk the steep, dirt switchbacks. The altitude made running especially difficult, and with no call boxes on the trail, a heart attack or asthma attack would be a near-death experience, if you were lucky.

As he ran through campus, he felt a cold wind on his face, but by the afternoon highs would be in the eighties. His feet thudded along the first switchback. The first three switchbacks, always the most difficult, were narrow and steep. He pushed himself with each step, hearing the knee-high, golden grass

rustling in the slight breeze. Mount Sentinel was green during
the spring, not as green as Ireland, but nice in the West. In
August, the mountain turned light beige in the dry weather,
which led to fire restrictions for the treeless mountainside.
When the grass turned beige, what looked like ripple marks
appeared on the face, from long-gone waves that had once crashed
against the mountain. Centuries ago, glaciers had melted into a
great lake, filling the entire valley. The mountain Ben was
running on had been a prehistoric lakeshore. He stopped to
breathe at the concrete M. Ben looked out over the valley, the
city, and the university, soaking in the view.

He sat on the concrete letter. *What do I do? Do I leave you
forever? Or do I follow my career and see where it goes?* He knew
what he wanted to do, but he couldn't convince himself to do it.
Gazing across the southern valley, he thought of his parents. As
he walked down the mountain, he decided to go see them.

After a long walk home, he backed out of the driveway and
began the forty-five-minute trip. The road leading out of the
city was a four-lane highway for fifteen miles, before it wound
through a small gap in the hills and turned to a two-lane road.
The hills opened into a wide mountain valley. The road was
bordered by fields of grass, with the spine of the Rocky
Mountains farther to the right and smaller hills to the left. As
Ben approached mile marker fifty-five, he put on his flashers

and pulled over. He lowered the window to see the marker clearly, breathing in the hot August air mixing with car exhaust.

He pulled onto the road again and soon found the turn to take him away from the Rocky Mountains, smoke still hovering about them. The car crested a hill and turned left. A hundred yards later, Ben approached a grassy plain full of loved ones laid to rest.

He closed the car door with a *thud* and began to walk toward the graves, the crunching pebbles of the trail turning to burnt grass. The cemetery was silent, only sporadic cries of a robin or a crow breaking the stillness. He found his way by memory to the flat granite stone, its inscription facing the Rocky Mountains. His parents had always loved those mountains. Ben kneeled and wiped bits of grass and willow tree seeds from the stone. "Hi guys, I know it's been a long time, but I just need some guidance." He put his hands on his knee and bowed his head. "I miss both of you. I hope you're proud of me."

As he spoke, the wind began to flutter in his ears.

"I'm sure you know I saw Alice, Mark, and the twins."

The wind grew stronger, then suddenly stopped.

"The twins are doing well. They will give Alice headaches. I wish you could have met them." He lifted his head, leaving his eyes closed. "Alice never liked Aine, but I am sure you would have. I think if you were alive, none of this would have happened. Alice wouldn't have acted the way she did. I wish you could have met Aine. You would have liked her. Now I don't know what to do. Give up my promotion? Try to forget her? Can I leave you here alone with the mountains? I feel so old some days. I want to fight for her, but I'm not sure I can."

The wind picked up again, and Ben finally opened his eyes. A green leaf rested on the tombstone. As he picked it up gently, he smiled. It was a four-leaf clover.

"I love you guys. I miss you every day."

***

As he entered his office, Ben could smell the sweat clinging to his skin, but there was no one here to object. His secretary wouldn't start for another week. He sat in his desk chair and looked up at the ceiling,

"Good afternoon, Ben."

"Alan, do you have an alarm system set to alert you when I'm here?"

"What is that smell?" Alan said, fanning his nose as he sat in the chair he'd claimed. He was still dressing for summer, a maroon polo and gray shorts.

"Funny, Alan. What are you doing here?"

"Can't a friend stop by, The president would like.."

"The President?"

"Yes, he'd like you to stop by. He needs to talk to you about your new position and--" Alan spoke to Ben in a way he rarely did--as a boss, not a friend. "Your last day in this office will be next Friday."

Ben's nerves tightened. "So I don't have a choice?"

"You are an asset to the university. Your new office will be in Main Hall. The chancellor wants you for this position."

He thought that if he had done the bare minimum, he wouldn't be in this situation. He wouldn't have this opportunity, to work and research without teaching classes.

"What are you doing tomorrow night, Alan?"

"Not much. Lisa is away for a conference."

"Let's go out and have some drinks. What do you think?"

"Drinks during the week? I'll pick you up at six."

The old wooden chair moaned as Alan departed.

Ben took out the leather-bound book, thinking of the last time he had opened it in this office. No matter his decision, this would be the last time he would open the book in this office. He ran his hand over his desk, the many grooves and ridges played back memories.

***

Ben felt energized as he traversed the campus in the afternoon sun, Ben heading to Main Hall, the oldest building on campus and the first to have been renovated. He entered the president's office through two thick glass doors. The security guard greeted him, wearing her usual smile.

"Good afternoon, Rebecca. Is the chancellor in?"

"I'm afraid he's gone for the day. He will be in tomorrow, or do you want me to call him?"

"Oh no, that's not necessary. I will be on campus tomorrow. Could you leave this on his desk for me?" His hand trembled as he passed her the envelope.

"Of course, have a good day."

"You, too."

As Ben headed to his car, he unlocked his phone and texted Aine.

We need to talk, I made a decision, I'm not sure if you will like it.

Ben stared at the screen. Even without her response, he felt a mountainous weight had been lifted.

***

Morning came early as always. As Ben moved through campus, he looked at the buildings, the cobblestone walkways, the pine trees, the flowers, and the ever-present *Go Griz* signage. He slid the key into his office door--already unlocked.

"Shit."

He opened the door and found President Leonard sitting at his desk, drinking a cup of coffee and perusing the morning paper.

"Ah, Dr. Meagher, good morning. It's nice to see you." Dr. Leonard was a tall, gray-bearded man in his mid-seventies.

His speech, dress, and presence all oozed academia. He stood and shook Ben's hand.

"It's nice to see you, too, Chancellor."

Dr. Leonard smiled and placed a large hand on Ben's shoulder, studying him like his shelf full of books. "I think the best conversation is done walking, wouldn't you say?"

"Yes, sir." Dr. Leonard gestured toward the door.

The morning was warm and bright, the sunlight reflecting off the maple trees dotting the walkways. Dr. Leonard reached inside his coat and produced a letter.

"Let's talk about this, shall we?" He looked down at Ben by his side.

"I have thought long and hard about this."

"Is it the stress?"

"No, sir."

"Have I not been a fan of yours?"

"Of course you have, with the new position."

"Would you rather teach?"

Ben stopped walking. They were in the middle of the campus, in the center of a cobblestone circle, each stone of which was engraved with names of individuals who had given their lives in service of the country.

The two men faced each other.

"It's not teaching. It's not stress. It's not the new position, for which I am extremely grateful. It's life. I have found something beyond work. I love this university, but over the last few months I have come to realize my life should be more than my work."

Dr. Leonard receded into his thoughts for a moment. "Come up to my office," he said.

In the president's office, a window overlooked the cobblestone circle. The pair sat in wooden chairs to the left of the desk.

"Gone are the days of smoking cigars, and it's too early for brandy." He smiled. "Do you see that picture in the bookcase?" A floor-to-ceiling glass bookcase, full of books, awards, and pictures, covered the far wall of the office. Ben stood up to get a closer look.

"It's you and your wife."

"That photo was taken this year, at my seventy-fifth birthday. Would you like to know how long we have been married?"

"Fifty-five years?"

The chancellor laughed. "Oh god, no. Try again." The wooden chair creaked as he shifted.

"Forty-seven?"

"Wrong again."

Ben shrugged and sat once more.

"Thirty-five years," the chancellor said, "I was forty. I had never been married, and neither had she. I never had any interest in a life beyond my career, until I met her." The chancellor's eyes became smaller. "Do what you need to do, but" He pointed a long finger toward the photo. "If someone told me I could trade my time with her for all the money and accolades in the world, I would tell them to--well, to go fuck themselves. Quite simply, life is too short, and for this--" Dr. Leonard went to his desk, the letter in his hand. He fished a silver lighter from his drawer, flung it open, and in one swift hand motion, burned Ben's letter of resignation. When the flame was almost to his fingertips, he dropped the charred page in the trash. "I do not accept your letter." Dr. Leonard wiped his hands with the handkerchief from his front pocket.

"Then I will just leave," Ben said.

"And give up? There are many avenues to enlightenment. Neither your career here nor your new position is bound to Missoula. We have a sister university in Ireland." He sat down across from Ben. "I will send you the paperwork. You are too valuable for us to simply let you walk away." He smiled and motioned Ben to the door.

"Oh, two more things." Ben turned around. "I have been asked by the athletic department to select a faculty member to present awards to our generous donors before the game tomorrow." Ben began to object, but the chancellor raised his voice ever so slightly. "I expect to see you at the faculty breakfast, as well. Also, would you tell Alan hello from me when you see him?" Dr. Leonard smirked and raised an eyebrow. Ben nodded and left.

* * *

Dinner arrived as quickly as the Concord had once flown across the Atlantic. Ben met Alan at the same sports bar where they watched English football. They found seats not far from the one in which Ben had seen Aine on the television screen. "So how did you know, Alan?" Ben took a swig of dark beer in his mouth.

"You know the chancellor beats everyone to work, even though he's older than the university. He read your letter at three thirty this morning and called me. I was on campus by five, and we talked about you. I'm sorry." Alan nervously sipped his beer.

"No, that's fine, really. It would have made me crazy if you'd told me."

"Are you going to do it, Ben? Are you going to leave?"

Ben thought. The word *leaving* seemed so final. He would never return to Montana or the university. He would never see Alan and Lisa again. He knew he would be back, and he would visit his friends, but the thought still stung.

"I think so, I'm still not entirely sure. What would you do?"

"This is a life-altering choice," Alan said, "It's your decision, and no one can help you make it." He took another sip of beer. "But what I can say is that I've never heard you talk about a woman like this."

Ben spun his glass slowly in his fingers and smiled. "How's Lisa?"

"The conference was good. She just got back, actually. She was too tired to come."

"Well, tell her hello from me." He glanced up at the TV screens. "So the chancellor chose me to present the donors' partnership awards tomorrow."

"Yeah, I know. Sucker."

They toasted to the first football game of the season, to the beginning of another school year, and to the decision Ben had to make.

* * *

Alan entered the house from the garage. He heard laughter
from the back deck, and as he opened the sliding glass door, the
found three women sitting around the outdoor table.

"You guys made it. This is amazing." Alan shook hands
with both redheads, kissed Lisa on the head, and pulled up a
chair. "I can't believe you're here. Aine, your daughter looks
so much like you. Man, this was a tough secret to keep."

In the setting sun, Aine's hair reflected the warm rays.

"It is very nice to meet you as well," Aine said,
brushing her hair back with slender fingers. "Billings is
beautiful, but this is amazing." Aine pointed to the Rocky
Mountains in the distance. She dipped her chin. "It would be
difficult to leave."

Alan looked to Ashling. "Are you in classes yet?"

"In a couple of weeks."

He nodded and asked about her studies. After they had
covered music and teaching, he gave Aine a small grin.

"Tell me about the first time you saw Ben."

"The first time? I had just left an education class
and met another volleyball player in the middle of the campus.
We saw a freshman stumbling around with a map of the campus.
Which is funny because campus had about ten buildings. Someone
helped him, eventually. I saw him in the pool a couple of days

after that. I didn't realize it then, but I think I already loved him."

Alan smiled. "He loves you too, Aine. There is no doubt about that."

Aine leaned across the table. "What is the plan for the game tomorrow?"

Chapter Sixty-One

Aine took off her hood connected to her silk white jacket. It had been weeks since Ben left. The day ran through her mind, work was *the* focus. Her pocket vibrated, the phone had come alive since he had left. Clouds enveloped the town, bringing wind and the occasional raindrop. Inside the grey blocked church complex, Aine noticed the lack of warmth compared to her old school. The school year *had* to work here, and she would do anything for that to happen. The headmaster waited for her in the foyer. He looked much older than when she had last seen him, only months ago. Deep groves covered his face, white hair, and facial stubble were visible. Hands held a dark, wooden cane.

"Headmaster it is so nice to see you."

He looked up at her and cleared his throat.

"Damn it Aine, how long have I known you, and it's Sean."

She placed her hand on his shoulder. Her fingertips could feel a small shoulder made of bone.

"Almost all of my life. So what do you want of me today?"

"No heels today? I guess this is informal. We need to walk and look at the rooms."

They began the tour of the facilities. Sean would use his cane to point out desks, carpeted floors and small rooms.

"What do you think?"

Aine sat across a desk from the headmaster. It was a small office, naked bookcases behind him.

"I think that the rooms will work. They are small, yet it's what we have."

"Excellent that is what I wanted to here."

"Everyone will make it work."

Aine noticed his eyes were studying her.

"How was your summer?"

"It was good, got to spend time with Ash. It was nice. Where are your books?"

Sean looked around and back at her.

"I'm resigning Aine. I've hung on too long. I want you to take my place."

"I, I only want to teach, I might be traveling some to the states. I don't."

He slowed his speech, into a methodical tone-one she had
heard many times.

"Aine, you have a couple of days to think about it. I
have watched you in school, playing volleyball and your career.
You will be great at it. You are a natural leader."

* * *

Aine looked over the parents that arrived for the
meeting. Her thoughts focused on the past. She was once one of
those young parents. Hopes and dreams of Ashling having a
successful path in school and life. She greeted every parent
with a handshake at the door. Sean had went home in the previous
hours. It was hers'. Aine hadn't given him a yes or no. They
both knew what the answer would be. Their bond was more of him
being her boss. Their ties grew after Aine had come back from
Montana. A time where she needed more than her mother. The frail
body of him at present was a shadow of himself when he was much
younger. Aine was younger as well. The days before time and the
throes of being an adult, and parenthood, took their toll on
mind, body and spirit. A time where Aine had to think of someone
else, reconciling of the days before Ash, the days of doubts.

* * *

Three letter-sized envelopes stained with tears
slipped underneath the light brown dorm door. Aine placed her

fingers along the letters attached to the door, *RA, she* feared

someone would see her, traveled left, down the staircase with

one suitcase. The cab waited for her. Aine packed everything she

could fit. The rest was left. Maybe she would return. Maybe she

wouldn't. Her mind was a forest of possibilities. Ben was gone.

Taken somewhere she did not know. Aine was going home. The plane

was cold, the seats harder than the wings submerged in below

zero air.

     Flight attendants and passengers alike could only

guess what was wrong with this tall young woman. No one asked.

Aine fought the feeling of loneliness. Yet she wasn't alone. Two

thoughts were with her, yet both couldn't react to them. Softly,

Air Lingus touched the pebbles and earth, she was home.

     The weather was cold and drab. Aine was just old

enough to rent a car. The long drive to her mother's house was

all that was left. She had let her mother know what had happened

to Ben. Aine had left some certain facts to herself. The last

living parent didn't know she was due at home today.

     Aine's hand knocked on the door. She waited on simple

white steps of the two-story house. She noticed the curtains

drawn on the windows that laid flat against the frame of the

house. It was early afternoon. Her mom was at school, working.

Why she had knocked she didn't know. The dampness started to

seep into her skin. The back door was unlocked, letting herself
in, the smells of home came to her. The house was old, yet
everything from the walls to the stove had a function, that kept
Aine warm through her life.

Hours passed, Aine took a restless nap on the sofa.
Car lights illuminated the drapes through the trees. A tapestry
of ghostly shapes projected onto the ceiling. Aine waited for
her mum as she parked.

"Aine?"

"Mum?" Her breath piercing the night air.

Aine moved toward her.

"I'm in a mess. I don't know what to do. I need
help, please."

The mum, who had always been there for her, reached up, and
soon her thumb was covered in wet salt from Aine's tears.

"It's cold out here. We need to go in."

The wood stove was lit. Aine never forgot the smell of wood
burning. The smell was the same in Montana, dark and rich. Both
soon found a spot on the sofa.

"Are you hungry?"

"Not really?" Aine brushed her long hair away
from her eyes.

"I'm surprised. I thought you were going to call today. Not be here. What has happened Aine?"

"Mum. I'm sorry. I have failed you."

"Aine you could never do that. What has happened, Aine?"

"Mum-I've quit school and."

"What? Why? School? Volleyball? Aine-."

"Because I'm pregnant, I'm sorry. I have lost Ben, I can never go back. I'm so sorry, I'm sorry."

Her mother's hair was long and grey. Her eyes dark.

"Aine, what are you to do?"

"I have been thinking I could help at your school. The headmaster will help me right?"

"Sean has many things on his mind. He might, but he will ask questions of you."

"I understand."

Sitting across from the headmaster while Aine was in school made her palms sweat. She was rarely in trouble, her mother made sure of that. This meeting was different, she would have to answer certain questions. Questions that she didn't know the answers to. Questions that through out her life she will answer.

"Headmaster it's nice to see you."

"Equally, yet what are we doing here? It's Sean, Aine. I've known you and your family for most of your life. "

"I would like to ask if I could help at the school-"

"What about your education in the States? Volleyball? I'm not sure what exactly is going on."

"Headmaster. To be honest I'm not sure what is going on either. I need time. Time to think."

"Aine I will allow you to be here. There isn't a question with that. What there is, is a question about your schooling. Being absent from here will not be tolerated. Also enrolling in evening classes will be something I would look into. If I see or hear that doing these will be a burden, you will not be allowed to be here."

"I understand, thank you Headmaster, you will not be disappointed."

Halfway out the door she heard his voice, frozen in time.

"Whatever happened, happened. I believe in you and that your destiny is here. You will be successful. Your family and myself will always be here for you. Pass on who you are."

* * *

The last words echoed through her mind. Words spoken over twenty years ago. Memories still fresh as the new school year.

"And with the new setting brings another new beginning. I will be the headmaster for this year. Thank you."

Many parents asked for a visit when the new year began. The night was soon over. Aine checked the rooms for stragglers, adults and children. One last person was waiting for her.

"Headmaster I thought you went home?"

"I did. Yet I needed to come back to see if anything happened."

Aine felt her lips tick up.

"Yes something did happen Sean."

Aine opened the door to Ash's room, flipped on the light switch, and sat at the edge of the bed. Every time Ash had traveled back to Dublin, it was the same feeling. The feeling of being alone. This time it felt dark, darker than the oak grove at night. Touching her daughters picture on her phone, Ash answered. "Hey Ash. I know, just wanted to talk for a second. How are you? I know, I miss him too. I've been offered the headmaster position. I'm going to take it, Sean has helped us.

Ash, I know. I miss him. We can't travel, not now. I don't know when we will. I want to see him too, but I can't leave now."

The conversation ended without resolution.

* * *

Ashling took the phone and slammed it on her pillow. *Why is this so hard?* She lay in bed, looked at the two nooks in her small flat. Inhaling and exhaling, she reached for the phone again. Opening up Google, typing Ben Meagher University of Montana, she examined the picture of him, and slowly felt sleep take over. First year students were arriving tomorrow to the Academy of Music. It would be a day of help and listening. No matter how confident a new student is, there was always a chance a new student would buckle.

The Music Academy, a collection of buildings on a small narrow street, had been Ashling's home for the last four years. Stepping into the building reminded her of home. The white walls and the red carpeting, chandeliers dangled from the low ceiling. The academy and the building had seen Dublin grow. It was a place where art and the outside world could mix, mingle and leave its mark.

Ashling traveled up the same stairs she had done many times. Feeling the worn oak of the banister on her palms and remembering her thoughts from her first intrepid steps up these same stairs. Talent and work ethic had taken Ashling to this point.

Today, she felt different, tired and the complexity of the past month entered the consciousness. What can I do? A voice brought her back.

"Ashling, so nice to see you."

The voice came from somewhere around her, she focused, cleared her mind and found the voice.

"Good morning, Professor Cahill." The professor, being the same height as her, longer dark hair and blue eyes. Through the last years, Ash felt she had been another mother and mentor. "It is nice to see you."

"Time off, I hope was inviting."

"It was, inviting to be back however."

"A consummate artist you are, come, I have someone that you should meet."

* * *

Ash entered the auditorium—the smell of fresh paint, carpet and air conditioning calmed her mind. She could feel a smile, how I love this, she thought. The lights dimmed, giving the stage definition and a piano began to be play with what Ash thought was perfection. The pair stopped short of the stage. She noticed a small young girl behind the piano.

"She is very good, how old is she?"

"Not much older than you when you first came to us."

The thought that she had been here for years covered her mind. It was home now; at first it was difficult-her passion, brought many dark nights into light.

"What do you need me to do?"

Professor Cahill looked at her, her blue eyes stern, her smile inviting. "When she is finished if you would talk to her? I have felt that she is having…difficulties."

"With playing?" She knew what the answer would be, also Ash knew that the professor knew she was a singer, and that her being brought here, to hear the girl and to talk to her.

Cahill's hand went to her defined cheek bone-voice soft and punctual. "Her playing is remarkable, she will only get better with age. She...has been having difficulties being away from home...much like someone I once knew."

"I will speak with her and talk to you what I find out?"

"Excellent, welcome back for your last year. I will miss you, nice to see you Ashling." A stern hand was placed on her arm as they embraced-the music stopped.

The sound of the stage, under her foot again made her smile. The wood planks making a slow, rolled noise as she approached the piano. The girl, flipped through the music book with care, and studied each page as she did so. Ashling took a knee next to her, she could feel the girl's battle in her mind.

"Hi, I'm Ashling, a friend told me to talk to you."

The girl continued to look through the book. "It was the professor, that told you to talk to me. She scares me. I'm Gina."

"It's nice to meet you Gina, tell me, how old are you?"

Gina turned to her, eyes sunken-body frail. "I will be 12 tomorrow...I want to go home."

"Well happy early birthday Gina...where are you from?" Ash could tell her accent was much different.

"Atlanta, Georgia."

"From the States, that's amazing." Ashling could feel her eyes glisten. "Would you want to walk with me?"

★★★

The sun was warm, the breeze carrying aromas from their destination. A block away from the academy was a large public park amongst the gray of city life. Paths led to beds of colorful flowers, and large trees intertwined the scenery.

"Let's stop at this bench." Ashling said. The area of the park she picked, was quiet, devoid of the surrounding area. "Do you like it here?"

"It's okay, I guess. I don't have many friends."

Ashling nodded her head. "But you will, how long have you been here?"

"Four days, I think."

"Things will slow down for you, just like they did for me, don't worry."

Ashling noticed something took Gina's attention. "You miss your parents?"

A breeze began to swirl, lightly brushing her face. "Yes. But they said I need to be here, my mom is from England."

"So you will see her more than your dad?"

Gina shook her head. "But I wish I could see him more."

"Could I let you in on a secret Gina?" Ashling placed her finger on Gina shoulder. "You remind me of...me...when I came here. You are here because you have a gift. Being away from your parents no matter, is hard. You will be fine. I will be with you this year. Find me whenever you need to talk and then next year, I will give you my number, and we can talk."

Gina looked up at her, color began to come to her cheeks. "Thank you."

Ashling smiled, "You will be great!"

"That's a really tall woman walking over here." Gina remarked.

"Where?" Ashling took her focus off of Gina, and to the path to her left. "Mum, what are you doing here?"

Chapter Sixty-Two

Thirty-thousand people would soon funnel onto campus for game day. The staff and faculty ate breakfast outside the stadium, each wearing a maroon and silver University Of Montana shirt with *Griz* stenciled onto the left chest. The breakfast was more of a press-the-flesh affair than a real meal. Alan found him before he'd reached the front of the line. They filled their paper plates with low expectations. Today, though, breakfast actually tasted perfect. Instead of bagels and coffee, they found bacon from a local meat company, sausage, eggs, and hash browns.

They sat on white folding chairs, eating from their laps.

"How's Lisa? Recovered from her trip?"

"She was sleeping when I got home. I stayed up and watched *Law and Order*. Is it just me, or is that show always on?"

Ben chuckled and gnawed at a piece of bacon. "Aine hasn't returned my texts for two days. I'm getting worried."

"Maybe there's something wrong with her phone. Have you tried to call her?"

"Yeah, I left messages."

"I'm sure everything's fine." Alan sipped his orange juice. "Just try to focus on presenting the awards."

Ben groaned. "A lecture hall is one thing, a stadium with thirty thousand people? I'm kind of nervous."

"Just hand over the awards and smile. I know you can do that."

"I don't really feel like smiling today." Ben took a deep breath, seeing a fleeting image of Aine walking away forever, from something he had done, or hadn't done quickly enough.

The crowd's anticipation was electrifying the crowd. Ben entered the stadium through the underground tunnels leading from the locker rooms. As he entered the field, the muffled crowd became a roar, echoing off the mountain and back into the stadium. At fifteen minutes to kickoff, the excitement was palpable. Maybe this year the Grizzlies would go all the way. With their first national championship in 1995, to their last in 2001, any year the Grizzlies didn't make the playoffs was seen as a failure.

Ben stood on the visitor's sidelines, with thirty thousand fans in the stands behind him. Above the alumni section, two small screens flanked a massive, high-definition video screen, the largest in their conference. Ben walked over the grizzly painted onto the midfield turf. Fans watched on, waiting for the formalities to end and the game to begin.

Alan had followed Ben onto the field. The cheerleaders and the band were in place, forming a tunnel for the football team to run through when the awards were finished.

"You ready, Ben?" Alan asked.

"Yeah. Did you notice the new athletic trainers when the walked by?"

"No, why?"

"One of them was really tall."

"I guess I didn't notice."

The announcer's voice quieted them.

"Welcome, ladies and gentlemen to a new season of University of Montana football." The crowd applauded. *"At the fifty-yard line are this year's donors, receiving a commemorative football from the math department chairman, Dr. Benjamin Meahger."*

Ben handed each a football and posed for a photograph. After the twenty footballs were in the hands of the donors, Ben sighed and headed toward the sideline. Before they were off the field, Alan grabbed his shoulder. "Look up at the board."

The announcer spoke over the music and the roar of the crowd. *"New this year to University of Montana football is the Cub Cam. Before each game, this drone will present special messages from around the university, and today it is live from the M."* The screen cut to two women in football jerseys standing beside the concrete letter. One was Lisa.

"Hello, everyone!" Her voice echoed through the stadium, but Ben's focus was trained on the beautiful redhead beside her.

"My god, Alan. She's here!" Alan smiled and gave Ben a shoulder hug.

Aine and Lisa shouted, "We are!"

The crowd finished the chant. "Montana!"

"We are!"

"Montana!" Fireworks ignited around the stadium, and the Grizzlies rushed onto the field. Thirty thousand fans gave battle cries as Ben and Alan watched from midfield. As the team ran past them, one of the trainers following alongside stopped and lifted her hat, looking straight at Ben.

"Dad, go and get Mum, please."

Ben reached the letter in record time. With each step up he felt his dreams of the past become the present and the future his future, with Aine.

He was out of breath when he made it to Aine. She put a
hand on his back.

"Are you surprised?"

"Of course I am. When you didn't."

"I turned my phone off. I didn't want to ruin it."

Ben stood up and hugged Lisa. "Thank you, thank you."

She grinned. "I'm going to watch the game with Alan. Dinner
tonight." Lisa pointed at Aine. "She is worth waiting a lifetime
for."

As Lisa started down the trail, Ben smiled at Aine. "I
know."

They sat together on the edge of the concrete letter.

"So how did that happen?" he asked. She looked so good
in that football jersey, mountains in the background.

"Ash and I were playing cards when the doorbell rang.
I peeked out the window and saw Lisa holding a pink sticky note
that read, *Hi! I'm not Alice.*"

Ben laughed and looked down at Lisa descending the
mountain.

"She is amazing," Aine said. "Alan's lucky."

"He is." Ben took her hand. "I'm luckier."

The game below was close, but with twenty-two seconds
remaining, a Montana wide receiver broke open, and seventy-five

yards later he scored the game-winning touchdown. The crowd ignited.

"Aine, in December, I'm leaving the university. I want to be with you and Ash." Her eyes shone a bright emerald green.

After the game, Ben and Aine walked down the trail and found Alan, Lisa, and Ashling, who had watched the game from the sidelines. For dinner, they went to a local favorite, a remodeled railway station. The restaurant's granite floors, dark wooden booths, and soft lights were a nod to the forties.

Ashling was excited about her first American football experience. "The crowd was so loud, I couldn't hear sometimes."

"I'm glad you liked it, Ash," Aine said. "The day was very nice from where I was." She squeezed Ben's hand.

Ben ordered rye whiskey for everyone, and Alan raised his glass.

"To new friends and old. And to my best friend, who has found his love and his daughter."

"Thank you, Alan." Ben said.

After they had all drank, Lisa said to Aine, "Thanks for not kicking my ass when I showed up at your house. I heard you kicked Ben's. At least twice."

They all laughed, and Ben gave a puckering smile. "Ha. Ha. Thanks, Lisa."

"Okay, okay." Ashling settled the laughter and spoke to Ben and Aine. "In all seriousness, both of you knew something better was waiting for you. I am so proud to be your daughter and grateful to have you--both of you--in my life."

***

Ashling stayed the night with Lisa and Alan, who showed her the city. Ben and Aine went to his house. Aine was leaving on Monday, a day and a half away.

"Wow, Lover," she said as they walked inside. "You don't believe in furniture, do you?"

"I never had a reason to." Ben grabbed her hand, and they started up the stairs, undressing each other before they hit the first landing. They slammed against the walls, finally making it to the bed, and Aine had her first orgasm of the night.

Afterward, Ben and Aine lay together in his bed, with him making constellations from the freckles on her back. He traced Andromeda with his index finger. "I love your body."

"Whatever," she said.

"You are beautiful." He bent over and kissed her back.

"Aine, do you ever want to have another baby?"

She rolled over and pulled the covers over her chest, propping the pillow behind her head.

"Why? I mean why do you ask?"

"I just feel like I have been left out of something. I wanted to be with you when you started to grow, when you bought clothes to fit you. To be there when Ash was born." Ben sighed. "I just want to be a dad."

Aine exhaled and sat up, taking the covers with her.

"Ben, you are her dad, biologically, emotionally. You. Are. Her. Father. What happened wasn't fair. We all know that. But we have to deal with the destiny we've got. I love you, with everything I am, I love you. Did I want this to happen? NO! But if it's a choice between a prefect life with someone else and *this* life with you, I pick you, Lover. Every time. You are the reason I have Ash, and being with you again is more than I could ever dream of."

"I know. I'm sorry, I just…"

"Being pregnant sucked." Aine laughed. "*If* we decide to have another child, we will. But I am getting older, and so are you. Maybe we should just enjoy what we have."

Ben lowered his head, ashamed he had questioned her love for him. Aine gently pushed his chin up.

"Lover, forever." She closed in slowly, meeting his lips.

When they pulled away, she squinted at his expression.

"What is it?" she asked.

Ben smiled, "I have an idea."

Chapter Sixty-Three

"Are you sure you want to do this?" Aine asked as they passed a green and white sign. "Three hundred and forty-three miles. Really, are you going to be okay?"

She glided her hand across the black leather console, onto his leg. Both of his hands were on the steering wheel. "It was nice of Alan and Lisa to let us borrow their BMW," she said. Ben gripped the wheel.

She glanced at Ashling in the backseat, listening to music through her headphones. "Hey Ben, are you okay?" She squeezed his leg and finally received a response.

"Ow, yes I'm okay. I really want to do this. It's three hundred thirty-six miles, now. I will get through this."

"Your palms are sweating."

"That's because of your hand on my leg."

He glanced toward Aine with a forced smile. She shook her head.

The interstate from Missoula to Billings had several rest stops, Deer Lodge, Butte and Bozeman. They stopped to stretch at each one, giving Ben time to calm his nerves. Along the interstate, they had driven sweeping curves and straight stretches. They'd passed canyons and two mountain passes--after the last of which they left the mountains behind, the land opening into the Great Plains.

"We are getting close. I remember this type of geography." Aine said.

"Yes, we are."

Ashling woke from a nap and yawned. "Where did the trees and mountains go? Isn't this Montana?"

Ben smiled and told her they were still in Montana. On the eastern side of the state, the Great Plains swelled the land.

By two in the afternoon, they reached their destination. After eight hours of driving, they were all thankful to pull the car into the college parking lot, behind the dorms Aine and Ben had once called home. Aine pointed out the marquee: Montana State University Billings.

"So they did it," she said as Ben shut down the engine. "It's not Eastern anymore, and the colors aren't black and yellow."

Years ago, there had been talk of the region's smaller colleges becoming part of the state's two biggest schools, the University of Montana and Montana State University. For some reason, Eastern was the only school to change its name--Northern and Western retained theirs.

Aine squinted. "Eastern's mascot was the yellow jackets. How can you have a blue and yellow bee?" Aine queried.

"I don't know, but let's go for a walk. Ash, you're coming with us, right?"

"Oh yeah, I'm comin."

They walked through the atrium separating the two dorms, down the concrete stairs, and outside to campus. Aine's pace slowed, and she found Ben's hand.

"It hasn't changed all that much," she said.

Grass and cottonwood trees surrounded wide concrete walkways. A warm August breeze nudged the limbs, and the older trees groaned. New buildings had been built on the fringes of campus, but the core buildings were unchanged. Aine stopped and squeezed his hand.

"What is it?" Ben asked.

Ashling watched her. "You okay, Mum?"

Aine's gaze fixated on one of the cottonwoods.

"I never told you, but this is where I first saw you. I think I loved you even then."

"I thought the first time you saw me was the day you hit me with a volleyball."

"No, it was here. I was with Amanda, and I had my chance to tell her I was interested in you, but I was too scared. Then I saw you again at the pool, and I told myself that I had to do something."

There was a long silence. Ash's eyes turned red as her mother's hair.

"Let's walk around campus for a while," Ben said, "and then we'll go."

Ashling wiped her eyes. "Let's go this way."

They walked a lap around campus. Ben and Aine showed Ashling where their classes had been. They pointed out the hospital where Ben had stayed and the athletic complex where Aine had spent so much time.

They made their way back to the car, and Ben turned the ignition to start the car.

"So where are we going?" Ashling asked.

"You'll see," he said.

They drove down the street connecting the valley to the plateau and parked at an overlook. Ben and Aine sat at the edge of the sandstone cliffs.

"The Rims. I really liked this view, but it's better at night," Aine said.

Ash yelled from behind them. "There is no way I'm putting my legs over that cliff. I'll stay on this boulder."

Ben laughed and looked at Aine. "This is where I began to love you. He reached into his pocket and produced a light blue box. "Now, all these years later, here we are again."

Ben placed the small box in her hand. The bow flickering in the breeze. She gently untied the ribbon.

Ash called from behind them.

"Oh, Mum."

Ben took Aine's hand and slipped the diamond ring onto her finger. The stone shimmered in the afternoon sun.

"I should have done this long ago."

"Yes, Ben, yes." Aine said, embracing Ben. She whispered in his ear. "December nineteenth. I don't care what day it is. We'll be back in December…I have an idea." Aine wiped tears from her eyes, and soon all three were in a family embrace.

Chapter Sixty-Four

Ben and Aine decided not to have a best man or bridesmaids. They had waited so long for this moment. The only ones beside them as the priest pronounced them man and wife, would be their parents, looking down from heaven.

Ben waited for Aine at the front of the church. The guests only filled four rows of pews, but this wedding wasn't for family and friends. It was for them. A small contingent of university string musicians--a harp, a guitar, two basses, three cellos, and three violins--began playing "Canon" in D. Ben smiled as the violins played in unison. Aine was heading toward him.

Her steps were slow and pronounced. She could reach the alter in ten steps with her natural stride, but she was savoring the moment. Ben stared as she walked down the aisle in her baby-blue dress, embroidered with deep purple leaves. Her train flowed behind her. She wore no veil, and her hair looked as red as Ben had ever seen it. He recognized Ashling's signature braid. When she reached the altar, the music quieted, and the priest spoke.

"Dearly beloved, we are gathered here today in view of the Lord to unite these two in matrimony. Lisa, a dear friend of both the bride and groom, would like to speak."

Lisa slowly covered the distance from her seat to the podium. Her hands trembled slightly as she unfolded her notes, but her voice was strong and confident.

"When I first met Ben, we were both much younger, and I couldn't understand how such a handsome man, sorry…Alan. I couldn't understand how Ben was single. At first, I assumed he must be a player, but that soon proved false. Now, finally, after years of being fortunate enough to call Ben one of my and my husband's greatest friends, I know now why he was always a self-imposed bachelor. Somewhere in the past, two people met and fell in love. Then they lost each other. Most people would have moved on, but these two couldn't. Their connection was too deep. And now, it's deeper still, thanks to a love that only a parent could know. Please welcome their daughter, Ashling, singing '*Prayer*.'"

Ashling walked toward the front, Ben and Aine knelt in front of Lisa, who tied three ribbons--orange, green, and white--around Ben and Aine's intertwined hands.

She began to sing, a tear dripped from Aine's eye, rolling down her cheek and falling to the floor.

Ashling's voice shook under the moment's emotions, but after the first line she gathered herself and sang with her strong and steady voice. The song ended, and she gently dabbed tears from the corners of her eyes. The priest gathered himself to perform the ceremony.

Aine and Ben didn't change clothes after the ceremony. The moment was too precious. The reception, like the ceremony, was small. They held it at the sports bar where Ben had seen Aine on the television screen, many months ago.

After Alan and Ben had finished a round of beers, Ben found Aine sitting with a white-haired young woman. He had never seen hair that color outside of old age--it nearly matched the snow

outside. He sat next to Aine and rested his hand on her thigh.

"Hello, husband."

"Hello, wife."

She gestured to the white-haired woman. "I think you two

have met."

"Hi, Ben. It's nice to see you again."

Ben tried to place her face, but couldn't. The woman spoke

with no accent. Perhaps with a different hair color? He looked

to Aine.

"Lover, this is Alec."

The woman smiled across the table. "Ben, I am so happy at

the way you fought all those years ago. Aine and I fought for

you every night."

A memory as sudden and violent as lighting shook his

nerves.

"You were in the helicopter with me. You saved my

life."

"It was my first night, and I tried my best. I'm a

doctor now, but I could never forget you and Aine. When she

found me, I had to come."

Ben shook his head. "How could I ever thank you?" He didn't

give her time to swat away his thanks. "Could I talk to you,

alone?"

"I get the hint, Lover," Aine said, standing. "You want to be alone with a beautiful woman one last time. Besides myself, of course." She left the table and found Lisa. Ben watched as they began to trade whiskey shots. He laughed to himself. Lisa was in trouble.

"Thank you," he said to Alec, "for taking care of her, when I couldn't."

"She had it rough. She was alone. Your--"

"I know Alice didn't make it easy."

"No, she made it impossible for her. I stayed around to help her, but also to protect her when your sister showed up." Ben smiled at this small woman who could take on anything.

"How was she when she found out about Ashling?"

"She was beyond herself. Depressed at times. She had so much to worry about, you, school, volleyball, and then a pregnancy. But Ben, everything happens for a reason. There are things in my life I wish I could change, but they make me who I am. You are happy now, and you have an extraordinary daughter. Live your life, and enjoy it."

"Thank you, Alec."

As Alec pushed back her chair, Aine walked over and embraced her.

"You're leaving?"

"God knows what trouble my daughters are getting into at the inn. Teenagers."

Alec reached into her coat pocket and brought out a small box, depositing it into Aine's large hands.

"I love both of you very much. Please keep in touch."

The night ended in a warm haze of joyful memories.

The next morning, Ben and Aine looked over their gifts.

"Don't these people know we have to get all this back to Ireland?" Aine said.

"I know, they are just being nice. What is that?"

Ben pointed to a small box with white wrapping paper.

"That's from Alec."

"Didn't she get us something?"

"She did. Something extra, I guess."

"Well, what is it?"

Aine slowly tore the paper and opened the box, "Ben, come here."

With a finger he brought the contents out. "Aine, it's your ring, she had it."

***

All three of them climbed in the car and drove down the valley, dusted lightly with snow. They stopped at the cross on the side of the highway. Each of them placed a single rose on the ground beside the cross. Aine closed her eyes, and Ben could barely hear her words.

"I forgive you, Alice. I forgive."

Ashling put her arms around her mother. The three of them sat together for another few minutes, then headed farther south into the valley.

Thankfully, the snow wasn't piled up at the cemetery. Only a thin layer of icy snow crunched underfoot as they approached the tombstones, their breath visible in the frigid air. Aine and Ashling placed red roses on each of Ben's parents' graves.

"Would they have liked me, Ben--Dad?"

"Yeah." Ben looked down at the graves, "They would have loved you. They would have loved your laugh and your smile. My mother would have loved that you drink coffee. She would have poured you a strong cup and sat with you in the mornings. My dad would have loved your passion for music. He would have passed down his vinyl collection to you." He paused. "You are my daughter, Ash. They would have loved you, for being you."

"I'm sorry I never got to meet them," Aine said quietly.

"I'm…" Ben fumbled for words. "I'm sorry, too."

Ben placed a silver picture frame between the graves. The photo was from his and Aine's wedding. The three of them kneeled as snow clouds gathered around the mountains. They held hands and closed their eyes, none concerned with the wet snow or cold ground.

"Mom and Dad," Ben said. "I will be leaving you. I have found who I want to be with for the rest of my life. Then, I will see you again. I love both of you. Thank you for everything you gave me."

Their new family stood up slowly and walked back to the car. They left for Ireland the next day.

Chapter Sixty-Five

The early-morning clouds left the Bitterroot Valley, south of Missoula. The night before those same clouds had been heavy with snow as they struggled to cross the Rocky Mountains.

A black-cloaked figure knelt beside two mounds in the snow. Gloved hands brushed away with powder, revealing headstones. Something clinked against the stone, and the slender fingers stopped. The hands slowly lifted a picture frame.

A sharp winter wind began to blow, and snow whipped around the graveyard. The figure grabbed both edges of the hood and flipped it back, exposing long, gray hair.

"You didn't even tell me," Alice muttered. "Without me?"

***

The office intercom buzzed, and Alan narrowed his eyes. The semester had ended weeks ago. *Who would have a problem with a professor already?*

His secretary began to speak. "Dr. Schliefer, you have a visitor. She says she's Dr. Meagher's sister?"

A chill ran down his spine. "Of course, let her in." He had been ready for this meeting, but Alan hadn't expected her to come so soon. Ben only left Missoula a couple weeks ago. The door opened, and Alan stood. "Hello, Alice." He extended a hand.

Alice took it. "It's been what, five years?"

"Yes. Since we helped your brother move. How are you?"

"We can cut the bullshit, Alan. Where is he?"

Alan gestured toward the seat across from his desk. Alice remained standing.

"I don't know what you mean," he said.

Alice's voice quivered. "I was at my parents' graves, and I saw a picture of my brother--and her."

He closed his eyes. "Yes, he is finally--"

"He didn't even tell me. My only brother got married, and he didn't even-- He was at mine. Without my parents, he is all I have." Alice turned her back.

"I know what happened all those years ago, and I am sorry, but he's happy with her. After all these years, he's happy. I don't understand why you tried so hard to keep them apart. He's thought of her all these years. We're lucky he didn't end his life over it."

Alice faced him, her eyes watering, her cheeks a volcanic red. Her eyebrows bent inward, and deep grooves formed under her nose and in the corners of her eyes.

"Aine was going to take him from me. I lost three people I loved dearly. I, too, think of people every day, who I can't touch or see. Only memories." She wiped away tears. "Now he knows what that feels like."

"Alice," Alan said slowly, "I won't pretend I know what you've been through, but I know what you've put *him* through. No matter how you feel about Ben or about Aine, seeing those two together would have made you proud. Maybe it would have relieved some of your spitefulness. If you want to find your brother, by all means, go find him. I'm not sure what type of reception you will receive, but just remember he has a family to consider now, a wife and a daughter."

Alice looked down at the wooden floors. Alan thought he saw shame in her body language, but he couldn't be sure.

Alice walked slowly toward the door, pausing with her fingers on the brass doorknob. "Alan?"

"Yes?"

She cleared her throat and pronounced each word carefully, "Let my brother know that Mark and I will bring the twins to Ireland for New Year's."

* * *

The stove was warming the house when Alan walked inside. He put his arms around Lisa, and she rested her head against his.

She squinted when she saw his face. "What's going on?"

"Long day. I had a visitor."

"Who?"

"Alice." The kitchen turned silent except for the sound of boiling water. "She wanted to know where Ben is."

"You didn't tell her, did you?"

"No, I didn't have to. She already knew, and they are going to see him."

"Did you tell Ben?"

"I texted him. No response."

Lisa placed her arms around him and whispered in his ear.

"Let's go out to eat tonight and have some fun."

He nodded. "You always know how to make me smile."

Chapter Sixty-five

Ben woke to what seemed like a dream. Aine lay on top of him, her back stretched, her eyes intensely green. He smiled and

signaled to be quiet. Aine laughed and motioned toward the
shower. Ben stepped inside and started the water.

"Good morning, Lover."

He pulled her long, wet hair across her shoulder.

"It's nice waking up with you," he said.

"Always."

Downstairs, Aine started coffee, sausage, and hash browns.
After breakfast, they would go for a walk through the oaks, this
time to her mother's grave. Ben and Aine were already sitting
down to eat when they heard slow footsteps down the stairs.
Ashling entered the kitchen in her pajamas.

"Enough already with banging pots and pans in the morning.
Or I might bang some pots and pans of my own."

"You better not," Aine said.

Ben stuffed hash browns in his mouth and pretended not to
hear.

After breakfast, all three put on winter coats and went for
a walk. As they strolled through the grove, Ben could see in his
mind the dress Aine had been wearing the previous summer and how
she had shone radiantly among the greenery. Today, in her white
winter coat, the green was subdued, but Aine was as beautiful as
ever.

Instead of turning left, as they had last summer, they
turned right onto a narrower path leading to the top of a hill

and a small cemetery. From the hilltop, Ben could see over the oak grove to the old sandstone. Each day he learned a bit more of his new home. With Aine as his tour guide, he was beginning to feel as though he'd always lived here. For the first time in his life, he felt calm. For the first time, he felt at home.

The cemetery was older than any he'd seen in Montana. Some of the headstones' dates were obscured by time and weathering. Others were large and ornate. The newer part of the cemetery was evident from the less-expensive grave markers. Simple headstones worked just as well--the family had the memories. Aine led Ben to her mother's grave, where he knelt, as he had knelt before his own parents' graves.

"I know I only talked to you a few times," he said, "but I feel that I knew you. Thank you for raising a daughter who is full of love and courage. I could barely live without her. Thank you." Ben looked at Aine. Her back was turned, facing the oak grove. He placed a hand on her shoulder, and she faced him, her eyes liquid green.

"Thank you, Ben. Thank you."

As they walked back to the house, Ben asked Aine, "Where do you want to be buried?"

"This is my home," she said. "Of course I want to be buried here. But if you don't."

"I want to be buried next to you. Here, or anywhere else."

Aine laughed through her tears, "I love you, Ben."

"I love you, too."

They were nearly to the house when he spoke again.

"What do we want to do about our visitors? They should be here today."

Aine inhaled. "I will try to be on my best behavior, but I can't guarantee anything. I still don't like this."

Ashling interrupted. "I think I'll just stay in my room."

"You will not." Aine said.

* * *

After shopping and cleaning all day, Ben slid a pan of homemade lasagna into the oven. Aine leaned against the counter, sipping red wine. "Maybe they won't show." she said.

"I highly doubt that, but you never know."

They heard a knock on the door and looked at each other.

"Here we go." Ben said. "I'm not excited about this either. But she's my sister."

"I'm just surprised she hasn't killed her offspring yet."

Ben chuckled. "Just remember, there's nothing she can do to us, now."

Ashling had already answered the door when Ben emerged from the kitchen.

"Mark, Melissa, Tiffany. Please come in. Ash, can you take their coats, please?"

Mark and the twins passed Ben, but he blocked Alice before she could enter. "We need to talk."

He led her down the porch steps and away from the house. Finally, he stopped and faced her. "Alice, what are you doing here?"

"I guess we weren't invited to the wedding."

"What was I supposed to do? You kept us apart for years."

"I know. But it's over. You're married, and you have a daughter I have never met."

There was so much he wanted to tell her, but he couldn't believe any of it would make a difference. "If you truly want this to be over," he said, "you need to talk to Aine, alone."

Dinner was full of awkward exchanges and small talk. Ben and Mark talked the most, mainly about Ireland and how much Ben loved living here.

After dinner, Melissa and Tiffany followed Ash to her room. Ben and Mark did the dishes while Aine and Alice headed outside.

Mark looked over at Ben, a freshly washed plate in his hands.

"Ben, I'm sorry."

"There's nothing to be sorry about anymore."

***

Aine and Alice sat on cold plastic chairs, on opposite sides of the table.

"It's funny."

Aine took a breath. "What is?"

"I never truly knew how much he loved you."

Aine sighed. "Alice, I've never known what your problem was with me. Or why you did what you did."

"I didn't know you were pregnant."

"So? You didn't have the right to keep him from me. Baby or not."

Alice rubbed her temples. "Do you remember Devon?"

"I don't know a Devon."

Alice placed her hands on the table, palms down, tapping both index fingers. "Your first year at Eastern, you were at the movies. You were talking to someone, a boy."

Aine thought back to freshman year. "I remember talking to someone for Amanda."

"Amanda?" Alice buried her face in her hands, her words muffled through her shaking fingers. "Oh, shit! It wasn't you." She lifted her head and met Aine's gaze with watery eyes. "You have every right to hate me."

Aine' shook her head. "You will never be one of my favorites. But you are his sister. You're my sister, now, too. Maybe some things happen for a reason."

Alice wiped her eyes. "Maybe."

* * *

Each December, before the New Year, Aine watched "Legends of the Fall." When Ashling was old enough to watch it, the movie became a family tradition. This year, the viewing was different. Ben, Aine, Ashling, Alice, Mark, and the twins all sat in the living room, watching the movie and warming the room with their body heat, if not with love. Aine and Alice sat on opposite sides of the room, but Ben noticed the hatred burning between them seemed to have dimmed.

"I don't know how you guys watched that in the theater," Ashling said. "So long and so depressing." The twins agreed. Soon after the movie ended, Alice's family left for the inn.

Aine spread a large blanket in the front yard. Before joining her, Ben went to Ashling's room.

"You want to come outside, Ash?"

"It's okay, I'm going to listen to some music. I think you and Mum need to be alone to talk."

The night was cold enough for Ben and Aine to see their breath. Their winter jackets kept them warm, but their feelings kept them warmer. Ben looked at his wife--at the freckles

across the bridge of her nose, at her green eyes that appeared

dark in the moonlight.

"Hey."

"What, Lover?"

"You okay?"

"Yeah, just thinking. About us, together. It's more

than I thought."

"You know you can call me something else, besides Lover."

"Nah," She shrugged and moved closer to him. "It gets

me hot."

Ben touched her face, and they fell into a slow, passionate

kiss. When their lips broke apart, they touched noses.

"Happy New Year. Lover. My life is so much better with

you in it." Aine looked up at the night sky. "Last year when I

looked at those stars, they were a lot dimmer."

They looked up at the brilliant opened sky, each star a

bright speck of burning light. Just like all those years ago, a

shooting star crossed the blackness.

"Make a wish, Aine."

Aine smiled and touched her ring. "I want us to go one

more…place."

Chapter Sixty-Seven

A rubber mallet pounded a steel stake into the ground, the sound of not one, but four stakes had reverberated off the walls of the mountains that surrounded them. Sweat, dripped from Ben's face.

"Wow, I thought I was in shape."

Aine smiled. "It's the altitude lover."

Ben felt his lips smile back, the October sun casted shadows during midday. Ben looked at the tent. It had been over twenty-two years since they had camped at the same spot. The small lakes and bear grass, told that years moved slowly in the Northern Rockies. The clean air went into his lungs as he breathed.

"I think the tent is big enough this time."

The laugh that Aine produced echoed. "Yes I think it is, even if it not, it would be great."

***

The stars appeared on schedule, bright and visible. The galaxy ring overhead, the wind quiet. Sitting with their backs to the tent, Ben held Aine, and looked at her.

"So this is your wish?"

Her eyes gleamed in the visible light. "Mostly."

"Mostly?"

With great care, Aine moved his hand slowly across her chest and then down further, while she placed her mouth close to his ear, and whispered, "Leannen…I'm pregnant."

The End

<<<<>>>>

Alec will return in *Snow on Glass*.

Made in the USA
Middletown, DE
10 July 2019